THE MIGHTY ADVENTURES
OF MOUSE, THE CAT

THE CALLING OF THE PROTECTORS: BOOK 2

LOUIS PAUL DEGRADO

iUniverse®

THE MIGHTY ADVENTURES OF MOUSE, THE CAT
THE CALLING OF THE PROTECTORS: BOOK 2

iUniverse books may be ordered through booksellers or by contacting:

iUniverse
1663 Liberty Drive
Bloomington, IN 47403
www.iuniverse.com
1-800-Authors (1-800-288-4677)

ISBN: 978-1-5320-6838-6 (sc)
ISBN: 978-1-5320-6840-9 (hc)
ISBN: 978-1-5320-6839-3 (e)

Library of Congress Control Number: 2019903620

Print information available on the last page.

iUniverse rev. date: 03/26/2019

To my daughter, Annalea, whom I love very dearly. She was the inspiration for many of the songs contained in these stories.

Special thanks to
Richard Wright for teaching me the guitar

Special mention for extraordinary support goes to the following:
Faith Bent
Jodi Bond
Shawn Cadwell
Naomi Hernandez-Perry
Judy Hudson
Christine Razo
Deanna Wakley

Also by Louis Paul DeGrado

The Calling of the Protectors: The Legend of Chief
Gold Award, Literary Classics, 2017
Editor's Choice, iUniverse

A small amount of courage has a giant impact in this book that is fun for the entire family. When a small, fluffy cat teams up with an advice-giving canary, a cockatoo, some jazz-loving alley cats, and a fancy mouse to protect their home from a villainous hoodlum rat, a hero is born.

Complete with eight original songs, this story is sure to inspire.

The 13ᵗʰ Month
Editor's Choice, iUniverse
Finalist, Foreword Review Book of the Year, 2015

Have you ever wondered why bad days linger or why moments of regret stick with you and bad situations seem surreal? What would you do if you found out that evil exists in these moments and forces of evil were working to control and extend them by warping reality? Would you have the faith to stand and fight?

Evil once controlled the 13ᵗʰ Month and is looking to do so again.

When revered priest Father Frank Keller investigates a tragic murder in his parish, he is thrust into a covert battle between the forces of good and evil. Seeking answers, Father Frank is contacted by a group consisting of a holy man from India, a Native American shaman, a college professor, and an attractive middle-aged psychiatrist. The group's mission is to fight shadows: parasitic creatures that lurk in moments of time and warp reality to take control of their host.

The leader of the group, Adnan, is convinced that the shadows, once banished from the world, are gaining a foothold. The only way to stop them is to go to the place where the shadows come from and turn the tide.

Father Frank must face his own insecurities and desires in order to find the faith to combat the evil that threatens those closest to him and help the group. To do so, he must prepare himself to cross through a portal where the shadows come from, a portal that might lead him directly to the gates of hell.

Savior
Finalist, Foreword Review Book of the Year, 2001

Glimpse the future in this exciting science fiction thriller.

How far will we go to save ourselves? Faced with its own demise, humankind turns to science for answers, and governments approve drastic measures in genetic testing and experimentation.

Battle lines are drawn when a religious crusader and the medical director of the largest research firm clash over thousands of people frozen in cryogenic stasis who are being used as human test subjects. Caught in the middle is Kyle Reed, the director of the company, who has been brought back after two hundred years to face his greatest dilemma: support the company he founded or expose the truth behind its plans.

The Questors' Adventures
The Round House and *The Moaning Walls*

This combo pack includes the first two stories in *The Questors' Adventures*.

What do you call a group of boys who set out to explore the unknown? They call themselves the Questors, and they're ready for excitement, adventure, and mayhem. Join the adventure as the boys, ages ten to thirteen, must overcome jittery nerves and active imaginations to investigate a haunted house in their neighborhood. An engaging series for young readers.

The People across the Sea
Editor's Choice, iUniverse

Within the towering walls of the city by the sea, a dark secret is kept. The city's history was wiped out by foreign invasion, and even now, the city stands poised to repel another attack from the dreaded people across the sea.

A culture based on fear and the threat of invasion has spawned a leader, a council, and the Law of Survivors. Aldran Alfer is now the Keeper of the Law and the council leader. He knows the hidden terror that threatens to rip the city apart.

The sons of Aldran, Brit and Caln, find themselves caught in a web of danger and mystery. Brit finds himself on the run from the Black Guard, veiled men who prowl the streets and crush any who oppose the council's will.

While Caln remains in the city, struggling to hold his family's position on the council, Brit heads to the forbidden desert to seek out the Wizard, a man with strange powers who was banished from the city. In the company of the Wizard and a mythical desert wanderer, Brit will find his destiny. He must cross the land of the Sand Demons, fierce predators who stalk the desert, where he searches for a way to carry out his father's plan to lead their people to safety and end the threat from the people across the sea.

www.literarylou.com

Home of
Author Louis Paul DeGrado

CONTENTS

PROLOGUE

"We have beaten the rat bully, Bragar," Mouse said. The alley went quiet as she spoke. "Let's not forget this night when we stood together as one. As we go back to being what we are—pigeons, cats, a mouse, a cockatoo, and a canary—we can take with us something greater because of this moment we shared."

"Well spoken," Carl said. He put his wing to his head and saluted.

Just then, Sam's truck entered the parking lot by the side door. The other animals left the parking lot as Mouse and Charlene ran to the end of the alley and watched Sam exit the truck, carrying something wrapped in a towel.

"Dad!" Mouse yelled out and ran to Sam, who carried her father, Chief, in his arms.

"What's going on here?" Sam asked, as Mouse and her mom, Charlene, approached him from the alley. "What are you two doing out here?" Mouse bumped Sam's leg. "Yep, I got your dad here. He's a little groggy, just got out of treatment, but he's going to be fine. Let's take him inside so he can get some rest."

Mouse and Charlene followed Sam to the apartment, where he laid Chief in one of the cat beds on the floor. Then Sam went into the kitchen. Mouse walked up to her dad and could see the stitches on his chest and a sling around his leg where he'd been hurt. Charlene licked Chief's head.

"I'm sorry," Chief said. "I should have paid more attention."

"Let's not worry about that now," Charlene said. "Let's just get you better."

"Mouse?" Chief said.

"Yes, Dad?"

"I need you to go get Baxter for me. He'll need to help us with our rat problem until I get better."

Mouse looked at her mom and then back to Chief. She wasn't sure how to tell him what had been going on. She was worried he would not approve and would scold her.

"There's no more rat problem," Charlene said. "Your daughter—your brave daughter—took care of the problem. So get some rest. Come on, Mouse. Let's get something to eat." Charlene headed toward the kitchen, but Mouse stayed behind.

Chief raised his head. "Just what has been going on since I've been away?"

"Lots, Dad," Mouse said. "Bragar is no more, and the truce with Wilber is back in place. The apartments are safe."

"I'm sorry I doubted you," Chief said. "I guess ..."

Mouse thought she spotted tears forming as Chief spoke.

"It's okay, Dad," Mouse said. "If I saw me coming, all fluffy and small, I would have doubts about my toughness too. But it's kind of like my camouflage. You see, I'm tougher than I look. I also learned that I'm stronger with my allies than by myself."

CHAPTER 1
A DARING RESCUE

At two minutes to midnight, the normally quiet street was suddenly full of movement in front of the Belaire Animal Control building. Three cats, ten pigeons, a mouse, a rat, and a sulphur-crested cockatoo took positions in the shrubbery across the road from the business and scanned the surroundings.

"Hold here," Colonel Wellington, leader of the Pigeon Brigade, called out.

Mouse, a small, fluffy black-and-white cat approached Colonel Wellington, who, although he was mostly gray and white like the other pigeons, was easy to distinguish by his large form and makeshift medal he wore around his neck. The medal was really a large, decorative brass button with a piece of twine through it.

"Are we ready, Mouse?" Colonel Wellington asked.

"Everyone's here," Mouse said. "We're ready."

"Recon patrol, launch," Colonel Wellington called out and waved his right wing in the air. Six pigeons took flight, lifting off with such grace that they were nearly silent. Mouse watched as they spread out, with two taking the right, two to the left, and the other two flying high to the front of the building and then going to the roof and around the back. Mouse knew she was built to see in the dark and could see farther from the ground than the pigeons could, but the view they had from above would be invaluable to the success of the mission. A small black-and-white mouse named Little Foot and a scrawny, unkempt rat named Streets flanked her as she patiently waited for the reconnaissance flight to return. The other cats and pigeons waited behind her.

"How exactly did you get the name Mouse?" Streets asked.

"It happened by accident," Mouse said. "When I was a small kitten with my family, the apartment manager, Miss Sorenson, told my mom and dad they could only keep one from the litter of kittens. I was what you call the runt of the litter, and my mom picked me because she worried I wouldn't make it without her looking after me. My dad told her I would be unable to take his position defending the building and that I wasn't even as big as a mouse. The name stuck."

"So, you have brothers and sisters?"

"I suppose so," Mouse said. "But I don't remember much about them or know where they are now. How about you?"

"I never knew my pops, but my mom—she was a real go-getter. She had a place where everyone came, and she would serve vittles, and that's how she got her information—by listening to the conversations. She would share it for the right price. I never could cook. So when she passed, I gave up that business. Since I knew so much about what was going on, everyone kept coming to me. With no place to go, I just roamed around the streets and soon learned where everything was and listened to what was going on. See, I know what's going down all around town."

"And that's why they call you Streets," Mouse said. "Makes sense."

"My real name is Benson."

"That's a great name," Mouse said. "Why don't you go by that?"

"I have a reputation. Here—let me put it another way." Streets took a few steps back from the road into the clearing, where the other animals waited, and started singing:

> They call me Streets;
> I know the town.
> I know what's up
> And what's going down.
>
> I might be a rat, but I never tell.
> They call me Streets.
> I got something to sell.

Uptown, downtown—
You can say I get around.
Any location is my vocation.
Gossip and lies, had no disguise—
I heard it all and have information.

The call me Streets.
I know the town.
If it's info you need,
I got the lowdown.
I might be a rat,
But I'll never tell.
You got something you need—
I got something to sell.

Streets moved around Mouse and the others as he said, "Do you know what happened on Forty-Second Street last night?"

Mouse shook her head.

"Well, I do," Streets said. "How about what's going down in LODO?"

Mouse recognized the slang word for Lower Downtown but shook her head because she had no idea what was going on there.

"I didn't think so," Streets said and started singing again:

I might share what I know,
And knowing's what I do.
Got something you need,
I got something for you.

Uptown, downtown—
You can say
I get around.
You think no one's watching.
You haven't got a clue.
Got something you need,
I got something for you.

After Streets finished his song, the others clapped, except for Colonel Wellington, who shook his head and ruffled his feathers as he said, "If we're quite done, I would remind everyone that we're on a rescue mission that we could jeopardize at any minute if we don't keep quiet!"

"Sorry," Streets said.

"I didn't know you could sing," Mouse said. "That was really good; wouldn't you say so, Carl?"

Carl, the sulphur-crested cockatoo, joined Mouse and Streets as they looked out across the road. "Yes, a very catchy song."

"I've been listening to the alley cats," Streets said. "That's why I'm helping you get them out. Life's been so boring without their music and parties livening up the alley. Only I'm not going inside with you."

"You don't need to," Mouse said. "You can leave if you want to."

"Oh no, I'm not going to miss this. I need to be able to tell an accurate story of everything that went on here. I'll wait until you're out."

The pigeons returned across the double-lane road and landed. Each gave a report to Colonel Wellington, who then came to Mouse.

"Mission Commander," Colonel Wellington said.

Mouse glanced at Streets and Carl, the cockatoo, but neither of them said anything.

"That's you," Carl said, raising his crest as he spoke.

"Oh," Mouse said. "What do you have to report?"

"It looks as though our planning has paid off. The building is clear of any human presence and ready to infiltrate."

"Thank you, Colonel Wellington," Mouse said. "What do you recommend we do next?"

"We should post lookouts along the alley and front while our infiltrator goes in."

"Please give the orders," Mouse said.

"Very well," he said and turned his head to one of the pigeons. "Private, take your position on watch. The rest of you, fan out as we planned." After he was done giving the orders, Colonel Wellington turned to Mouse. "It's clear to move in. You're the Protector here. Would you like to give the order?"

"You have so much more experience than me," Mouse said. She glanced at Carl, who nodded his approval. He had advised her to make sure she was polite to Colonel Wellington, whose reservation with helping cats was overcome by his ego and desire for adventure.

"Yes, well ..." Colonel Wellington cleared his throat. "Right flank patrol, launch to position. Left flank, launch."

Mouse watched as two sets of birds took off from the area to keep watch on both sides of the building. Colonel Wellington looked to Little Foot. "Now it's up to you, my little friend."

"You understand I can't go with you," Carl said. "I spent the better part of five years in a cage and don't even want to be near a place like that."

"I understand," Mouse said. "Someone needs to keep the rendezvous area clear." Carl saluted her, and she did her best to salute back by raising her paw to her forehead.

Mouse knew how dangerous it was to cross a street. She had spent time with her father, Chief, watching the front street of the apartment complex. Her observations led her to believe humans were often careless in their actions and even more so when they got into a car. "Ready?" she asked Little Foot and lowered her shoulder to let the mouse crawl on her back.

"Hold on tight. I'm going to go fast," Mouse said. She looked around to see if any cars were coming before she took off across the road. Two cats, Sikes and Rascal, followed her, and the four made it across without incident. They approached the door of the animal control building directly from the front. Mouse could see the small space between the bottom of the door and the floor. Little Foot jumped down off her back.

"You sure you can fit through that gap?" Mouse said.

"I have a very flexible body," Little Foot said as she stood on her hind legs and stretched to the left and to the right. She popped her neck and then went to the door.

Mouse and the other two cats kept watch as Little Foot squeezed under the doorway. The door was solid, so once Little Foot was through, Mouse could no longer see her.

"Okay, go to the window," Little Foot said from the other side of the door.

Mouse went to the side of the building where they had spied a window that they had planned to be their breach point into the containment facility. Sikes and Rascal were already in place. As the three cats watched, Little Foot appeared on the other side of the window, clicked the latch, and opened it. The three cats jumped and were inside the building.

As they came down from the window onto the floor, Mouse's senses alarmed her. "There's something dangerous here," she said. "Let's stick together."

"Where do you thinks we should start?" Sikes said.

Mouse sniffed, and Little Foot raised her ears.

"They're in the back," Mouse and Little Foot said in unison.

The group headed down a dimly lit hallway to a large room. A smell of animals permeated the air, and Mouse stopped suddenly, causing the group to stop.

"What is it?" Rascal asked.

"I've got Scratch's and Dazzle's scents, but there's something more."

Rascal sniffed the air. "I smell a dog. Multiple dogs. They're just in here like the rest of the animals."

"I've never met a dog," Mouse said.

"Trust me," Rascal said. "They're trouble. I think it's because they're jealous."

"Jealous?"

"Yes. See, they have to be enclosed or on leashes. They don't get to roam free like us. And lots of them are put outside on purpose. Some even have jobs and aren't really pets but work for a living."

"I see," Mouse said. "But there's one loose in here."

"Probably a guard dog. That's why there are no people here at night. The dog does the job. He might get in our way."

Just as Mouse was about to reply, she heard a deep, low growl and turned to face a brown-and-white bulldog at least six times her size. Its sharp teeth were bared. Mouse's stomach lurched in fear, but she tried not to let it show as the dog stared her down.

She said, "Nice doggie," in a weak voice, eliciting three loud barks that sent chills through her and made her fur stand on end.

Then the bulldog fell onto the floor and started laughing. "Forgive me," he said, "but I've never heard a cat use the words humans say to me when they're about to wet their pants." Then he stood and came nose-to-nose with Mouse. "Now, get out of here before I make you wish you had."

Mouse stood her ground. "We're here to get Scratch and Dazzle free."

"As much as I'm touched by your story, I can't let that happen. See, I'm supposed to protect this place. If I let them escape, it'll look like I'm not doing my job."

Mouse had calmed a bit and noticed the name *Butch* engraved on the tag that hung from the bulldog's collar.

"I understand," Mouse said. "See, I'm a Protector."

Butch raised his eyebrows. "A Protector?"

"That's right," Scratch said. "So you just better move aside."

"I can't do that," Butch said. "I have a job to do, and that's the only reason they keep me around. If I don't do my job, it could be me they dispose of next."

"Oh, that's terrible," Little Foot said.

"Hey, cat," Butch said.

"It's Mouse," she said.

"I know it's a mouse," Butch said. "I just didn't know if you knew it's on your back."

"No," Mouse said, "my name is Mouse. And yes, the mouse on my back is my friend. Her name is Little Foot."

"My name is Butch," he replied.

"I know," Mouse said. "It's on your collar tag."

"Oh my," Butch said and scratched the side of his head. "A cat who reads and makes friends with mice. This happened to me once before when I ate some bad dog food. I must be having a bad dream or something."

Mouse and her friends pushed past him, entered the back area, and went down a central hall that was lined on both sides with cages. Mouse could see through the bars; she spotted dogs, cats, a few animals she didn't recognize, and a raccoon.

"Wow," Mouse said. "I didn't know there'd be so many. How could this be?"

"Takes it from me, kid," Sikes said. "Peoples just don't care sometimes. And this is where whatever they cast away ends up."

Sikes and Rascal lived in the alley by the complex that Mouse patrolled. She learned from Rascal that Sikes hadn't always been an alley cat but had once been a house cat; he left his home to take care of the others.

"What's going to happen to them?" Mouse asked.

"If no one comes for them"—Sikes put his paw across his throat in a slashing motion—"it's the end of the road."

"Don't," Rascal said.

"Don't what?" Mouse asked.

"We can't take all of them with us. We came for Scratch and Dazzle."

"We just can't leave them behind."

"How would you explain this to Chief? He's already going to be mad that we didn't tell him about this. Besides, where would they go?"

They had turned around and had gone back to a side room they'd passed along the way when Sikes spotted Scratch and Dazzle in a cage. "There they is," Sikes said and pointed with his right paw.

Scratch was a mostly gray cat with some white stripes and white feet. Dazzle was white with gray stripes and had some black on him, including his feet, which were colored in such a way to make it look like he wore dancing shoes.

"Oh, look at them; they look all well fed and groomed and all." Sikes got as close as he could to the front of the cage. "Psst! Wake up, yous guys."

Scratch slowly opened his eyes and spotted the group in front of him. He tapped Dazzle on the shoulder, and he woke up as well.

"My, oh my," Dazzle said. "Looks like a rescue party and just in time. I was thinking we'd never get out of this place."

Little Foot went into the cage. In a moment she had pried the door open, and both cats came forward. The noise of the door opening caused the cat beside them to wake.

"Jinx," Mouse said to the black-and-white cat in the cage next to Scratch and Dazzle.

"How did you know my name?"

"It's written on your cage," Mouse said.

"You can read?"

"Yes. Can't you?"

"No. I never learned what the letters meant."

"How did you end up in here?"

"That's my whole story there in my name," the small female cat said. "No matter what I do, something always goes wrong. I had an owner, and I broke some stuff, so she gave me away. Then my next owner left me in her car with the sunroof open. I saw this butterfly, and I just wanted to take a look, but it kept flying so I kept following. Next thing I knew I couldn't find my way back."

"Maybe we can …" Mouse didn't get to finish her sentence as Sikes patted her on the head.

"Come on, kid," Sikes said. "We's gots to go now before something goes wrong."

They were about to leave the room when they heard another low growl. Butch, who had obviously taken another route through the building to head them off, was blocking their way. His lower teeth were exposed through folds of skin.

"Just what is going on here?" Butch said. "I told you I can't let you take those cats."

"This is a rescue," Mouse said. "These two cats have a home, and we've come to take them back."

Rascal, Scratch, and Dazzle slowly stepped to the side and started to move around the bulldog.

"Wait a minute here," Butch said. "Where do you think you're going? Want me to put you in the hospital?"

Rascal said, "Hey, we're just like you, cast aside, no family. But we stuck together and made ourselves our family. We just came to get them because they don't belong in here."

Before Butch could respond, Carl flew around the corner and buzzed Butch's head with a loud squawk.

"Now's your chance," Carl said as he did an aerial U-turn and headed down the hall. "Sikes has the front door open."

The diversion caused Butch to turn, and the three cats ran past him. Then Butch recovered his position and stood squarely in front of Mouse. Mouse, not wanting to truly hurt the dog, retracted her claws and took a swipe across his face so she could escape.

Eyes wide, Butch's head went to his right as Mouse hit him. His body didn't move, but as soon as his jaw went to the side, Mouse and Little Foot ran to his left and went past him.

"Ouch, that hurt."

Mouse stopped, worried because she'd hurt him.

"What are you doing?" Little Foot said.

"I'm sorry," Mouse said as she turned to Butch. "I tried to not hurt you, but you've got to understand. These are our friends, and we had to do something. I hope we don't get you in trouble."

"Well," Butch said, rubbing his face with his back paw. "It didn't really hurt as much as it surprised me. For someone so small, you pack a pretty good right cross."

"My dad taught me," Mouse said.

Butch moved his jaw around. "If your friend opened the front door, it set off the alarm, and someone will be here in a few minutes."

"Will that get you in trouble?"

Butch tilted his head to the left. "You know, if we clean the cages your friends were in to make it look like no one was in them ... well, there are so many animals in here they probably won't even notice those two are gone. Will you help me?"

Mouse and Little Foot went back down the hall and helped Butch make the cages look like no animals had been in them by emptying the dishes and straightening the toys. Standing beside him, Mouse noticed how large Butch actually was, compared to her. His brown and white colors ran along his sides and down around his face. Overall, he looked rather pleasant to her with his floppy folds of skin.

"The only reason I do this job is so they don't get rid of me. I used to be in a house—comfortable carpet and couch to lie on. They feed me good, but I don't really get to play anymore, and floor is hard."

"Why do you stay?" Mouse asked.

"I have nowhere else to go." Butch pointed to the cages. "You see, animals with no place to go end up here. Most don't make it out."

"Oh."

"You're really a Protector?"

"Yes, my father is too," Mouse said. "You know about the Protectors?"

"Just stories, mostly, about how they are supposed to be good and all," Butch said. "But I've never met one. I mean, for the most part, dogs and cats aren't usually in the same crowds."

"Well, I can be your friend," Mouse said.

Butch turned and looked at Mouse. "Do you know your eyes are different colors?"

"Yes, I know," Mouse said. "My mom tells me that's what makes me unique and not to let it worry me."

"Sounds like good advice," Butch said. "I always get made fun of because of all this extra skin hanging down." He put his paw to his face and flexed his cheeks.

"I think it looks marvelous," Little Foot said. "Compared to all of the other dogs I've seen, which isn't many, it gives you a unique character, just like Mouse's eyes make her unique."

"She's a polite little mouse, isn't she?"

Mouse nodded.

"You don't want to be my friend," Butch said. "The other animals in here don't like me because of the job I have. My advice to you is to stay as far away from this place as you can." The group started walking to the door. "By the way, how did you get in here?" Butch asked.

Mouse nodded and glanced to Little Foot.

"I'm very flexible," Little Foot said. "I crawled under the front door and unlocked a window."

"Oh no," Butch said, and they heard sounds from the front of the office. "That means the silent alarm went off when you got here, and someone's already here."

"What do we do?" Mouse said.

"Come on," Butch said. "There's a back way out of this place."

Mouse and Little Foot followed Butch as he ran back down the hall, past the cages of animals, to a back door. Mouse felt the excitement of a chase build inside of her, and her heart pounded. At the same time, she couldn't help but take a good look at her surroundings, something her senses did automatically. In doing this, she noticed the animals in cages were all awake and watched as she went by. It bothered her to see them locked up.

"There," Butch said. "That's my little door to the back. It opens by a signal from my collar." He went and stood next to the door so it would open for them. "Do me a favor, and keep your friend safe. I don't want to see any of you here again." Butch turned and went back to the hallway, barking as he did.

"Thanks for the help, Butch!" Mouse called out as she went through the back door and ran around the side to the alley.

"They're over here," Mouse heard one of the pigeons call out. She ran down the alley and carefully crossed the street back to the rally point, where the rest of the group waited.

"We were about to mount another rescue," Colonel Wellington said.

"No," Mouse said. "We're fine. Is everyone else out?"

"Yes. They've already started back," Carl said. "I think Sikes and them were so caught up they didn't even notice you weren't out yet."

"Then it's time to go."

"Well," Colonel Wellington said, "it was an honor to join you and your team in an adventure once again." He saluted Mouse, and she did her best to salute back as the pigeons took flight. Only Carl remained.

"Thank you for the help, Carl," Mouse said.

Carl raised his crest and cleared his throat. "Well, seeing as how a new strategy needed to be implemented immediately, I couldn't help but intervene. After all, Colonel Wellington and his brigade are a fine specimen of order and execution but not really adept at improvisation."

"What does all of that mean?" Little Foot asked.

"I think he means when things don't go exactly as planned, he's not good at figuring stuff out."

"That's it," Carl said. "Now, if you won't be needing me any further, I would prefer not to be out at this time of night." Carl took off, flying toward the apartment complex.

With Little Foot on her back, Mouse headed back to the apartment complex, catching up to Sikes, Rascal, Scratch, and Dazzle. She could hear the alley cats talking and celebrating.

"It was Mouse's idea," Rascal said. "In fact, she's kind of a hero now. She took on Bragar and all of those bad rats back at the place, and now everything is back to normal. Even Chief is okay."

"Is that so?" Dazzle said. "Maybe we'll have to write a song for her to celebrate."

"Speaking of celebrations," Sikes said, "yous guys missed old Paggs retiring. Now Chief is patrolling what used to be Paggs's building, and Mouse here has her own building, and Baxter is still doing his. Isn't that right, kid?"

"That's right," Mouse said, flexing her shoulders up as she did so. "I'm officially a Protector, just like my dad."

"Hey, where is your dad anyway?" Scratch asked.

"He doesn't know about this," Mouse said. "I didn't want to worry him."

"Don't you think he's going to find out?"

"I came up with a plan to keep him busy so he wouldn't notice I was gone." Mouse walked along with the other cats, hoping her plan to keep her dad occupied would work until she returned home.

High on the roof of the apartment complex, Chief crept slowly along the edge, watching and listening for movement. He'd been on top of all three buildings of the apartment complex, which he guarded with the help of his daughter, Mouse, and another adult cat, Baxter. Baxter was a muscular, black, short-haired male cat with a single spot of white on his chest. He had several ear scars, indicating he had seen action. Although he had been at the complex longer than Chief, he had bowed out of taking charge because of Chief's reputation as the "Bronx Bruiser" and because Chief was a Protector, a special kind of cat descended from an ancient line.

He could hear Baxter moving on the other side across from him but sensed no other presence. It seemed to Chief that what they were after was more ghost than real.

Chief jumped across several cooling towers and landed in front of Baxter. "You sure you saw something up here?"

"I thought so," Baxter said.

"Well, we've been looking for hours and haven't seen anything."

"You sure there wasn't anything on that side?" Baxter asked.

Chief noticed Baxter looking down at the alley between the buildings, and his eyes widened.

"Did you spot something?" He tried to get close to the edge, but Baxter moved in.

"I thought I saw it again, over there." Baxter pointed to the other side of the building.

This time, Chief didn't run or respond. He wondered how Baxter had spotted something on the other side when he had been looking down in front of where they both were standing. Still, Chief decided he'd check. He moved his ears and reached out with his senses; he had a keener set than most cats, which now told him there was nothing there. "Okay, what's going on?" Chief said as he nudged past Baxter and looked down to the alley. There, he spotted a group of cats coming in from the street.

"Nothing," Baxter said. "Hey, let's go check my place one more time and call it a night."

"It's too late," Chief said. "I've already seen them." Chief trotted along the outside of the roof toward the fire escape and started heading down to the alley.

"Look," Baxter said, keeping stride with him. "I can explain."

"You mean you can explain how my daughter went out on one of her adventures again, and you tried to cover for her but blew it?"

"Uh, well," Baxter said.

"Look." Chief stopped for moment. "You should have just told me."

"Oh, right," Baxter said.

"What does that mean?"

"You remember how upset you got when you found out Mouse took a trip to see the motel you stayed at before you ended up here? And when you found out she was going to see Wilber?"

"He's a rat!" Chief said.

"But he's an ally and keeps the sewers clear around our buildings because of your daughter."

"She actually goes to the sewer and eats spaghetti with him," Chief said.

"I think it's cool," Baxter said, "although I don't know much about spaghetti."

"Well, maybe when you have your own kids to worry about, you'll understand."

"Mouse is like my own kid," Baxter said. "And she's a great one at that."

"I know," Chief said. "But she's got to learn that our priority is taking care of these apartments and that her running all around town on these adventures is a distraction." Chief started down the fire escape stairs again.

"I think you'll approve of this adventure," Baxter said.

The two cats made it to the bottom of the ladder, which was about eight feet from the ground, and jumped the rest of the way, landing in front of the group of cats coming down the alley.

"Well, I'll be," Chief said, surprised. "Scratch, Dazzle, is that you?" He looked upon two lanky cats, one that was gray with white stripes and the other white with gray stripes. The only difference between the two was their feet and that Scratch had a fluffier coat.

"You bets it's them," Sikes said. "The group's all back together."

The four alley cats walked by Chief and Baxter, saying hello as they passed, and went to the dumpsters they called home, leaving only Mouse and Little Foot in front of Chief.

"Hi, Dad," Mouse said.

"You can go, Baxter," Chief said. "Maybe you should go check around for that phantom you had me chasing all night."

"Sorry, kid, I did my best," Baxter said and disappeared down the alley.

"Hi, Mr. Chief," Little Foot said as she crawled down off Mouse's back.

"You should run along too, Little Foot," Chief said.

"Well, it's late, and I don't want Mom to worry," Mouse said and tried to get away.

"Just a minute, you," Chief said.

Mouse turned around slowly. "Don't you think Mom's going to worry about our being out so late?"

"I think she'll be fine," Chief said. "We're going to take a little walk around the perimeter. Who knows what all of you stirred up with your little adventure?" Chief started walking, and Mouse fell in beside him. The alley they were in ran between two of the fourteen-story towers that were part of a three-building newly developed apartment complex. The third building was behind the first two to the east. The main building, where Chief and Mouse resided, had another alley behind it, where the dumpsters were located and where the alley cats lived. Bordering this alley was a tall, six-foot concrete wall that ran along the entire back of both buildings, with a single gap where it opened to the third building. The main building, where Chief and Mouse resided, differed in that it was the model for the other two and had a larger lobby for receiving people.

The two cats headed around to the back of the complex and the third building, which was Baxter's building now. So Baxter had moved to that building, leaving Chief in charge of the first two.

"We don't have to do a patrol, Dad," Mouse said. "We can just talk if you're mad at me."

"I'm not mad at you," Chief said. "In fact, I'm very proud that you managed to execute a plan to free Scratch and Dazzle. I'm sure they're very happy to be back together. I just wish you would have told me."

"If I had told you, would you have let me go?" Mouse said. "Because when I told you about going to see Wilber, you didn't seem to like it."

"Those are two different things," Chief said. "Going to save cats is a lot different than you putting yourself in danger by visiting the sewers to see the head rat in this area."

"But I'm not in any danger," Mouse said. "I can take care of myself." She put out her right paw, claws extended, and slashed it across her body. "I learned that from you."

"Yes, very formidable," Chief said. "Still, the sewers are full of vermin, and Wilber has a darker side than you might know. You think he's in charge of all of those rats because they had a popularity contest, and he won?"

"I guess not," Mouse said. "Since Bragar is gone, Wilber is in complete control, and they kind of like me down there. I'm like a calibrity."

"You mean *celebrity*," Chief said.

"Oh, I guess that's right."

"It's still dangerous," Chief said. "And so is what you did tonight. You not only put yourself in danger but a lot of your friends." The two finished circling the last building and headed back along the alley behind the first two buildings. "Who else was with you besides the alley cats and Little Foot?"

"Carl, Colonel Wellington, and some pigeons," Mouse said.

"Ladie didn't go?"

"Ladie's afraid to leave the building," Mouse said. "She doesn't like to leave her room unless it's something important."

"Little Foot is pretty small to be running around out there; don't you think so?"

"But I'm there to protect her," Mouse said.

Chief tried to hold back his sigh. His daughter was putting up a good fight in the conversation, making points, but he felt she just didn't understand how small she was as a cat. He didn't want to say anything that would hurt her confidence.

"Besides," Mouse continued, "without Little Foot, we would have never got the door open."

"Hey, there's the hero!" Sikes and Rascal came out to greet Chief and Mouse as they passed the dumpsters. "Hopes you isn't bein' too hard on her an' all," Sikes said. "I know the boys appreciate it an' all. I would have never figures out how to do all that. I probably would've got myself captured."

Chief stopped and sniffed the air. "Where are they?" he asked.

"Ol' Scratch and Dazzle were so exhausted and worried from being in that place that as soon as we got back, they sacked out. I don't think the trash truck coming through here would wake them up."

"Okay," Chief said. "Well, it's good to have you all back. Now remember, the key is to keep a low profile." Chief knew Miss Sorenson, the complex manager, would immediately call animal control if she knew Scratch and Dazzle were out in the alley. Chief didn't mind that they were there, as long as they kept a low profile. They were an extra tier of security against other alley cats and vermin that threatened the complex.

Chief and Mouse rounded the building through the parking lot, which was quiet at this time of night. A few cars went by on the usually busy four-lane street that ran in front of the complex. He noticed Mouse was going slower.

"Are you tired?"

"Yes," Mouse said. "It's been a long day. I'm just glad you aren't that mad at me."

"Getting mad wouldn't do me any good," Chief said. "The truth is that as you get older, you have to start making your own decisions. I just want you to respect my advice and keep me informed. That's the same thing I would expect from Baxter and Sikes."

"Oh, I will next time. I promise I will," Mouse said as she pranced around her dad.

Chief put his paw out on her head and stopped her from circling him again. "That's not the point of our doing this patrol," Chief said. "I made you walk the perimeter of the complex tonight so you could understand how big this place is and how much territory falls under *our* responsibility. See, there are a lot of people depending on us, Mouse. Not just them but all the animals that call this place home, including Little Foot, Ladie, and your mom. There's no telling what may come along that will be the next test. You've got to realize your first responsibility is to your home and your family. Your running off on adventures can take you away from your duties here and put the place at risk. If you can't understand that, then maybe you aren't ready to make your own decisions."

As he stood facing Mouse, Chief also faced the road, while Mouse faced the large buildings behind him. He watched as her eyes went from one side of the complex to the other.

"I'm sorry, Dad," Mouse said. "You're absolutely right, and I'll be more careful."

"Thank you," Chief said. "Now let's get back inside for the night and get some sleep."

"Dad?"

"Yes, Mouse."

"You don't mind if I still go see Wilber, do you?"

"No," Chief said. "We need his support. It makes it a lot easier around here. I just want you to be careful; especially if you notice any changes in his behavior or if he's not in charge anymore."

"I'll be careful," Mouse said. "I hope nothing goes wrong, though. I would miss the spaghetti and meatballs."

Chief laughed. "I've never tried any."

"Maybe you should come with me one of these times when I visit him. I'm sure he won't mind. Also, you and he think alike in the way you run things."

"Really?"

"Sure. You're both organized and in charge, making sure everyone does his or her tasks. And you say a lot of the same things about respect and responsibility."

"I never imagined," Chief said.

CHAPTER 2
STRANGERS IN TOWN

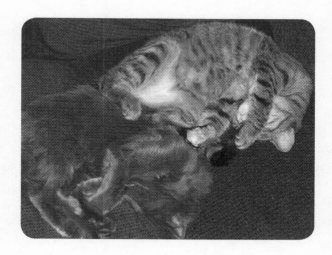

M oats shook his head and looked at Rocko, the large black cat, beside him. "Did we see what I think we did, Moats?" asked Rocko. "Yes, we did," Moats answered. The two cats sat in the bushes that lined the street across from the apartment complex that Chief and Mouse patrolled. After witnessing the group in the park and then watching the scene at the animal control center, they had followed the cats and their companions back to the complex.

"I don't believe it, but I've seen it," Rocko said. "A cat with a mouse riding on its back, talking and being friends with birds."

"See, I told you this neighborhood was different, Rocko," Moats said. "They probably have so much food here they don't even need to eat the mice and birds."

"You said it would be better coming this way," Rocko said.

"I did," Moats said. "Don't you forget whose idea it was either."

"Should I go tell the others?" Rocko asked.

"No," Moats said. "We followed them here for a reason. We won't tell the others until we know we have it all worked out."

"What if we run into trouble?"

"Did you see any cat in that group bigger than me?" Moats asked, flexing his shoulder muscles.

"No, I guess not."

"All right, then. Keep your head down, and be quiet. Let's just watch and see what else goes on." The two cats found it easy to follow the other group of cats, who had talked all the way back to the high-rise buildings and were too distracted to notice they were being followed.

"Looks like an expensive neighborhood," Rocko said. "Let's get a closer look." He had started to move forward when Moats put his paw out in front.

"Wait a minute."

"Sorry," Rocko said. "You first."

"Shh, that's not what I mean. Get down." The two cats went prone and watched the complex. "See?" Moats pointed his paw forward to two cats who had come around the parking lot of the buildings. One of the cats was the small black-and-white cat they'd seen earlier. The other, a large yellow-and-orange striped cat, moved with skill. "Look how that orange cat moves. He's observing even as he's talking to that little one. His steps are careful and calculated. He's no housecat with those muscles. I bet you he's the one who runs the joint. He's the one we'll have to deal with."

"I bet you there's all kinds of food behind these buildings," Rocko said, "just waiting for us. You think he'll be a problem?"

"When we bring our three pals back, there'll be five of us and only one of him and that smaller cat," Moats said. "There may be some others too, but they'll be weaker cats. I think we can handle them. Remember what we just witnessed—a cat being friends with rats and mice. For all I know, the rats run rampant in this area, just like they run the rail yards. We might have more problems with the rats than these cats, so we'll have to teach them a lesson and make sure they know who's in charge."

"Look, they're going in between the buildings now."

"Good," Moats said. "Let's take a look around. You take that side"—he pointed to the left—"and I'll take the far side. Stay back so no one can see you, and just look around to see if there are any more cats. Then we'll meet back here."

Moats watched Rocko for a moment before he went on his route to the far right of the complex. After crossing a double-lane road that wasn't too busy for the late hour, he made his way to a field of dirt. While there was nothing but a large abandoned lot on this side of the building, behind it there was a lot of construction equipment and materials. As he approached the back part of the building, he sensed the other cats from earlier in the evening and kept back. He could see the back alley between the first building and the construction site but couldn't see any cats.

"Hmm, they must be in that alley somewhere," he said to himself. He didn't linger long before returning across the road to find Rocko.

"I didn't see anything," Rocko said, coming back to the bushes where Moats waited.

"What about smells?"

"I could smell cats and just the one rat from earlier tonight. The place seems awful clean."

"I went around the other side," Moats said. "There's no sign or scent of any rats. That can't be happening unless they've paid them off somehow."

"Or maybe that cat is just that good," Rocko said.

"No way. Not with just a few cats. There're just too many vermin for a place to be this clean. There's something going down."

"We should take it over like we did the last place," Rocko said. "This time your son isn't around to sell you out."

Moats tackled Rocko and held him down with the claws of his left paw above his face.

"Hey," Rocko said, "take it easy, Moats. I was just suggesting."

"I'm going to suggest we take it slow," Moats said. "We went too fast last time, and look where it got us—back out on the street. This time we're going to do things my way."

"Sure," Rocko said as he slowly slid out from under Moat's grasp. "We'll do it your way. I'm sure we have plenty of time. So what do we do now?"

Moats went back to his prone position, where he watched the complex. "Let's settle in and observe some more. Once we know for sure what's going on and that there are only a few cats running the place, we'll head back and get the others."

"What about the rats?"

"They must be coming from that side"—he pointed to the side Rocko had investigated—"probably in some of the older buildings down that way or in the sewers. We'll find some of them and make sure they know who's in charge."

"Oh, I can't wait until we get into that alley and get some food," Rocko said.

Moats lowered his eyebrows and showed his teeth as he glared at Rocko. "But only when you say we can."

Mouse rolled out of her bed early the next morning in the two-bedroom apartment where she stayed with Chief and her mom, Charlene. Sam, their owner and the maintenance man for the complex, lived in the other room. Located on the first floor of the main building in the complex, it was down the hall from the lobby and conveniently located close to the elevators and stairwell. She went to the water dish to get a drink and overheard Sam talking in the hallway to Bill Ryan, the owner of the complex.

She peeked through the partially opened door to see her dad standing by Sam as he talked to Bill Ryan. Sam was a six-foot strong man with calloused hands, who usually shoved his mat of black hair under his hat but had reformed to combing it more often in the past few months. Bill Ryan, a suit-and-tie guy with city shoes, always had finely combed hair and was clean-shaven. She listened to the conversation.

"You've done an excellent job here with the complex, Sam," Bill Ryan said. "I would have never thought it possible when my wife insisted we try to go green and use cats to maintain the buildings. The construction workers couldn't believe we wanted pet doors on all of the apartments, and some of the tenants couldn't believe it was in their agreement. Mrs. Ryan told me cats had overtaken dogs as the number-one pet, and she was right. I've got to tell you; we've got a reputation as one of the safest and cleanest complexes in the city."

"Thank you," Sam said, smiling through his capped front teeth. He bent down and patted Chief on the head. "I owe it all to Chief, here," Sam said. "He's the one that keeps the vermin out."

"It's not just that, Sam," Bill said. "We need to continue a high level of maintenance and upkeep. And that's why I'm here."

"I'm sorry, sir," Sam said. "It's been really busy, and I'm trying to keep up. Did I miss something?"

"No, Sam, you're doing great. Now that all three buildings are nearly full of tenants, and a fourth building is underway, I can only imagine your schedule is full. I wanted you to consider bringing someone on to help you with your duties. I'll post the job in the papers and such, and you just think of some questions you can ask so you know you get someone who's qualified.

When you pick someone, send that person to Miss Sorenson, and I'll make sure she arranges an apartment and gets all the paper worked signed."

"You mean …" Sam hesitated. "You want me to do the hiring?"

"That's right, Sam," Bill said. "It comes with the territory. I'm promoting you to facilities manager of the complex now."

"Facilities manager?" Sam whispered.

"Oh, and there will be a raise with your new position as well. I hope I covered everything. Do you have any questions?"

"No, not at all, sir," Sam said. Bill shook his hand and headed down the hall to the lobby.

Mouse moved out of the way as Sam and Chief entered the apartment.

"Oh, hello there, little cat," Sam said as he reached down and patted Mouse on the head. She purred and rubbed against his leg. "Chief, we've just been promoted. We sure have come a long way from our motel days. I guess I'll have to figure out some things, like who to hire and how we're going to celebrate. He or she will have to be able to fix things and be on time. No smoking or bad habits like that and must love cats. Right?"

Chief purred and rubbed against Sam's leg.

"Maybe I can finally start thinking about buying a new truck. Well, I better get started on today's chores, my boy. But as soon as I get someone hired, I'll spend more time with you and the family." Sam grabbed his Colorado Rockies baseball cap, shoved his hair under it, and disappeared down the hall.

"Are you happy, Dad?" Mouse asked.

"Yes," Chief said. "I'm glad Sam will be getting some help because he seems tired all of the time."

"Just like you would be if I wasn't helping you, right?"

"That's right," Chief said and pounced over Mouse, landing right beside her.

She was ready for him, and as soon as he landed, she pounced and tackled him to the ground.

"You're so quick these days," he said and smiled. "Do you need any help?"

"Nope," Mouse said. "It's all under control. I'm going on patrol now, Dad." She headed out the door to the elevator. She would start her patrol at the top floor and make her way down, checking to make sure everything was in order. The elevator had an attendant for a large part of the day, but it was before eight o'clock, and he wasn't on duty yet. Mouse jumped and hit the button to signal the elevator. Once inside, she considered what else she was going to do during the day and how happy she was with the events of the morning. Seeing her dad and Sam happy made her feel happy, and she was still elated by the successful mission the night before.

One of her favorite places to go was Miss Doris's place because of her pet bird, Ladie. Miss Doris was an elderly woman who lived by herself on the fourteenth floor. Ladie was a pure-yellow canary that had a wonderful voice and lots of friends. Mouse exited the elevator on the fourteenth floor and headed down the hall to the apartment. She entered through the pet door and went to the bedroom and listened for Doris. Once she could tell her breathing was normal, Mouse headed to the living room, where Ladie lived in her cage. The cage was up on a high round table across from the window.

"Good morning," Mouse said. She jumped on the wooden stool that was across from Ladie's cage. Later in the day, Mouse knew the stool would be used for Ladie's clients, pigeons that would come to her for advice.

"Good morning, Mouse. I was hoping to see you this morning. One of my friends stopped by yesterday and said she had some good news about Paggs. But first, tell me how last night went."

"The mission was a success. We were able to get Scratch and Dazzle out of the animal control building," Mouse said. "They're back in the alley at this very moment. I also made a friend there, a bulldog named Butch."

A flutter of feathers distracted both Mouse and Ladie as Carl flew in through the open window.

"Yes," Carl said. "Another mighty adventure of Mouse, the cat! Pretty soon you'll have a bigger reputation than your father."

Mouse blushed, but seeing Ladie sitting in her cage set off a reminder, and her heightened feeling was tempered by the memory of the night before. In all her celebration for the success of the mission and the fact that everyone around the complex seemed happy, she thought about the animals they'd left behind at the shelter, sitting in their cages, and it bothered her.

"I can't believe it," Mouse said. "How could all of those animals need homes?"

"What's that?" Carl said.

"The animals at the shelter," Mouse said. "I didn't know there would be so many other animals there. Where do they come from? How can that many need homes?"

"I don't know," Ladie said.

"I'll tell you," Carl said. "I've been around, and I'm not so fond of it, I tell you. I had a great family and life where I was from, and they dragged us out to sell us as pets. Then people don't take care of us anyway. The best thing I ever did was get out of my cage. No offense, Ladie."

"It's okay, Carl. I have a good owner."

"Why don't you go back to your home?" Mouse asked.

"Oh, my home is really far away. I'm not sure I could find my way there. Besides, what would you do without me around to help you?"

"He's got a point, Mouse."

"You're right, Carl." Mouse said. "But there's still something we could do."

"What do you suggest?"

"We go back there and break those animals out," Mouse said. "Just like Scratch and Dazzle."

"Hmm." Carl tapped the end of his wing to his chin. "That does seem possible but not too simple."

"Carl," Ladie said, "even if you could get all of those animals out of there, where would they go?"

"Yes, that's the issue," Carl said. "That would be a problem. Quite a situation. I don't like situations that I can't solve. Where could all of those animals go? They wouldn't be able to stay here, and I suppose taking all those cats down to the theater wouldn't please Colonel Wellington. It's a tough situation, kid, but one we're unable to resolve at the current moment."

"If you think of any ideas, please let me know," Mouse said.

"I will inform you immediately," Carl said.

"You said you had some other news?" Mouse asked.

"Did you want to tell her the news about Paggs?" Ladie asked.

"Well, yes," Carl said. "One of the pigeons that reported to the theater this morning said he'd heard through the pigeon network that Paggs is settled in out there in the country. Found a farm and a barn full of—" Carl stopped and scanned the room.

"What is it?" Mouse asked.

"Little Foot isn't here, right?"

"No," Mouse said. "I can't take her on my patrols anymore. My dad says it's too dangerous that we might be seen together. She's in the furniture storage room."

"Okay, good. Well, I was telling you we received an update on Paggs. He is doing well and says there's plenty of—forgive me for saying—tasty field mice there and lots of space to relax."

"Hmm," Mouse said. "Have you ever been to the country, Carl?"

"I've been one better," he stated. "When I was as young as you, I lived in the forest. It was completely free of humans and buildings. Full of space where we could fly and be free. Of course, I couldn't fly yet, but I remember seeing hundreds of birds just like me. Oh, it was true freedom."

Carl was still talking as Mouse stood and walked out of the room to continue her patrol, so consumed in her thoughts she forgot to tell Ladie and Carl goodbye. She went down each floor from one end to the other, smelling and listening for any sign of trouble, until she settled on the fifth floor, which held the laundry room and a large furniture-storage room, where Little Foot lived. Mouse went to the end of the hall and entered the storage room.

"Little Foot, I'm here," she called out as she entered through the pet door. The furniture-storage room was the same size as all the other apartments but had no interior walls and was just a large, empty room full of couches, chairs, and a few bed frames and mattresses. Mouse and Little Foot found it a convenient place to play and train, as it was usually free of people.

Little Foot emerged from behind a couch pillow on the floor. She walked straight up to Mouse and poked at her paws. "You know, I thought once you got older your paws wouldn't be so fluffy, and I would be able to hear you coming down the hall better. I can hear Baxter and your dad and all those people"—she stood on her hind legs and raised her front paws, walking in big steps—"stomping around with their big feet. Stomp, stomp, stomp. But I still can't hear you."

"That's because I'm stealthy," Mouse said. Little Foot stopped her display of stomping and turned to Mouse. "I guess it's good I to have some advantages since I'll never be as big and strong as my dad."

"Did you get in trouble last night?" Little Foot asked.

"No, not really. My dad just wants me to focus on taking care of my responsibilities first and not worry about everything else."

"You mean being a Protector and all?"

"I guess so," Mouse said. "I just wish I could figure out what to do about all those other animals we saw last night."

"I know," Little Foot said, twitching her whiskers. She sat back and put her right paw to her chin.

"You mean it's bothering you too?"

"I can't figure out how that could happen."

"What do you mean?"

"I came from a pet store. And I'm sure there were lots of animals just like those we saw last night, except people would pay for them. Why would there be a place where people pay for animals when they can get animals at a shelter? It doesn't make sense."

"As I get older," Mouse said, "lots of things don't make sense. Do you think all those animals we saw last night were lost pets?"

"It could be," Little Foot said. An intense look of concentration overtook her as she glanced toward the ceiling and tapped her fingers along her chin. "Maybe Butch knows. We could go see him again and have another adventure."

"We can't," Mouse said. "After the talk I had with my dad, I think I should stick around here for a while and do my patrols. Besides that, Scratch and Dazzle are supposed to have a homecoming party tonight."

"Good," Little Foot said. "Maybe they'll play a song like they used too. What are we going to do until tonight? Can we do some training today? I've really been practicing my pouncing and my tracking skills."

"I have to finish the rest of my patrol first," Mouse said. "Then I'll come back. Until I do, please stay out of sight."

Mouse continued her patrol through every floor and then headed out to the side alley and back toward the new construction site, where the alley cats hid during the day. She let her nose lead her to the nearest scent of cat and found Scratch sitting among some stacked pallets on a tarp.

"Hey, what you doing out here?" Scratch asked. "You usually don't patrol out here; only your dad does. Is it part of your new duties?"

"No," Mouse said. "I usually just patrol the building, but I was curious and had a question for you."

"What is it?"

"When you were in the animal control building, did you get to know many of the other animals?"

"Sure, we didn't get out of our cages much so there wasn't anything to do but talk."

"Why were all of those animals in there? Did any of them have owners that were coming to get them?"

"No, I don't think they had owners, not anymore anyway. Some of them had been taken there by their owners who were moving or didn't want them anymore. It's a sad story, I'm afraid."

What Scratch told her only made her feel worse about the animals she had met.

"I'm working on a new song for tonight. Dazzle is going to sing it, and he's working out some dance steps back there in that construction site."

Mouse knew Scratch got his name because he could scratch out a tune on a guitar. Dazzle was a dancer who could dance and sing. The two often performed in the alley after all the people were in bed.

"I'm looking forward to it," Mouse said. "I'll see you tonight." She was heading back to the side of the building when she heard Scratch.

"Don't forget to come tonight. You're the guest of honor."

Mouse walked back to the apartment complex, troubled by the news Scratch had given her about the animals and irritated that she could find no plan of how to help. She entered her apartment to find it empty. Sam and her mom and dad were all gone. She went to one of the many pet beds and lay down. She wasn't sure if it was the late night yesterday or the weight of the problem she carried that made her tired, but Mouse slept.

"Time to wake up." Mouse heard her father's voice and opened her eyes. "Scratch and Dazzle are going to be sorely disappointed if you don't go to their party tonight," he said. "You must have been tired from last night's adventures."

"I was," Mouse said as she stood and stretched. "I haven't done my second patrol yet."

"Then you better get to it; you're already late," Chief said.

"Are you going?"

"I might stop by," Chief said. "Sam's been working on some stuff in the basement, and I will probably stay close to him until he's done."

"This late?"

"Yes. That's exactly why he needs to get some help around here."

"I'll see you later, Dad," Mouse said and headed out to the hall. She wasn't sure of the time, but the lack of traffic in the hallway and the fact that the elevator attendant was off duty let her know it was late. She started on the top floor this time and knew she needed to hurry, not only to get to the party but because she was sure Little Foot would be upset that she never returned to play.

Mouse exited the elevator on the fifteenth floor. There was only one apartment on this floor, and it was currently vacant. It had been the apartment where Bill Ryan and his wife lived while the complex was being finished, but they had moved out. Mouse sensed her mom had been up on the floor recently. Her mom once lived with Mrs. Ryan in the apartment and sometimes visited her old home.

"I guess I don't have to check the place if my mom's been here," Mouse said and headed down the stairs, floor by floor, doing a quick check, until she ended up at the furniture-storage room. She entered the door in rush and immediately spotted something coming at her from the left.

"Ha!" Little Foot yelled. She jumped at Mouse but overshot her, as Mouse ducked and Little Foot flew across, tumbling onto the floor. She lay there for a moment before turning over.

"Are you okay?" Mouse asked.

"Just give me a minute," Little Foot said. "I practiced that move all day, but that wasn't what I planned."

"You came really close to getting me," Mouse said. "You probably just got too excited at the last moment and jumped too far. But it was an impressive distance."

Little Foot stood and shook her head. "You think so?"

"Definitely," Mouse said. "Sorry for not coming back sooner. I fell asleep."

"Me too," Little Foot said. "We were out kind of late last night."

"Then we should be well rested for the party tonight." Mouse smiled. "Do you want to go?"

Little Foot clapped her front paws together. "Yes!"

Mouse stuck her head out of the pet door and scanned the hallway. "Okay, the coast is clear." She stepped out into the hallway, with Little Foot crawling under her. Since they were both the same color, it was nearly impossible to see the little mouse. They went to the end of the hallway, down the stairs to the second floor, and out the window. From there, Mouse let Little Foot go on her own to the alley. The two rounded the corner to find the alley cats, along with Chief, Charlene, Baxter, Carl, and Colonel Wellington, already assembled. Everyone cheered when Mouse entered the alley. She smiled at her dad, who surprised her by being there.

"There were many involved in getting us back home," Dazzle said. "Without Mouse to lead the planning and convince everyone to go, we might still be in those cages. Thank you, Mouse!"

Scratch and Dazzle lived up to their names that night in the alley as they performed their songs, and Dazzle sang and danced. He stopped only to introduce his new song.

"This song goes out to a cat who has her own groove and knows where it's at," Dazzle said. "She's someone near and dear to all of us, and although she often thinks she's too small, she is really a giant when it comes to having style. This song is dedicated to her."

All the cats and Little Foot gathered around. Scratch started playing the guitar, and Dazzle danced out in the middle of the group and started singing.

> You can have fortune and fame,
> And everyone knows your name.
> Without this one quality,
> It won't last long, you see.
>
> *Style—*
> It's always in.
> You can always win with
> *Style.*
> It's all the rage.
> You can't take the stage
> Without style.
> It's not just a material thing,
> Not that you dance or you sing,
> Not the clothes you wear,
> The way you do your hair—
> It's more of a natural thing,
> *Style.*
>
> Actions and reactions can create distractions.
> Don't let it get the best of you.
> To yourself always stay true
> With style.
>
> When someone sees
> It's the things you do
> When no one's watching you,
> That's your style.
>
> It's all about who you are.
> Without, you won't go far.
> It's in all the raves—
> Everybody craves
> *Style.*

It's not just a material thing,
Not that you dance or you sing,
Not the clothes you wear,
The way you do your hair—
It's more of a natural thing,
Style.

Applause erupted from everyone in the alley as Scratch took a bow.

"Thanks, guys," Mouse said. "That song means a lot." She felt better than she had earlier in the day but still needed a place to think. The excitement of being recognized a hero was still dimmed by the feeling of those she couldn't help. She decided to go to the roof of her building to get away from everyone. To do so, she climbed the fire escape

Mouse walked along the outer edge of the building. When she was learning how to patrol, her father had taken her to the top of the buildings to show her the view; now she came here when she wanted to be alone and think. The lights of the distant city and its tall buildings were beautiful, but the view couldn't match the other one she preferred, that of the stars above. Suddenly, her instincts kicked in, and she whirled around, sensing something was on the roof with her. She lowered her ears and listened. In a moment, she relaxed, recognizing the black form that approached her.

"I wish I was all black," Mouse said. "It sure works good for sneaking around."

"I thought I might find you up here," Baxter said. "You left Scratch and Dazzle's party kind of early, didn't you?"

"You don't think I was rude?" Mouse asked.

"No," Baxter said. He sat down beside her. "Wow, there's a great view from here at night, wouldn't you agree?"

"That's why I came up here," Mouse stated.

"Is that the only reason?"

"No. I needed to think."

"What's on your mind? You've been sort of quiet since you came back from rescuing Scratch and Dazzle. Did that run-in with the bulldog shake you up?"

"You heard that part?"

"Carl has told the entire neighborhood about his daring rescue and how he swooped in to help you."

"No," Mouse said. "Butch, the bulldog, was actually really nice and just doing his job. It was what I saw when I was in there—all the other animals in cages." She remembered Jinx the most. The face of the small black-and-white cat reminded Mouse of herself, including that Jinx had a confidence problem, which Mouse often had struggled with herself since she was small.

"Yes, it's a problem. People used to keep pets as part of the family, part of the household. Little Foot, Carl, Sikes, and even your mom, Charlene, were all forgotten by their owners."

"How can that be?" Mouse asked. "How can people just forget about their pets?"

"I don't know, kid. You and your dad are lucky to have Sam; he's a great person. Paggs and me, we were just around because we did a job. When I see how these people treat each other sometimes, it's no wonder we're becoming less important when we can't even talk back. I wouldn't let it get you down."

Mouse didn't respond, but she couldn't help but think about the situation and worry. She wasn't good at accepting bad situations and that's what usually got her into trouble. Somehow she knew, as she sat and watched the stars, that this would be no different.

> Look up at the stars so bright—
> I make a wish,
> A fantastic wish, tonight.
> Places to go,
> Things to see—
> Countless adventures
> Are waiting for me.
>
> Calling out to me,
> Calling out to me.
> I open my eyes—
> What will I see
> Calling out to me?
>
> I walk along the edge
> Of a great unknown.
> Take a step past the walls,
> I might find I'm on my own.
> Should I stay, or should I go?

Part of me doesn't know.
Frightened and excited,
Maybe so.
Doesn't change the way I feel—
Voice that seems so real
Calling out to me.

Tells me of all the things I'm going to see,
Glorious places waiting,
Waiting for me.
Countless wonders
Just beyond
That boundary.

Take a step;
Take a leap.
Just wait and see
All of the wonders
Waiting,
Waiting for me.

Calling out to me,
Calling out to me.
I open my eyes—
What will I see?
All of the wonders
Waiting … waiting for me.

Mouse knew she needed a plan. The best person to talk to would be Carl; he was always creating plans and coming up with ideas. "That's it! I'll find him in the morning."

The next morning, Mouse started her day with her normal patrol but decided she'd begin at the bottom and work her way up. She wanted to spend additional time at Miss Doris's apartment so she could talk to Ladie, who was always someone who could cheer her up. It was also the place where she was most likely to see Carl. She hoped he'd come up with a plan, and if not, she was forming a plan that would involve enlisting the help of Butch, the watchdog at the animal control office. She was heading out of the apartment when Chief caught her.

"Wait a minute there," Chief said. "Where are you going in such a hurry?"

"To do my morning patrol," Mouse said.

"Without any breakfast and without saying good morning to your mom? I don't think so. I know I taught you to stay lean and fit, but totally skipping breakfast will make you sluggish later."

"Sorry," Mouse said and went to the food dish. In the evening, Sam usually fed them fish. In the morning, they ate dried food. Mouse crunched down a few mouthfuls and, with her mouth still slightly full, peeked in to where Charlene sat in the second bedroom. "Hello, Mom. I'm going on patrol now and wanted to wish you a good morning."

"Thank you, Mouse," Charlene said. "Say hello to Ladie for me."

"I will," Mouse said and started toward the door. She turned to her father. "Was that better?"

Chief nodded and grinned.

"You have a good morning too, Dad," Mouse said and hurried to the stairs. She normally took the elevator but kept with her decision to start at the lower floors today. She liked riding the elevator when it was early in the morning, before the attendant arrived, because she didn't have to worry about the awkwardness of riding with him in the elevator. He had once tried to shoo her out of the elevator, and she reminded him that she was the Protector of the building by showing him her claws. Since that time, she always felt a little uncomfortable with him in the elevator, although he now left her alone and even stepped to the back when she got in.

Mouse did her patrol while constantly considering plans on how to help the animals she'd seen in the animal control building. She couldn't remember half of what she had done before she ended up on the fourteenth floor and ran down the hallway to Miss Doris's apartment. She was surprised to find that Miss Doris had already left the apartment. She went to the living room to see Ladie.

"Miss Doris is eating breakfast at the cafeteria," Ladie said. "She got up early today for some reason. I think it's because her niece called last night and is planning on stopping by today. She seems to be happy to have a visitor and got up early and started cleaning and straightening everything."

"That's good," Mouse said. She moved from her position on the floor to the stool by Ladie's cage. "My dad told me I'm always to begin my patrol by checking on her. I guess if she got up early and is already eating breakfast, then she is fine."

"It's good that you check on her," Ladie said. "I enjoy your visits as well. Did you have fun at the party for Scratch and Dazzle last night?"

"Sure," Mouse said. "They even did a new song for me about style, and it was great."

"It's good that everyone is back together and things are going so well around the apartment. We all owe that to you and your dad."

What Ladie said should have made Mouse feel great, but it didn't. She looked to the windowsill. "Has Carl been by this morning?"

"Not yet," Ladie said. "He usually comes when Doris is at breakfast. He might be here any time now. Did you want me to tell him something?"

"Something's been on my mind lately. I've been thinking too much about the other animals at the center. I can't get them out of my mind, no matter what everyone tells me. I still feel like there's something I need to do. There was a cat—her name was Jinx—that looked like me, just a little bigger is all. She could have been my sister. Everyone keeps telling me that those animals aren't my problem and that I need to worry about the apartments. It just doesn't feel right. I was hoping Carl might help me with a plan."

"You have a compassionate heart," Ladie said. "It's hard to turn away when you see something that isn't quite right, but we can't always change the world. It's too big of a place. Sometimes all we can worry about is just our little corner."

"I feel helpless," Mouse said.

"There are many times we feel down, and it affects us to the point that we even get depressed."

"Even you?"

"Even me," Ladie said. "I live with an elderly person whom I care about a lot, but she has many health problems and is often in pain. I give advice to pigeons who are often brokenhearted and feeling helpless, just like you."

"I guess I can see why you would get down," Mouse said.

"That's when I say turn it around."

"What?" Mouse asked.

"Turn it around," Ladie said and started singing:

> Sometimes I just wanna cry.
> I don't know why.
> Got sand in my eyes.

I turn away
So no one sees.
I just can't be me
When I'm feeling down.

I turn it around;
Turn it around.
I'm not getting lost in the crowd.
I'm going to shout out loud
And turn it around.

Don't let what's wrong go unchanged
Because you look away.
It's time to stop the pain
And come in from the rain.
There's got to be a better way
To turn it around.

This world can push us all too far.
Stand up for who you are.
What you do is up to you.
Time for us to see this through.
Turn it around;
Turn it around;
Turn it around.
Don't get lost in the crowd.
Stand up and shout it out loud
And turn it around.

Sometimes I just want to cry.
I don't know why.
It's just the way I feel
When things get me down.
Turn it around.
I'll turn it around.

Carl, who had come in during the song and sat on the bench beside Mouse, joined Mouse in applause as Ladie finished singing. "An inspiring song, if I may say so," Carl said. "I may have to learn that one. Wouldn't you agree, Mouse?"

"Yes," Mouse said. "A wonderful song." The words inspired Mouse, and she knew she must undertake another adventure to help the animals she'd seen at the center. It was the only way for her to make a difference. She turned to Carl. "I have another mission and need your help."

"Oh?" Carl's voice raised in tone. "Another adventure!"

"Not the kind I would like, but one we need to do. We need to help the animals that are stuck in that place, but it will take a lot more time to rescue all of them," she said, pointing in the direction of the animal control building. "I can't just do *nothing.*"

"Hmm." Carl put his wing to his chin. "It sounds like a complex mission. I'll have to think about this. We're going to need air support again. But it can be done. Anything can be done if we put our minds to it."

"Carl, do you think you can get a message to Colonel Wellington for me?"

"Sure. What do you suggest?"

"If we get him and some others I have in mind together in the alley, we can convince them to help us. We need to keep it confidential."

"No problem," Carl said. "They'll just look at it as another of your adventures."

"The most challenging one yet!"

The night was dark, with clouds covering the moon and stars, as Mouse made it out of the building and went around the corner to the meeting place. After a few minutes of being in the alley, she heard the distinct flap of two sets of wings. Carl and Colonel Wellington made their landing in front of her. The noise brought Scratch and Dazzle out from the dumpsters and into the alley.

"Hey, what you two doing here at this time of night?" Dazzle asked.

"Mouse asked us to come," Colonel Wellington said. "I do hope it's for another exciting mission."

"It is," Mouse said. "Scratch, Dazzle, I wanted you to be part of this meeting."

"Sikes and Rascal are down at the park," Dazzle said. "They like to go down there and stargaze."

"That's okay," Mouse said. "This is just for your ears. You see, I think that you, Dazzle, and Carl—more than anyone—can empathize with the pets we left behind in that building."

"Yeah," Dazzle said. "It's too bad for them. If our alley was bigger and we weren't always afraid of being discovered and such, maybe we could've taken a few of them with us and all. Hey, don't let that get you down."

"What do you mean?" Mouse asked.

"I could tell you were a little down at the party. Is it because of the animals at the shelter?"

"Yes," Mouse said. "I keep thinking about them."

"I see," Dazzle said. "There's a whole big world out there. Too big for us to change everything or worry about everything. If we try, it could crush us. That's why I say you can't worry about all of that. It's too big for you to control. Just worry about your little corner."

"That's not a good attitude," Mouse said. "I've been feeling bad for days, and Ladie recommended I find a way to turn it around. It starts by not looking away."

"What do you mean?" Dazzle asked.

"Ladie agree that we need to make a difference where we can. I think the reason I keep thinking about those animals at the shelter is because I'm supposed to help them—just not by myself. Won't you help me?"

Dazzle took on a serious look. "Sure, kid. You don't have to do things on your own. We're all here to support you."

"Then we're going back. We're going to break them out."

"Like you did for us," Dazzle said. "That's probably impossible, you know."

"No, it's not."

"I don't think you've fully thought this out."

"What? What is it?" Mouse asked.

"I was just wondering if you've thought about what we're going to do once we get all of them out."

"We're going to take them to the country," Mouse said.

Scratch and Dazzle looked at each other and then back to Mouse.

"There's supposed to be plenty of space there and plenty of ..." She hesitated and looked at Little Foot, who smiled at her. "Uh, food," she finished. "That's what your message from Paggs said, right, Carl?"

"Yes, but—"

"That sounds like an idea," Scratch said. "I've never been to the country. Is it far away?"

"Sounds far away," Dazzle said. "How do we get there?"

"Maybe we can ask someone," Scratch said. "Do you know how to get there?" He looked at Mouse.

"No," Mouse said. "I was hoping you guys knew how to get there."

Both Scratch and Dazzle shook their heads.

"Paggs!" Dazzle said. "He was going there; he would know."

"Except he's already gone there," Scratch said.

"Good point," Dazzle said. "What else do we have?"

"I don't know. Rascal and Sikes come from the city, so they won't know how to get there."

"I haven't been there," Carl said.

"Neither have I," Colonel Wellington said. "But we do have outposts clear out by the farms. We could send word back along our way to keep everyone informed."

"We still need to know how to get there," Mouse said.

"What about Streets?" Little Foot said.

"Yes," Scratch said. "The streets must go there if we can just find out which one to follow."

"Oh, definitely," Dazzle said. "And we should travel by night; it's safer."

"No," Little Foot said. "That's not what I meant."

"What about Baxter?" Mouse asked.

"He comes from Queens," Scratch said. "That's definitely not the country."

Little Foot walked in front of Mouse and reached up, grabbing her whiskers and pulling Mouse's face in front of hers.

"What is it?" Mouse asked.

"You aren't listening! Streets knows everything that's going on," Little Foot said. "Remember his song? He helped Paggs get to the country and might know how to get us there."

"Of course!" Mouse said. "I'll find him. Until then, we need to keep this between us. Agreed?"

"Agreed," Scratch and Dazzle said.

CHAPTER 3
SPAGHETTI FOR DINNER

"I'm going to see Wilber today," Mouse said to her dad before she left for her morning patrol.

"Be careful," Chief said. "Remember the other day when Baxter was leading me around, chasing shadows?"

"Sorry," Mouse said. "He was supposed to be diversioning you so you didn't know I was gone."

"You mean *diverting*," Chief said. "My senses usually tell me if something is going wrong, and that night I couldn't find anything, so I knew we weren't in any danger. Baxter should have known he couldn't fool me."

"So why did you go along with it?"

"I thought it might be something else—you know, like Little Foot running around on the roof or something out of place that he really did see."

"What's that got to do with Wilber?"

"Nothing," Chief said. "It's just that last night when I was walking the parking lot, I had a strange feeling at the edge of the property, like something was watching me. I'm hoping it was something that will pass, but I would just ask that you be extra careful."

"No problem, Dad," Mouse said.

Mouse went about her patrolling as normal that day and even spent part of the day sitting with Little Foot in the sunlight that came in through the window. It was late afternoon when she headed back to the furniture-storage room on the fifth floor to get Little Foot, who often accompanied her to see Wilber and eat spaghetti. She caught the elevator to the floor and went in to the storage room but couldn't find Little Foot.

"Come out if you're hiding," Mouse said. She felt sure she would sense Little Foot but also knew how well her friend could hide. "Okay, I'm leaving without you." When there was no response, she left and headed down to the bottom floor and out the side door. She had barely stepped out on the sidewalk when she heard Little Foot.

"I thought you forgot me."

Mouse looked to see the small black-and-white mouse on a windowsill. She stood on her hind legs, holding her tail in her front paws.

"I went to get you, but you were already gone," Mouse said. "Remember we have to wait until it's almost dark, or people might see us. Besides, I think you were just restless."

"I was," Little Foot said, coming down the wall to where Mouse stood. "It gets boring waiting in that room all day. I have an adventurous side, and I think it's a very big part of me, probably my entire right side."

"That adventurous side is going to get you in trouble or hurt," Mouse said. She was about to bend down and let Little Foot on her back but stopped.

"What is it?" Little Foot asked.

"I think I just realized something."

"What?"

"How my father feels when I go out on my adventures. I just felt the same way about you." She knelt down, and Little Foot climbed on her back.

"You're starting to sound more like him," Little Foot said. "You shouldn't worry. I can take care of myself."

"That sounds exactly like something I would tell him," Mouse said. "Now I know he really cares. Because I wouldn't be worried about you if I didn't care."

"Oh, that's a nice thing to say. Thank you."

"You're welcome. Now hold on!"

Mouse ran down the alley and across a set of new buildings that were under construction. Given that she and Little Foot were the same color, she didn't worry too much about anyone noticing the mouse riding on her back. Most of the buildings were still empty or were closed at this hour, and she rarely ran into anyone. She headed down to the building where Streets usually kept himself. He wasn't there, so she knew he was out or visiting Wilber, which he did often to pass along information.

"Streets?" Mouse called as she entered the building through a broken window in the back. He didn't answer.

"He must be out tonight," Little Foot said. "Probably wasn't expecting us since it isn't Thursday."

"That's okay," Mouse said. "I don't think they'll mind if we come down, even if it's not Thursday."

Mouse found her way to a floor drain and down into the sewers. She kept going down to the tunnels underneath the building that led deeper into the drainage system. Wilber was the boss of the rats in this area. He had been for some time, until Mouse came along. At about the same time Mouse was learning how to be a Protector, a hoodlum rat named Bragar organized a group of vile rats and challenged Wilber's territory. Bragar would have won if Mouse hadn't found a way to defeat him. Since that time, she and Wilber had become allies and friends. Two to four times a month, on Thursdays, Mouse visited Wilber at his headquarters, which was located underneath an Italian eatery. There, she sat and had spaghetti and meatballs with him. Although it was only Tuesday, Mouse didn't want to wait two more days for her plan and thought if she couldn't find Streets at his place, Wilber might know where he might be.

After a few turns, they found the point where they had to cross to the other side of the water, where there was a secret entrance to Wilber's headquarters. The water was deep here, and the only way to cross was a secret bridge that the rats raised from the opposite side.

"I know you're over there," Mouse said. "You're good at hiding, but I can smell you. It's just me, Mouse, and Little Foot is with me. We came to see Wilber."

"It's not Thursday." A large rat came out of the darkness and spoke. "Didn't you know that?"

"I know," Mouse said, "but I have something to ask him and needed to do it today."

"You got anyone else with you?"

"Just me and Little Foot, like I said." Mouse watched as the rats pulled on a cord and raised the bridge through the water. "Thank you," Mouse said. "Is Wilber in?"

"Of course," the rat said. "He's in there with Streets."

"Oh, that saves us from finding him," Mouse said. "Looks like we're in luck."

Two doors led to a pipe that Mouse went through and emerged inside a room that was two and a half feet high, seven feet long, and five feet wide. The room had lights, and just inside the opening there were several dozen rats sitting at makeshift tables, eating pasta.

She spotted Streets at the end of the room, where Wilber sat at the main table. Streets was standing as he talked to Wilber.

"Did you ever notice how different Wilber and Streets are, given that they're both rats?" Mouse asked Little Foot in a hushed voice. "I mean, Wilber is big and round. His fur is nice and well groomed, and he doesn't slouch. Even his teeth are clean. Streets is skinny, and his eyes are shifty. His teeth are crooked, and he always looks like he just stepped out of the shower and didn't fully dry his hair."

Little Foot laughed.

"What's this?" Wilber said. "Mouse, you and your friend come to visit me on a Tuesday. That's all right. I understand you couldn't wait to have some pasta; is that it?"

"Yes, that's right," Mouse said as she walked down the aisle that led to the head table where Wilber sat. "I was in the neighborhood and thought I would stop by. I hope you don't mind our coming."

"Ah, this neighborhood," Wilber said. "Always under construction. I think more and more people are moving here to the outskirts of the city. Hey, Quido," Wilber called out. A tall, fit rat, dressed in a black outfit resembling a tuxedo, moved forward from the background. "Get a plate for the hero here. Of course, kid, you're welcome any time. If it wasn't for you, we might have lost everything." Wilber gestured with his hands to the left and right, where other rats were sitting. "Now we have peace; we have family; we have respect; and—most important—we have pasta!" He laughed as he rolled some long spaghetti noodles onto his fork and ate them.

Mouse sat down across from Wilber. She noticed that all the rats had stopped eating. Although she'd been visiting him for four months, the rats still looked at her like they didn't trust her. Quido put a plate of noodles in front of Mouse, who started eating, knowing it wasn't polite to talk business before eating. Little Foot took a seat beside Mouse and helped herself to some of the noodles.

"So what brings you to the neighborhood and why you decided to stop by?" Wilber asked.

"I was looking for him," Mouse said, pointing to Streets, who remained standing to the right and slightly behind Wilber.

"What did you do, Streets?" Wilber said.

Streets dropped his ears and lowered his head. "I didn't do anything," he muttered.

"No," Mouse said. "He didn't do anything wrong; in fact, he's been a great help."

Streets's ears raised, and he straightened his shoulders.

"We just needed to get some information," Mouse said.

"Oh," Wilber said.

Not wanting to hurt Wilber's feelings, Mouse added, "We wanted to talk to both of you, actually, because we need some help, and you both know so much."

She could tell her words had the anticipated effect, as Wilber slurped his pasta confidently and then took a piece of tissue and wiped his face. He moved his plate away a little so his paws fit on the table, where he folded them together.

"What is it, kid?"

"We wanted to know if either of you know how to get to the country."

"Why do you want to go there?"

"We have some friends who need to get out of town, and we heard there's plenty of room out there where they could roam around."

"Yes," Wilber said. "There's plenty of room out there, but why would they want to go there?"

"They're cats," Mouse said. "And they're locked in cages. We're going to break them out."

"I see," Wilber said. "You're determined to do this?" Mouse nodded. "Then I'm determined to help you. Not only because of our alliance but also because the thought of having any more cats around than necessary just"—he put his paws together and stretched them outward, cracking all of his knuckles—"doesn't feel good. No offense, kid."

"Oh, don't worry," Mouse said. "We can't have any more cats in the apartments or in the alley. I need to get them somewhere safe."

"Streets, you helped get someone out of the city before."

"Yes," Streets said. "Just not all the way. I can get you to the edge of town. After that, you'll have to see a cat named Midnight. He's smuggled others out of town. But he ain't easy to deal with."

"Why is that?"

"He's hard to find."

"Oh, Streets, I have confidence in you." Wilber glanced up at Streets. "Well, you aren't going to find him standing there."

"Yes, sir," Streets said and left the room.

"So it's settled, then," Wilber said. He put his napkin back on this lap and started eating. "Why don't you stay awhile and tell me about this adventure of yours. I heard you stood up to a bulldog. Is that so?"

Mouse and Little Foot told Wilber the story of breaking the animals out of the center and then finished their meal before heading back to the apartment.

On the other side of the doors from where Wilber and Mouse were eating, two rats were in the kitchen, cleaning.

"Psst," Slouch called across the kitchen, where his buddy, Slim, was doing dishes, whistling as he did so. Slouch finally went over and hit Slim on the back.

"Why did you do that?" Slim asked.

"I've been trying to get your attention over there for like an hour."

"What is it?"

"You didn't hear that conversation out there?"

"No, I'm doing dishes. I can't hear anything but soap and water. What did you hear?"

"That character Mouse was in eating with Wilber and Streets."

"Mouse? It isn't Thursday, is it?"

"No, that's not the point."

"Oh, it's not Thursday."

"No, it's Tuesday. Did you hear what they were talking about?"

Slim raised his sponge and squeezed it so soap and water ran out; he shook his head.

"You know how we've been talking about leaving this place. Well, a plan just came to me."

"I don't know," Slim said. He put down the sponge that he was using to wash dishes. "We have plenty of food here and our own room, and we don't have to worry about someone pushing us around because Wilber and his boys protect us."

"Sure, but all we do is work. Besides, you could do with a little less." He poked Slim in the stomach. Although both rats were the same height, Slim was heavier than Slouch, who, despite what he ate, remained extremely thin.

Slim looked at the pile of dishes he had finished and compared it to the few Slouch had finished. He raised an eyebrow and frowned while shaking his head.

"Slim …" Slouch went over to him, put his head next to Slim's, and gestured across the room with his hand. "You're missing the big picture."

"What's that?" Slim looked but didn't see anything.

"We used to be free spirits. We ain't meant to be tied down. It's a philosophy," Slouch said.

"Oh, one of those again," Slim said.

Slouch leaned on his broom and started to sing:

> I'm a free spirit;
> I can't be tied down.
> When someone says they have a goal,
> You can bet I won't be around.
> I'm a free spirit,
> Don't want nothing to do.
> You say you got high standards;
> I say adieu to you.
>
> Lotsa people take their time
> To make something grow,
> But I say it's better
> To just get on with the show.
> If you work all day,
> There's less time to play.
> That just doesn't seem right.
> Why work all day
> When there's so much to do,
> Like staying out all night?
>
> I just don't want to compete.
> Don't need a lot, you see.
> Living on the street
> Where I am free.

I'm a free spirit,
Can't be tied down.
When someone says they have high goals,
You can bet I won't be around.

No one tells me where to go
Or tells me what to do.
Life's free when it's all up to you.
I have no job,
No worries,
No need to be anywhere,
No reason to hurry—
I'll be there when I get there.

I'm a free spirit.
I've got plenty of time.
You can have what's yours;
I'll take what's mine.

Slouch smiled as he finished the song but didn't get much time to celebrate before the door behind him came open.

"Hey," Quido said as he entered the kitchen. "What's all this singing in here? You two have work to do."

"What do you want?" Slouch said. "Can't a rat sing while he's working?"

"I want you to keep it down in here. The boss is having an important meeting out there."

"How long we gotta be in here?" Slouch asked.

"I don't know," Quido said. "I suppose until the boss thinks you learned your lesson. He didn't like it none that you two ran out on him last time, especially when you ended up on the side of them hoodlum rats and all."

"That was a mistake," Slouch said. "We were just trying to be free spirits and all. That Bragar made us be part of his group."

"Just get back to work, and keep it down in here. *Capisce?*"

Slouch grabbed the broom and started sweeping as Slim went back to doing dishes until Quido left the kitchen.

"What does he know?" Slouch said. "See, that's why we've got to get out of here."

"I don't know, Slouch," Slim said. "I'm pretty sure it was one of those philosophies of yours that landed us in trouble last time. Didn't we almost die?"

"Don't be so dramatic. We were in top leadership until things went bad."

"No, I'm not going," Slim said. "I think if we're going to go on this trip, it should be to help Mouse. If it wasn't for her, we'd still be serving Bragar and his goons."

"Okay, okay. But say we help her on this trip. At the end of it, if we find a better place to go, can we stay there?"

Slim turned and looked at all the dishes in front of him. "What? And give up all of this?"

They both laughed. Slim grabbed the broom from Slouch and handed him the sponge. Slim started sweeping, and Slouch started doing dishes.

"I'm glad we're out of the sewers," Little Foot said. "I don't know how those guys can live down there."

"Don't mice live in sewers too?" Mouse asked.

Little Foot stopped and shook her head. "I wouldn't think so, but I don't know any other mice so I wouldn't know."

"Come on, Little Foot," Mouse said. "Time to get onboard."

Little Foot jumped on Mouse's back and grabbed onto her fur. The two headed down the street toward the park. Mouse was worried as she changed direction because, unlike last time, she had no pigeons circling above, looking out for her.

"Where are we going?" Little Foot asked.

"We're going to see Butch and let him know the plan."

"Isn't that dangerous?"

"Not if he joins us."

"Oh," Little Foot said. "How do you plan on that?"

"You're going back in to get him to talk to me."

"Me?"

Mouse continued her journey at an increased pace, stopping only at the road to cross into the park and then again as they approached the street that crossed over to the animal control center. She took a moment to catch her breath.

"Yes, you. You're simply so polite and convincing that I'm sure Butch will want to hear what we have to say." She looked for cars and quickly ran to the front of the animal control center, letting Little Foot off at the front door. "Tell him I'll be out back," Mouse said. She waited until Little Foot squeezed under the door before heading to the back, where she easily scaled the small fence and waited by the back door. It didn't take long before the bulldog came out. Little Foot was close behind.

"What you doing here again?" Butch asked. He looked around suspiciously.

"Hi, Butch," Mouse said. "It's just us tonight. I wanted to talk to you."

"Are you trying to distract me while you're little squeaky mouse friend goes in there to let more animals out?"

"Hey," Little Foot said and marched over to stand by Mouse. "I'm not squeaky."

"No," Mouse said. "I wouldn't try to trick you. We're friends now. I've come to make you an offer."

"Yeah, well, you're taking a big risk coming down to this area," Butch said. "It's not safe."

"I want to help the animals in there," Mouse said. "And you too."

Mouse could see the exposed teeth in Butch's lower jaw as he raised one eyebrow and lowered the other and then switched them.

"What do you mean?"

"We're going to break them out of this place. And I want you to come too."

"Come with you? Where?"

"Have you ever been on a farm?"

"No. Can't say that I have."

Mouse walked over to stand by Butch. She looked to the stars and gestured with her paw across the sky. "Imagine a place where there's a lot of room, and it's not so crowded with people, cars, and buildings."

"You've been there?"

"No," Mouse said. "I've heard about it from a friend."

"Sounds like a dream."

"It is," Mouse said. "That's the point. We can save all those animals in there and take them to a better place."

Butch turned around and started heading back to the pet door. "I'd like to help you, but I'm too old for adventures, kid."

Little Foot ran ahead to stand in front of the pet door so Butch couldn't enter. It delayed him long enough for Mouse to get in front of him.

"Just hear me out," Mouse said. And suddenly she saw the way to get around the alarms.

Butch tried to move around Mouse on the side, but Little Foot didn't get out of the way; she folded her arms until Butch turned and faced Mouse.

"We have a plan that can help these animals. You don't have to go if you don't want to, but we're going to make a difference here. You know what happens to them if we don't get them out of there, don't you?"

Mouse thought she could see a tear in his right eye.

"You've got a point, kid. Life here isn't the best. Tell me what you have in mind."

Mouse laid out her plan for Butch. "So as soon as we hear back from Streets, we'll be ready to go."

"Sounds like you've thought it through," Butch said. "I won't stop you when you come, but don't forget you might have a tough audience in there." He gestured to the building. "Some of those animals have lost all hope. Others have been caught multiple times. I don't know how many of them will be willing to run around the city at night and take a chance to go to this place in the country that they've never seen."

"Leave that to me," Mouse said. She was confident, after all her conversations with Ladie and her dad, that she would find words of inspiration when the time came. "However, I could use your help to keep those alarms from going off. Can you stand near your pet door when we come back so it will let us in? We'll make enough noise out here so you can hear us when we come."

"Sure, kid. I suppose that's the least I could do," Butch said as he turned and walked inside.

"That went well," Little Foot said.

"Yes, it did. Now all I have to do is figure out how to tell my dad," Mouse said. "Come on; let's get back before he wonders why I'm out so late."

The next day, Mouse did her normal patrols and stopped in to see Ladie and Little Foot. Luckily, Miss Doris had company, a young couple who appeared to be staying the night, as they had suitcases. Mouse considered it was the niece that Ladie had spoken about the day prior. Due to this, Mouse didn't go all the way in but simply peeked in to see that Miss Doris was okay. She also wanted to dodge any questions from Ladie until her plan was ready.

She spent most of the day with Little Foot as they played hide-and-seek and sat in the sun most of the afternoon. Little Foot kept asking her what was on her mind because she seemed distracted; she was, but she didn't want to discuss it. It was during one of their breaks when the two were sitting on a comfortable chair, soaking in the sun, that Mouse opened up to her friend.

"You seem distracted," Little Foot said again. "Is it something I've done?"

"It's nothing with you," Mouse said. "I just need to find a way to tell my dad, and it's really on my mind."

"You're going to tell him this time?"

"Yes. I think it's important to him. And this time we aren't just sneaking out for a few hours, like we do sometimes. I think we'll be gone for a few days. That's also why I haven't told Ladie." She knew she needed to tell Chief what she was planning, especially after the conversation he'd had with her after the last mission; it was a matter of trust. She just didn't know how.

As the sun set, Mouse went on her next patrol. "I know," she said to herself in the middle of the fifth-floor hallways. "I'll ask him to go to the roof tonight to our special place. He likes it up there, and it always puts him in a good mood." She bounced down the hall, happy that she had made a commitment to a time and place to reason with her dad. She was thinking about the words she would say and found herself being led to the lobby by her senses. She noticed a lady who had just come in; for some reason, Mouse was drawn to her. The lady was tall, with sandy-blonde hair and blue eyes. She took a seat in the lobby as though waiting for someone and soon noticed Mouse watching her. She smiled at Mouse.

Mouse decided to go over to where the lady was sitting. She sensed another cat, not one in the building but on the lady's clothes. She rubbed against her leg, and the lady reached down to pet her on the head.

"Well, aren't you just a little darling," the lady said. "You must know I like cats."

"Pretty amazing," a man said as he approached the lady from the cafeteria. "The entire complex is patrolled by cats. There are pet doors on every apartment, and the cats keep all the vermin out. At least that's what my fiancée's Aunt Doris says. She calls that one Mouse. I'm Samar."

Mouse turned as she recognized her name.

"Yes, I remember you from the coffee shop. I'm Claudia Walden," the lady said, shaking the man's hand. "It makes me wonder."

"What's that?" Samar said.

"In the line of work I used to be in, cats played an important role. I was wondering if whoever runs this complex is in the same line of work."

"I wouldn't know. There's a cafeteria in here if you would like to sit and talk. Ira and I were just getting something to eat ourselves," Samar said. He and the lady went into the cafeteria, which caused Mouse to think of food.

She headed down to her apartment and went inside to eat. Luckily, her dad was there.

"Finished with your evening patrol?" Chief said as Mouse approached the food dish.

"Yep," Mouse said. "Just a few more things to check."

"Oh?"

"Miss Doris has some visitors," Mouse said. "I just want to check on her one more time. Then I was going to hang out on the roof and watch the stars." Chief didn't say anything, so Mouse prodded him some more. "You know, like we used to go to that place where you would take me? That we haven't done for a while."

"I have to patrol the perimeter, and then I'll come meet you there," Chief said.

Mouse smiled. "That would be great!" She knew it would be easier to tell him about her plan when he was on the roof and in a calm mood. "Gotta go," Mouse said. She exited the apartment and headed down the hall, where she ran into the lady she had seen in the lobby and the man staying with Miss Doris. They were waiting at the elevator, so Mouse joined them. When the doors opened, the elevator attendant noticed Mouse and backed away as she entered. *Guess he still remembers who's in charge,* Mouse thought. She watched the lights on the buttons to make sure they were going to the fourteenth floor.

Once the elevator stopped, Mouse didn't want the people to get too suspicious, so she headed down the other way until they were inside Miss Doris's apartment, and then she went there and stood outside the door, listening. She lost track of time and suddenly felt a presence behind her in the hallway.

"Hi, Mom," Mouse said and turned around to see her mother, Charlene, coming down the hall. Mouse thought her mom, a white Persian cat, looked beautiful and graceful as she approached.

"What are you doing outside the door?" Charlene asked.

"I was listening," Mouse said. "Why are you up here? Are you checking on me?"

"No," Charlene said and came close enough to nuzzle Mouse on the head. "I'm not checking on you. You forget I used to live in the penthouse.

Before Doris and Ladie were your friends or even your dad's friends, I knew both of them."

"Oh," Mouse said. "They have company, and I was just making sure Miss Doris was okay."

"Is she?" Charlene asked.

"She's not even there," Mouse said. "But they are having an interesting conversation about evil and shadows and other stuff. Hey, Mom, do the people have Protectors too?"

"I don't know," Charlene said. "I suppose maybe they do. Should we go back to the apartment? It's getting late."

Her mother's words reminded Mouse of somewhere she was supposed to be. "Sorry, Mom," she said as she started down the hall. "I forgot I was supposed to meet dad on the roof. I'll see you later."

Mouse hurried down the stairs to the second floor, where there was always a window slightly open at the end of the hall. There, she made her way to the fire escape and to the roof. Chief was already there, walking around the perimeter. Mouse went to their spot and sat down, waiting for her father.

"There's such a great view up here. I think I'll just start coming here to do my perimeter check of the building," Chief said as he approached.

"You seem happy, Dad," Mouse said.

"I am. Now that Scratch and Dazzle are back, and Sam is hiring some new help so he isn't so busy, things are just as good as could be. I guess there's no reason not to be happy. What a beautiful night!" Chief sat down next to Mouse and looked at the stars.

Mouse sighed and thought about the words she was going to say. Her dad was so happy that she didn't want to spoil the moment. But something inside of her couldn't let what was on her mind go unsaid.

"We have a good life, don't we, Dad?"

"The best," Chief said. "Believe me, I've been there in the city and know."

"Were there a lot of animals without homes there?" Mouse asked.

"All over the place," Chief said. "I was one of them. If Sam hadn't had helped me, I'd be in the shelter or worse."

"It's too bad for those animals in the shelter, isn't it?"

Mouse's comment got the reaction she wanted.

Her dad looked over at her. "Is that what's had you down?"

"You know?"

"Everybody knows you haven't been yourself lately. You're usually so spunky and cheerful. I thought it was because of the talk we had the other night."

"No," Mouse said. "You were right about all you said during that talk, Dad. And you're right to say we have a good life. It's just …"

"What?"

"I can't get it out of my mind. I close my eyes, and I see all the faces of the animals we left there in cages, especially one that I talked to. Her name was Jinx, and she looked a lot like me."

"That's why, then," Chief said. "Your mind has you thinking that could just as easily have been you in that place."

"I guess so," Mouse said.

"It's tough being a Protector," Chief said. "There's a part inside of us that wants to fix everything that's wrong and doesn't want to give up. That's the hardest part, realizing what we can and can't control."

"I can't just leave them there," Mouse said. "We're supposed to be Protectors. We're supposed to be the ones who do something about the bad conditions and protect."

"Hmm," Chief said. "And I suppose the reason you've been running everywhere and visiting everyone is that you're trying to find a way."

"I have a plan."

"I thought you would," Chief said, "and you decided to tell me this time."

"Yes," Mouse said.

"Is it because you need my help?"

"A little," Mouse said. "I need you to watch my building while I'm gone. That's the other reason I'm telling you. This mission will be longer than a few hours."

"If I say no, are you still going to sneak out and do it anyway?"

"Probably," Mouse said. "The feeling is too strong to ignore."

"Who knows about this, and who's going?"

"Right now," Mouse said, "Carl, some of this pigeons, Scratch and Dazzle, and Streets."

"The rat?"

"He's the one who knows how to get to the country."

"The country?"

"That's where we're taking them. We can't keep them here."

"You're right about that."

"Paggs said the country has farms where there's lots of room and food. You know what happens to them if we don't get them out?"

"I know," Chief said. "It just sounds dangerous."

"Do you trust me, Dad?"

"It's not you," Chief said. "It's the world out there I don't trust. One day you'll understand how hard it is to let go of something you care about and watch her go into the world when you no longer have the ability to watch over her."

"So, does this mean I have your approval to go?"

"Not exactly," Chief said. "I need to find out more details first, and … you have to tell your mom."

"But she'll never understand," Mouse said, stomping her foot. She looked down at her foot and could see that her father noticed what she'd done as well. *Act like an adult!* she told herself.

"What are the other things you want to know?"

"I want to know the route you're taking from Streets in case I have to come to find you. Arrange a meeting with Colonel Wellington. If we can get some of his pigeons to send back a status report so I can keep track of your progress, that would keep me from worrying so much, and if you get in trouble, Baxter and I can come to help."

"Wow, you're really smart, Dad. I guess that's why you're in charge of everything."

"So tell me what you plan to do."

Mouse outlined her plan from the start. She told Chief that she would use Little Foot to get into the animal control building and break out all the animals. After that, Streets would lead them to the edge of the city. This is where her story got a little sketchy because she knew nothing about the contact, Midnight, Streets had mentioned. She decided to leave that aspect out of her story and instead told her dad that a reliable cat named Midnight would help them get to the farm and back.

Chief frowned.

"What?" Mouse said when she finished describing the detailed plan. "Did I say something wrong?"

"No," Chief said. "You just reminded me how smart you really are and how proud I am to be your father. Sitting under the stars reminds me of how big the world really is. It keeps me from getting upset about petty things." Mouse felt her dad's lower chin as he nuzzled the top of her head with it. "What you did to save our place and to save Scratch and Dazzle took courage, and if we had more of that, the world would be a better place. I've learned from you. You showed me that just because something is a certain way or is supposed to be a certain way, it's still up to us."

"You're confusing me, Dad," Mouse said.

"I told you birds and mice were prey, yet you managed to make friends and allies of them, which helped you achieve what I could not. You taught me that just because something's bad, it doesn't have to be that way in our little corner of the world. We can make a difference."

"So I have your support?"

"Hold on a minute. Before you go, I suggest you figure out how to tell your mother. After you survive that, you get our team together and go through every detail of your plan, step by step, including what-ifs."

"What-ifs?"

"You know, what if something doesn't go exactly as planned. What if this character, Midnight, decides not to help you? Things like that."

"Oh," Mouse said. Things suddenly got more complicated to her. "Is that what comes with experience, Dad? The ability to know more about things?"

"Yes. It's good, and it's bad. Some experiences make us better because we understand and see things in a new light. Others experiences can make us afraid, which isn't always bad but sometimes can lead to us to not taking chances."

"Like sitting in a cage all day because it's safe?"

"Exactly," Chief said. "We should really go back now." The two began the trek back to the apartment. "One more thing—I'd reconsider taking Little Foot with you. I know you need her to get into the animal control building and all, but I heard the message from Paggs as well. Ladie told me. I heard the entire message, and while I don't know much about farm life, I know what the cats on a farm eat—mice. That, and you can't be sure all of the cats you break out will have the same soft spot for her that you do."

Mouse reconsidered Little Foot's going when she thought about what might happen to her.

"Now I don't think this mission will be hard at all," Mouse said.

"Why's that?"

"After I have to tell Mom what I want to do and after I have to tell Little Foot she can't go all the way, everything else will seem easy. I think I'll wait to tell her in the morning."

"Good idea, kid."

CHAPTER 4
A Daring Plan

I t was early in the morning at the apartment complex. Chief waited in the apartment while Mouse told her mom, Charlene, the plan she had outlined to him the night before. While Chief supported her plan and didn't want to protest and create conflict, he was hoping Charlene would find some way to reason Mouse out of it. Instead, she surprised him and went along with it all the way.

Mouse smiled at him as she passed by and left for her patrol. Chief knew she would be gone for several hours and maybe longer with all the diversions she had in visiting Ladie and Little Foot. It was the perfect time for him to visit with Charlene without Mouse's hearing.

"I can't believe you," Chief said. He and Char were in the living room of the apartment which, other than a plethora of cat toys, had but one chair, a small coffee table, and a television on a stand.

"What are you talking about?" Charlene said.

"I can't believe you're going along with her plan?"

"*You* did," she said. "Besides, many times she has proposed stuff, and then, when she really thinks it over, she realizes it's not what she wants."

"So by letting her get her way, you avoid the conflict and hope that in the end, she'll reason with herself and realize the plan is dangerous?"

"Yes," Charlene said. "If I were to be against it right away, it would just strengthen her resolve to go through with it, regardless. It's the same for everyone who is stubborn."

"Now I see." Chief paced in front of Charlene. "All these years you just pretended to let me have my way to give me a false sense that I was in charge. Is that it?"

Charlene didn't respond but simply sat and groomed her hair by licking the sides of her paw and brushing the sides of her face.

Chief stopped his pacing. "I never would have thought you were so cunning. It seems like a fitting strategy, but what if Mouse really goes through with this plan?"

Charlene stopped grooming. "You think she will?"

"Oh yes," Chief said. "I think she has had a lot of success in her adventures and is only getting bolder. She already snuck down to the place where Sam and I used to live, and that's a tough neighborhood. Whether it's luck or skill, I couldn't say, but she's feeling invulnerable. I know because I've been there and seen it, and it doesn't end well. It took a dramatic failure before I realized I wasn't invulnerable."

"What do we do, then?" Charlene asked.

"You're right that if we tell her no, she'll probably only resist and be even more stubborn. We have to support her."

"You mean, let her fail?"

"If that's what it takes."

"What if she gets hurt?"

"I don't intend to let that happen," he said and walked toward the door. "We can support her by being ready if she does fail."

"How?" Charlene asked.

Chief spotted a flash of black peeking in the pet door. "Come on in, Baxter," Chief said. "Anyone see you?"

"No, I kept it discreet, just like you told me," Baxter said. "Oh, hi, Charlene."

"Hi, Baxter," Charlene said. "Can I get you anything?"

"No, not right now. I'm curious to see what's going on here. Chief?"

"I called you here for a reason," Chief said. "A very important one."

"Please," Charlene said, "what is your plan?"

"You all know of Mouse's intention to save the animals in the control center and take them to the country, right?"

"I still can't believe you're letting her go," Baxter said.

"That's exactly my point," Chief said.

"Wait," Charlene said. "You're *not* letting her go now?"

"Just hold on a minute, everyone. Let me explain, and hold your questions," Chief said, raising his paw. "It think the mission my daughter has outlined is a worthy mission. I think she has allies to help her succeed, and we should support her. I think if we don't, we'll let her down, and she'll probably find a way to go unless we lock her up." He nodded, confirming he had made his points.

"So what do you need?" Baxter asked.

"Isn't it obvious? One of us has to go to keep an eye on her, and it should be me," Chief said.

"Why you?" Charlene said.

"I think Sam will notice if you're gone for a couple of days," Baxter stated. "Besides, you've never been out of the city."

"Have you?"

"*No*, that's not the point. I'm better equipped to sneak around." He feigned sneaking around by circling Charlene and Chief. "My black coat lets me blend into the background. At night, I'm practically invisible."

"You have several good points there," Chief said.

"Besides, your father instinct will kick in, and you'll probably jump in and interfere before you're needed. She won't appreciate that. I'm going, and that's final."

"Nonsense," a voice came from the hallway. Sikes peeked his head through and walked into the apartment. "No worries, Chief. I ain't been seen by nobodies." Sikes pointed at Chief and Baxter. "Yous two ain't going nowheres. I've been in and out and all abouts. I've been hiding out in alleys and roaming around this town most of my life withouts anyone noticin' me. You might be a Protector, Chief, and you might be bigger than me, Baxter, but you both have jobs. So, do your jobs and stay. I'm the only one qualified for this here mission. And I ain't taking no for an answer."

Chief glanced around at the others. He knew Sikes was right. "Then it's settled."

Mouse entered Miss Doris's apartment to find that the visitors had left, and Doris was sleeping soundly in her bed. She walked into the living room and jumped to the stool across from Ladie's cage.

"Good morning, Mouse," Ladie said. "You seem in a cheery mood today. Much better than yesterday."

"I am," Mouse said. "That's what I wanted to talk to you about." Mouse looked to the window. "How come the window is closed?"

"Doris closes it at night," Ladie said. "She always does. She opens it when she gets up. Why?"

"I was expecting Carl," Mouse said. "I guess I can tell you."

"Tell me what?"

"We're going tomorrow," Mouse said. "I'm just waiting for Streets to confirm his contact."

Ladie turned her head to the side and moved closer to the door of her cage. "You told your dad?"

"Yes." Mouse nodded. "And my mom. I was surprised they both agreed."

Ladie fluttered her wings, turned, and flew the small distance to the bar that went across the center of her tea-cup–style birdcage. "I guess you'll be gone for a while, then."

"Probably a few days, maybe more," Mouse said. "Scratch and Dazzle are coming along with Carl and Little Foot, although I've got to find a way to tell Little Foot she's not going all the way."

"Why is that?" Ladie asked.

"It's too dangerous for her."

"Darling, anything beyond the walls is this apartment complex is dangerous."

Mouse sat and thought for a few moments. "Do you think it's too dangerous? For Little Foot? For all of us?"

"Yes," Ladie said.

Mouse hung her head and looked at the floor. She always came to Ladie when she was feeling bad because Ladie was always happy, and not only gave good advice but usually had a song to sing. Mouse didn't want to make her feel bad.

"I think it's dangerous for all of you," Ladie said, "which is why I'll wish you the best and tell you to be careful."

Mouse jerked her head up and looked at Ladie. "You mean you're okay with it?"

"Yesterday you moped around all day because you felt you couldn't change what was happening to those animals. Today you're happy and vibrant because you were able to find a way to *make a difference.*"

"I guess I do feel better now that I have a plan," Mouse said.

"I'm worried, just like your parents and friends should be," Ladie said. "But you, Mouse, have something special about you. The world is a difficult place. If you just stood by and let the bad things be, you'd be like everyone else who doesn't get involved. You have the ability to turn things around."

Mouse smiled. "You always have such a wonderful way of putting things. Thanks, Ladie. I've got to go finish my rounds. Tonight we're all meeting to finalize our plans."

Mouse raced out of the apartment and headed down each floor, doing her checks until she arrived at the furniture-storage room. She waited before she went in, trying to find the best way to tell Little Foot about her role in the plan. A small head peeked out of the door.

"Little Foot?" Mouse said. "What are you doing?"

"I was wondering why you're waiting out there," Little Foot said.

Mouse used her paw to shove the little black-and-white head with a pink nose back in the room as she entered. "I forgot you have such good ears. Did you hear me outside?"

"Yes," Little Foot said. "When you got to the door you were breathing heavily because you must have been running." Little Foot walked toward the end of the room by the window, where the two usually hung out. "Are we going to do some training today?"

"I don't know," Mouse said as she followed Little Foot. "I have lots to get done. We're meeting in the alley tonight to finalize the plan. Everyone has agreed that we should go. I'm just waiting for Streets to make sure he got hold of the cat that's helping us get out of the city."

Little Foot climbed a cloth-covered recliner and sat down on the seat. Mouse jumped to the seat and sat beside her.

"There's one thing I wanted to talk to you about before we get with the rest of the group."

"Great," Little Foot said, throwing her front paws in the air. "You don't want me to go. I suppose it's too dangerous for little, tiny, eeny-meeny-miny me." She flailed for a few seconds. "What?"

"I just wanted to see how long you would go on looking ridiculous," Mouse said. "You're wrong, you know."

"Wrong?"

"You're essential to the mission," Mouse said. "Of course you have to go."

"Then it's settled," Little Foot said.

"No," Mouse said. "There's more. You see, we're breaking out a bunch of cats. I don't know all of them, and I don't trust them. I need to keep my eyes open, and I won't have time to look out for you or Carl or anyone else."

"I can look out for myself," Little Foot said.

"But I want you to help look out for someone else," Mouse said. Little Foot's ears rose, and Mouse could tell she had her full attention. "After we break the animals out and start our way to the country, I want you to come back. With all of us going, my dad is going to try to take on too much. As a junior Protector, it falls on you to help out around here. I expect you to watch out for him and even help patrol."

"Really?"

"Really," Mouse said. "I want you to do so in stealth mode."

"Why?"

"Because my dad has a habit of thinking we can't handle things because we're small," Mouse said. "But that's our biggest advantage because we can move about unnoticed. That's going to be your job."

"Okay," Little Foot said. "I guess that seems to make sense. It's just—"

"What you would be doing is important."

"I'll miss you."

"Me too," Mouse said.

The window faced the back of the apartment complex, which had become a busy site. The empty lot behind the main building that had become a junkyard was busy and full of workers clearing away the scraps and beginning work on the foundation for the fourth apartment building in the complex. The two sat there together, enjoying the warm sun and the silence, as they watched the workers move about at the construction site.

"Excellent," Carl said. "Your dad, that great Protector, was right. We need to get together and dissect this issue, to look at it from all angles"—he moved his head to look at Mouse with one eye and then the other—"and then formulate options. Yes, we must have options. Without options, we get ourselves stuck. We must be flexible; that is the key."

The group, which consisted of Mouse, Little Foot, Carl, Scratch, and

Dazzle, had met out by the dumpsters, once it turned dark, to finalize the plans for the raid.

"What kind of flexible stuff do we need to take, then?" Scratch asked.

"It's not stuff," Carl said. "It's a state of mind. In case something doesn't go as planned, we need to be able to come up with a new plan."

"Oh, I see. You mean, like, we need to be on our toes and stuff."

"That's it," Carl said.

"You're sure Colonel Wellington is ready?" Mouse asked.

"The colonel will meet us in front of the animal control building, as he did last time. And Streets?"

"Right here," Streets said. "I hope you'll forgive my coming into your alley, but Wilber told me I needed to get word to you right away."

"Is everything ready?" Mouse asked.

"I sent word to Midnight," Streets said. "He'll meet us at a place outside of the city and take you to the country."

"How about you?"

"I'll meet you at the prep point."

"How do we know we can trust Midnight?" Mouse asked.

"Oh, I can vouch for him," Streets said. "He's helped me out of several scrapes in the past."

Mouse glanced at Colonel Wellington, who said, "If Streets trusts him, that's good enough for me."

Streets grinned and then turned and disappeared down the alley.

"Who knows?" Mouse said. "If this mission goes well, maybe we can find some other shelters."

Carl raised his wing. "Wait a minute. Hold it right there. We need to focus on one thing at a time here. Otherwise, we'll get distracted. How about we wait until the mission is over and successful before we discuss what happens next?"

"How will we know when it's over?" Dazzle asked.

Carl looked at Mouse, but she didn't know what to say.

"How about when everyone returns back here safe and sound?" Carl said.

"Agreed," everyone responded.

"Let's meet back here at two tomorrow, and we'll go together," Mouse said. With that, the group went their separate ways.

Off in the distance, a different set of eyes watched; hiding in the construction and building materials adjacent to the alley. Moats remained still as he lay in a new sewage pipe, close enough to see what was going on but hidden by the darkness. "Looks like some of them are moving out. That will make it easier for me and the others to move in!"

From the other end of the pipe, he heard movement.

"Hey, Moats, you in there?"

Moats went to the end of the pipe, where Rocko stood with his front paws up, peering into the pipe.

"Call out louder next time," Moats said sarcastically. "Not everyone could hear you."

"Sorry," Rocko said. "What's the plan?"

"Watch and wait," Moats said. "We watch and wait. Looks like some of the cats are going on a journey, and then we'll have less of them to deal with. When the time is right, I'll have you get the others. Now, come on. I want to find out where that rat that was talking to them is heading. He might lead us to the rest of the rats, and we can pay them a visit."

"Let's do it," Rocko said. "I gotta say, it's not like you to be so patient, Moats. Usually you're wanting to rumble."

"I'm just trying to make sure we're prepared is all. I don't want any surprises. Once we move in, then I won't hold back."

"That's what I like to hear, Moats. With all those dumpsters back there, I think we're going to like it here."

CHAPTER 5
JUST ONE PATH

"**D**éjà vu," Carl said.

"What?" Mouse asked.

"Déjà vu. It's when you feel like you've been somewhere before. We just did this a few days ago, and we're back again so soon that it seems like the first time was a dream."

"It's like today went so fast that I don't even remember it," Mouse said. She stood with Carl, late at night, in the bushes on the other side of the road from the animal control center.

"Let's just hope everything goes as well as last time."

Colonel Wellington had already signaled the pigeons to do a reconnaissance flight, and they had taken off to circle the building. As they came back in and signaled all clear, Little Foot jumped on Mouse's back.

"Okay, everyone," Mouse said. "We're going around to the back this time and through the door. Butch is going to let us in. That way, we avoid any alarms. Once inside, everyone remember your positions and start unlocking the cages. Hey, Sikes."

"Yo," Sikes said.

"Remember not to let any of the dogs out unless they agree to a truce," Mouse said.

"Gots it!"

"I'll be overhead," Carl said as he took flight.

The group—consisting of Mouse, Little Foot, and the alley cats Scratch and Dazzle—headed across the road to the back of the animal control center. Mouse was the first to approach the pet door. "Butch!" she called out. She heard the clear patter of footsteps as the bulldog approached.

"We're clear," Butch said. "No one's here but us tonight. Make sure no one in your group opens the front door or a window, and you should be fine."

"Hi, Butch," Little Foot said as she jumped down off Mouse's back.

Butch nodded.

"Are the animals ready?" Mouse asked.

"I talked to them and let them know you were coming. Some of them are too scared to go," Butch said. "And that weasel is saying he's going to tell on us. I'd watch out for him; every time the animal control officers are out front, and someone is doing something, he makes noise to get them back here like it's his job."

"I sure do," the weasel said. Mouse turned toward the long, thin, furry creature with big black eyes. "You're all going to get it. I'm going to tell them what you did."

"Wow," Mouse said. "He has good ears."

Then Little Foot demonstrated her technique for opening cages to Mouse, and she and Butch opened the cages of the animals that were willing to go. There were two rooms of animals, one with dogs and the other with cats, a raccoon, and a weasel.

Mouse went to the middle of the room where the cat cages were located. "My name is Mouse. I'm here to take all of you to the country where there's plenty of room for you to live free. I have a friend named Paggs who has already gone there. If you want out of here, all you have to do is agree to a truce with the animals helping us."

"Who would that be?" a cat asked.

"In addition to any of you who want to come, we're going to be traveling with some pigeons, a cockatoo, a rat, and some dogs. They're all helping, and you must agree to my terms or you can't go with us."

"Agreed," several voices rang out.

"Sikes, you take Butch and go to the dog kennel. Give the dogs the same instructions. Butch will look out for you."

The two went to the other room while Mouse and Little Foot continued releasing the cats. Mouse went to Jinx's cage. "Remember me?"

"Yes, from the other night," Jinx said. "You've come back to get the rest of us out. We thought Butch hit his head or something when he told us you were coming."

Mouse opened the door, but Jinx didn't move. "Let's go," Mouse said.

Jinx reached forward and pulled the door shut. "If you want to succeed, you would be better off without me."

Mouse didn't know what to say at first. The image of Jinx sitting in her cage had been her main motivation for coming back.

"You're the reason I came back here," Mouse said. "I can't leave without you." She opened the cage and went inside, closing the door behind her. "So if you aren't going, I'll just have to stay too. Little Foot," she called out, "you and the others are going to have to go without me." She winked at Little Foot as she said this.

"Okay," Little Foot said. "It's going to be hard, and we might not make it without you since you're the leader, but we'll try our best."

"What are you doing?" Jinx asked. "You can't stay in here with me."

Mouse lay down. "Hey, if it's good enough for you, it's good enough for me. Besides, who wants to go live in the country where there's plenty of space and food and freedom?"

"But you don't understand. I want to go. I want to be free. It's just …"

"What?" Mouse stood.

"Everything I touch goes bad. That's how I ended up here in the first place. I had a home, but every time I went somewhere, I broke something. So my owners threw me out. If I go with you, I'll just cause problems."

Mouse opened the door to the cage and went out. She left it open as she turned around to face Jinx. "It appears to me that you don't know who I am. I'm Mouse. I'm a Protector."

Jinx's eyes grew wide when Mouse said this.

"I don't believe in bad luck, and even if you have it, it won't last long in my presence. I've had many successful adventures. Trust me. Please."

Jinx slowly moved out of her cage. She was slightly larger than Mouse but colored very similarly. "First time I cause problems, I'm splitting from the group."

Mouse was about to reply when she noticed many animals were not getting out of their cages.

Butch came around the corner with only one dog and shrugged his shoulders. "They aren't up for the trip," Butch said. "They think that the animal control officers will be here any minute."

"Tell them to come in this room and at least listen to what I have to say," Mouse said. "Everyone gather around. If you're afraid to get out of your cages, just listen to me." Once Butch returned with the dogs, about twelve in all, Mouse went to the center of the room. "Please, I know some of you are worried about getting out of here. We've made sure no people are around, and we have a place where a friend of mine lives. We have a good plan to get there, and we're on a schedule. I'm not going to force anyone to go, but this is your best chance to have a better life."

"Why should we trust you?" asked a beagle.

"It's too dangerous. What if we get caught?" asked a small black dog.

Mouse closed her eyes for a moment and searched for words to say that would help inspire those around her to take a chance. "You're right," Mouse said. "You don't know me. But these two cats do." She pointed to Scratch and Dazzle. "They were just in here, like you, and we managed to get them to freedom. We came back to offer you that same choice—live in a cage and await your fate, or come with us and take your chances. We have a plan and a path to get you to a new home."

None of the animals moved. She suddenly thought of Ladie, became inspired, and started singing:

> There's just one path—
> One road we need to know,
> One way forward
> We need to go.

She headed over to some of the cats who were hesitant to move and signaled with her paw. They came out of their cages.

> It takes one step,
> Two steps—
> Now we're on our way.
> There's just one path;
> There's just one way.
>
> Make time;
> Take time.

No matter what they say,
Just do it your own way.

Not everything comes easy.
The journey tells a tale
Of those who endure
And those who fail.

Don't give up too easily.
The mighty brave come through.
Win or lose,
It's up to you.

More animals came forward and gathered around Mouse. She continued her song.

There's just one path—
One road we need to know,
One way forward
We need to go.

It takes real power,
Faith in who you are,
To stand with the righteous,
Rise up to the stars.

More animals headed toward the back door, and Mouse knew she was getting through to them as she continued her song:

There's only one path—
One way we need to go,
The true way forward
We need to know.

It takes one step,
Two steps—
Now we're on our way.
There's just one path,

There's just one way.

"That was very touching," Butch said. "Count me in." He headed to the back door and went outside.

"That was groovy," Dazzle said as he came forward and patted Mouse on the head with his paw. "You and I are going to have to talk about performing together with that voice of yours."

"Thanks," Mouse said. "Now help me get everyone outside." She raised her voice as she said, "Anyone who's willing needs to follow Butch and go outside now. We're on a tight schedule." Most of the animals started coming out of their cages and followed Butch outside. She helped a few more animals out of their cages until only a raccoon and the weasel were left.

"You're going to get us all in big trouble," the weasel said, shaking his head.

Mouse passed by the weasel and went to the raccoon, who wasn't much larger than she was. "Don't you want to come?"

"I do," the raccoon said. "I just didn't think you would take me because I'm different."

"What's your name?"

"I'm Tristan."

"I'm Mouse," Mouse said. "I've never met someone like you. But I don't think you belong in a cage, and I think it would be great to have you along. We're getting out of this place, and you're coming with us."

"You said you're going to the country?" Tristan asked.

"Yes."

"That's where I'm from. I just wandered too close to some houses. You know, they have good treats there, but I got caught." He took a few steps forward and cautiously came out of the cage. "I guess I learned my lesson." He smiled at Mouse and then went to the door, leaving Mouse and the weasel as the only animal occupants in the building.

"I'm going to tell. I'm going to tell. You're all going to get in trouble. Yep, you're all going to get in trouble," the weasel kept repeating.

"Who're you going to tell?" Mouse asked. "Butch is on our side."

"I'll squeal until the people come."

Mouse, finally tired of the weasel's talking and realizing her polite manner wasn't working, went to the front of the cage. She stuck out her right paw and slowly revealed her claws. "Look," she said in a low voice, "you can come with us and be free or stay here all by yourself. But know this: If I hear that anyone says anything to anybody about what's going on here, I might have to"—she swiped the claws across her body—"start cracking skulls. You know what I mean?"

The weasel stopped pacing around his cage and stared at Mouse.

She returned the best solid stare she could, narrowing her eyes. "Capisce?"

The weasel fluffed its fur, backed up, and nodded.

"Everything okay in here?" Butch asked, coming back into the room. "Everyone is outside waiting."

Mouse jumped down from the shelf and onto the floor. She took one last look around. "I think we're clear. Now let's get out of here."

Upon exiting, Mouse found the dogs gathered together. She approached the one who was out in front; she assumed he was the newly elected leader of the pack.

"Look, it's Mouse, right?" a large brown-and-white Great Dane said as Mouse approached.

"Yes," Mouse replied, trying not to be intimidated by the sheer size of the dog.

"What you did is righteous, and me and the others are going to tell everyone about you so you won't have any trouble along your way. Just tell them King knows your name."

"You're King?"

The Great Dane nodded. "We appreciate what you did for us. Now that we're out, we can make our own way from here. Besides, we don't want to be impolite, but we can move a lot faster on our own."

"If that's what you want," Mouse said. "But I'm not coming back tomorrow to save any of you, so don't get caught."

"Good luck with the rest," King said and turned around. "Anyone who wants to get out of here fast, come with me." All of the dogs, except for a short, black, shaggy, older-looking dog and Butch, fell in line, and they started trotting away. "Suit yourself, Yorkie."

"Aren't you going with them?" Mouse asked Butch.

"They don't want me with them," Butch said. "My breed isn't known for speed. Besides, they think I'm a traitor because I was on the outside. They didn't know I was trapped just like they were."

"What about that dog?" Mouse pointed to the black dog.

"Let's go ask."

"Name's Jochs," the dog said. "He called me Yorkie because that's my breed."

Mouse immediately noticed his accent.

"Aye, lassie, I'm too old to go with that pack and too old to outrun one of the animal control officers. I'll be right back here in a week."

"Well, I'm Mouse," Mouse said. "If you want to come with us, you're welcome."

"In my eyes, you're the biggest one here," Jochs said. He saluted with his paw. "If you're leading, I'll follow and be of service."

"It's a deal," Mouse said. "Carl," she called out.

The cockatoo came in fast and landed right in front of Mouse. "What do we have?" Carl said.

"Looks like we have seven cats, one dog—two, counting Butch—and a ..."

"Raccoon," Butch said.

"Raccoon," Mouse said, "and a weasel."

"What?" Butch asked. Mouse pointed to the back door, where the weasel was standing.

"I'm sorry," he said. "I won't tell anyone what you're doing. I want to go with you." The light–brown-and-black weasel stood and looked around the group. "Besides, I'm a good lookout, and I can get into anything."

"What's your name?" Mouse asked.

"I don't have a name," the weasel responded.

"We'll call you Tattle," Jochs said. He turned to Mouse, adding, "If that's good with you."

"That's a fitting name," Mouse said.

"Well, if you're all quite finished," Carl said, "Colonel Wellington is ready with Streets at the rendezvous point. Shall we get started?"

"Everyone!" Mouse called out. "This is Carl. If I'm not around, he's in charge. Got it?"

The animals nodded.

"Give me a minute," Mouse said. She stepped away from the rest of the group with Little Foot. She could tell by the lack of energy in Little Foot's step that the little mouse was unhappy.

"This is the part we spoke about earlier," Mouse said. "I want you to go back and keep an eye on things until I get back. I've even asked one of the pigeons to fly you back."

Little Foot's face lit up. "What? Fly?"

"I told him you wouldn't mind because you're so brave and all."

"No, I guess I wouldn't mind. It's probably safer than trying to walk all the way back," Little Foot said.

"Safer?" Mouse said. "You're going to be clear up there"—she pointed to the dark sky—"above the building. It's faster but definitely risky."

Carl and a pigeon landed right by Little Foot.

"This is Private Sean Donry. He's here to escort you back."

Little Foot moved forward, grabbed Mouse's whiskers, and pulled on them so Mouse was looking right at her. "You better come back."

"I promise," Mouse said.

Little Foot stepped back, and the pigeon took flight, grasping her with his talons. He flew off toward the apartment complex as Mouse watched.

"I heard what you said," Carl said. "You know, she's not in any danger. That Private Sean—he's one of our best flyers."

"I know, Carl," Mouse said. "I told her that so she didn't think we were treating her like she was too small and weak to come along because I know how that feels."

"It's the right thing," Carl said. "No telling what we might run into out there. We don't need any more to look after."

"Let's just hope we can look out for ourselves," Mouse said. "Okay, Carl. Lead the way."

Carl took flight. "Everyone follow me."

The hardest part of the journey, to Mouse, was crossing all of the streets. Luckily, Scratch and Dazzle were experts and helped coach the other animals. Traffic was light, as it was between two and three in the morning. Mouse grew alarmed when they started getting into a populated area where the streets were closer together. In the distance, she could see groups of high-rise buildings like the apartment complex buildings, only more of them and taller. She came to a stop in a small playground.

"Everyone take cover for a moment," she said as she went to an open grassy area, hoping Carl would see her. Butch came beside her.

"You should stay back with the others until I make sure the coast is clear," Mouse said.

"Don't worry, kid. People are used to dogs being out. Is everything okay?"

"I just need to check on something," Mouse said. Just then she spotted Carl, swooping in.

Carl came in for a landing with one of the pigeons. "What is it?" Carl said. "Why did you stop?"

"Are you sure you're going the right way?" Mouse asked.

Carl turned and looked at the pigeon next to him. "Corporal, is this the way?"

"Yes, Sergeant Major. This is the way to the train station. That's where we need to be. Is there a problem?"

"I thought we were supposed to head away from town," Mouse said. "This area looks like it's busier, and the direction we're going in just doesn't seem right. The country is supposed to be full of open spaces."

"Corporal?" Carl said.

"I was told we needed to get to the train station; it's farther downtown. From there, I don't know what the plan is," the corporal said, gesturing widely with his wings. "Streets is there, and he has the plan of where to go, once we get there. All I was supposed to do is get you to the train station. Now, if you don't mind, can we please continue? I'm a little nervous being on the ground with all these cats around."

"Let's continue," Mouse said. Inside, she felt the sensation of fear and excitement. She normally handled situations like this with confidence, but she sensed danger.

"You sure about this?" Carl said.

"We're getting pretty far away from home," Mouse said. "I'm just taking precautions because it's unfamiliar. I sense a lot of dogs around. I can see them in the yards of some of these houses behind fences."

"We've got a long way to go still," Carl said.

"I hope not too long."

Carl looked behind Mouse to the other animals that had taken cover under a large set of plastic slides on the playground. "All those animals over there are looking to you to get them to a safe place. Now, come on. I know you have it in you."

"Right!" Mouse said loudly. "Lead the way, Sergeant Major."

"Geez," Sikes said, "for such a small cat, she sure is keeping a fast pace."

"She's got those pigeons helping her and all," Rascal said. "I can see them flying around everywhere. Maybe we just haven't kept in shape since we quit chasing pigeons at the park."

Sikes thought about that. After they joined Mouse's alliance, which included the pigeons, to rid the complex of the hoodlum rat Bragar, Sikes and the alley cats had agreed to stop chasing the pigeons in the park.

"You gots a point there," Sikes said, nodding. "Maybe when we gets back, we goes and talks to that Colonel Wellington and makes a deal. See, I sees how some of his pigeons are also getting outta shape, seeing how's we ain't chasing 'em around and all. Maybe he would let us chase 'em if we just don't hurt 'em. That way, we stay fit and they stay fit."

"He should agree to that," Rascal said. "It sounds reasonable."

"Just make sures you remind me," Sikes said. "I gots a lot going on for this trip and all." He peeked around the fence. "I can't figure out where they are going. Deeper into the city is where we's going now."

"Yep. I thought we was going out of the city."

"Chief said she had a plan," Sikes said. "He said Wilber's helping her."

"Oh no," Rascal said.

"What?" Sikes glanced around quickly to see what was wrong.

"I just hope we don't end up in the sewers—you know, since the rats are helping her out. Last time I was down there, it took me weeks of grooming to get the smell out of my coat."

"If we dos, we dos. I guess we just stay close. Heck, I'm hoping Mouse is right about everything, and then maybe we alls move out to the country too."

"You would give up the city?"

"You bets I would," Sikes said.

"Sure would be nice not to have to keep a low profile and all," Rascal said. He peeked around the corner next. "Looks like they are heading out again."

"Okay, let's not let Chief and Baxter down."

"You still see the rest of the group, Dazzle?" Mouse called. She, Dazzle, and Scratch had pulled out in front of the group to scout the area ahead. They entered a section of town with lots of houses and were now getting into an area full of old abandoned buildings with large open yards around them.

"You sensing something?" Scratch asked as he ran alongside Mouse.

"Yes," Mouse said. "This area reminds me of the lot behind our complex—lots of junk and places for things to hide. I don't know if it's because we're getting so far away and I'm not used to it or if there really is something wrong. Also, I've lost sight of Carl." Suddenly, Mouse came to a stop, causing Scratch to do the same as Dazzle caught up to them.

"What is it?" Dazzle asked.

Mouse's hair stood on end, and she raised her tail. Three large dogs appeared from abandoned cars that lined the area in front of them. The largest, a black-and-brown Rottweiler, was flanked by two pit bulls. There were several other dogs in the background, circling around, but Mouse couldn't make them out, just that they were large dogs.

"Look what we have here, boys," the lead dog said. "A group of kitty cats."

"Hey," the pit bull to the right said. "It looks like that little one in the middle is leading them. That one's mine."

Without hesitation, Mouse walked forward, right in front of the lead dog, still keeping her fur fluffed and making sure she was ready to pounce. "I'm Mouse, a Protector. I'm leading a group of animals to safety. We're short on time so, if you would, just let us pass."

"You? A Protector? I thought that whole line about cats was a myth," the lead dog said. He leaned down, bared his teeth at Mouse, and growled. "Now I know it is." He stepped forward and snapped his jaw, but Mouse was too fast for him and hit him across the face with her right claws. The dog jumped back and squealed from the sudden pain. The two pit bulls didn't move and appeared to be in shock.

"There's more where that came from if you don't let us pass," Mouse said. The rest of the group had caught up to them, and all of the cats formed a circle, hissing at the dogs, who now numbered eight and stood in a line in front of them.

"Allow me," Butch said as he put himself between Mouse and the Rottweiler. "What seems to be the problem here?" Butch said.

Mouse noticed Butch's bottom lip got lower as he clearly bared his teeth.

"Nothing we weren't handling," the dog said. "Are these ... *cats* friends of yours?"

"They are," Butch replied. "They just helped free a bunch of animals from animal control, including dogs. Now, we're sorry we entered your territory, but we'll be out in a moment if you let us pass."

"Well, isn't that nice. But this ain't your territory, and I can't just let anyone cross."

"No?" Butch said, raising his voice. "You're right." He flexed his muscles as he marched in front of the dogs, keeping his head pointed slightly toward them. Mouse recognized this as a defensive posture her father had taught her. "Now, we're just passing through tonight. And we don't want any trouble. See, my usual territory, since you brought it up, is working with animal control, making sure strays like you aren't out running the streets, threatening people and bullying other animals." Several dogs' ears raised as Butch said this. "And, well, if that's what you're doing"—he stepped back beside Mouse and looked at the leader—"then I'll just have to start cracking skulls!" Butch moved his head to the right, and his neck made a cracking sound. Jochs also made it to the front and stood next to Butch and Mouse.

"Hey, wait a minute," a black, medium-size dog said. "I recognize you from the control facility."

"Yes," Mouse said. "You were there."

"This cat helped us escape," the dog said. "That's not all. King was with us."

Mouse noticed the comments caused a lot of conversation between the other dogs. She tried to remember what the Great Dane had told her. *Yes!*

"King told me to tell anyone that gave us trouble that he knows my name."

"That's right," the black dog said. "I don't have any beef with this cat. Come on, fellows." He and the other dogs turned and left, leaving the Rottweiler by himself.

The lead dog raised his ears. "We were just checking; that's all."

"Looks like more than that by the scratches across your face," Butch said. "You aren't letting just anyone pass. This cat is a Protector, and you just got lucky. If word got out you were tangling with a Protector, one that knows King … well, that would just cause all kinds of bad, wouldn't it?"

Butch moved straight forward and made the Rottweiler step sideways out of his way. Mouse let Butch lead the group out of the lot, while she stayed behind until the last of them was through. Jinx and Tattle were in the back, and Mouse hurried them along. Carl swooped down to where Mouse stood.

"You're falling behind," Carl said.

"Sorry," Mouse said. "I lost sight of you for a minute, and then we had a slight delay."

"You better get your group together and pointed in the right direction," Carl said. "We only have a few hours before daylight."

"Lead the way, Carl," Mouse said, and as he took flight, she ran to the front of the group, where Butch and Jochs were.

"That was some sight," Jochs said. "You two were excellent there!"

"I didn't know you used the term 'cracking skulls,'" Mouse said.

"I don't," Butch said. "I heard you use it back at the shelter on the weasel, and it seemed effective. I was just trying to sound tough so we wouldn't get our butts kicked. And we would have."

"I guess so," Mouse said. "I got that saying from the leader of the rats, Wilber. He's a pretty tough character."

"You were pretty tough yourself," Butch said.

"And you were very brave," Mouse said.

"That had nothing to do with it, kid. After all this running we've been doing, I was just too tired to outrun them and too old to care. We got out of it, right?"

"We did," Mouse said.

"I'll bet you that dog won't forget the swipe you gave him for some time."

"I hope not," Mouse said. "This is a round trip for me, so we have to come back this way."

The group picked up the pace and trotted along for much of the distance. Mouse stopped one more time for a break, only to be prodded on by Carl and the corporal, who promised rest once they were at the train station and who told them they needed to get there before daylight was upon them. Mouse let Butch and Jochs take the lead while she went up and down the line and checked on the other cats.

"Everyone doing okay?"

"When we going to pick up the pace?" one of the cats replied.

Mouse noticed Jinx and Tattle were in the back of the group. She ran alongside them. "You two doing okay?"

"I'm doing fine," Tattle said, "but she's a little insecure. She keeps telling me about the time she knocked over a lamp and something about a broken vase and a kid's balloon."

"Tattle, stop," Jinx said.

"Just saying," Tattle said.

"Well, nothing like that's going to happen on this trip," Mouse said. "I'm going back to the front. You can come with me if you'd like."

"I'll just stay back here," Jinx said. "That way I won't be in anyone's way, and no one can blame me if something happens."

"Suit yourself."

Soon, Mouse spotted a large opening in the houses and buildings and could hear large equipment moving about. As they approached this area, a peculiar scent crossed her nose. *Rats!* She came beside Jochs and Butch, who were setting a good pace.

"You smell that?" Butch asked.

"Sorry," Jochs said. "I'm afraid that my sniffing ability was eclipsed when I hit sixty. That's in dog years, laddie."

"Who you calling laddie?" Butch said. "I'm fifty years old myself."

"Well, I must say you're keeping fit for an old-timer."

"Oh, thanks. I haven't felt this good and this free for a long time," Butch said.

"Yes," Jochs said, "it's kind of exciting to be on the run."

"What's that smell?" Butch asked.

"It's rats," Mouse said. "We're getting ready to meet one, but that smell isn't him. This place is infested with them."

"Are they any trouble?" Butch asked.

"Depends on what kind of rats they are and if we're out of Wilber's territory. But yes, they can be a problem."

"I guess it's a good thing we got all these cats with us, then."

"Maybe, but there are a lot of them out there."

In front of them was a tall fence, and Mouse brought the group to a halt. Carl landed above them on top of the fence and pointed with his wing. "Down that way, you'll find a water pipe, and Streets is waiting there."

Mouse led the group through side streets and back alleys to the rendezvous point—the train station.

"Over here." She heard Street's voice as they approached. He was hiding in the water pipe that went under the fence.

"I see you got quite a crew," Streets said. "Not many dogs, though; that's good."

"The dogs wanted to go on their own," Mouse said. "Streets, meet Butch and Jochs." Mouse pointed to the two dogs.

"A rat?" Jochs said. "I'm glad I don't have many acquaintances. No one would believe the story I'm going to have to tell after this journey."

"What's the plan?" Mouse asked.

"We're going to the rail yard," Streets said, "but you've got to make sure your friends won't harm any of the rats in there."

"Is that what I've been sensing?" Mouse said.

"Hey," Streets said, "us rats been running this rail yard and shipyards for years. I've got rats stationed all over the place, on Wilber's orders, to secure your safe passage. There's a train car in there, see?" He pointed to the center of the yard where the tracks merged. "We get on, and it'll take us to the edge of town."

"We've been going at a good pace," Mouse said. "Some of these animals need a break."

"Once we get to the car, they can sleep in there," Streets said. "We're in the middle of the city now, and it will take a long time to get out near where the farms are. But we got to get on quick before the train leaves and before it gets light."

"Lead the way," Mouse said.

Streets led them through a water pipe that was nearly too small and narrow for Butch to pass through, and he had to crawl through much of it. When they exited the pipe, they were inside the rail yard. Streets looked to the sky.

"We're cutting it close," Streets said. "Colonel Wellington is overhead, making sure the coast is clear of people. Now, see that car over there on the tracks?" He pointed to a large boxcar attached to a long line of cars. This one had the door cracked open, and a board ran down from the opening to the ground. "That's our ticket, kid. We gotta get all these … uh, is that a weasel?"

"Yes," Mouse said. "Just don't tell him anything unless you want everyone else to know. He blabs everything he hears."

"Got it."

"Continue what you were saying."

"We need to get inside that railroad car. It will take us reasonably close to the farming area where Paggs lives. We should break up into groups and take a few at a time. I'll take the first group."

"Scratch, Dazzle, and I will take three more groups," Mouse said, turning to the other cats. "I'll lead the last group."

Mouse watched as Streets led the first group, which had Jochs and Butch with it, across the tracks and up a board to an open railroad car. Then Scratch and Dazzle went with their group. Mouse turned to her group of two cats, including Jinx, and Tattle.

"Okay, let's go, and keep it quiet," Mouse said. Then she heard a noise. A train horn sounded, and the car that they were supposed to get in jarred forward suddenly.

"Run!" Mouse called out as the group made haste to the railcar. The board fell to the ground as the train began to move along the tracks. The cats ran alongside and jumped to safety, but Tattle could not make the jump.

"Just leave me behind," Tattle told Mouse. He remained on the ground beside Mouse and started slowing down.

Mouse looked to the railcar and spotted Butch at the edge. "Butch, get ready to catch," she called out.

She grabbed Tattle at the top of his neck, the same spot where her mom used to carry her when she was a kitten, and with her best effort, she turned her head one way and then back to the other, flinging him into the air. Butch caught him and hauled him into the car. *It worked!* Mouse celebrated inside but noticed the train was gaining speed, and she was having trouble keeping up. With great effort, she hurled herself in a pouncing motion toward the opening, only making it with her front paws. With claws out, she grasped tightly as the rest of her body hung perilously out of the car. Mouse spotted Butch, but he was still setting Tattle down. She felt her grip slipping when a mouth closed over her neck and pulled her to safety.

"Thanks, Jochs," Mouse said as she shook herself, trying to clear her head from the close call.

"You're something, kid," Streets said and put his fist toward Mouse. She bumped his fist with her paw. "Now, you can all settle in for a while and get some sleep. We've got a long ride ahead of us before we get to our exit point."

"Good," Mouse said. "Do we have everyone?" She scanned the car where the animals had spread out among some boxes and wooden crates. She spotted all seven cats (including Jinx, who nodded at her), Tattle, Jochs, and Butch, along with five of Colonel Wellington's pigeons, who stood in line. Carl and Colonel Wellington had not made it to the car yet. Mouse also spotted several rats, including two that looked familiar.

"Hey, what are you two doing here?" She went over to the rats.

Slim nudged Slouch in the side with his elbow as Mouse approached.

"I told you she would recognize us," Slim said.

"Did Wilber send you?" Mouse asked.

"Yes," Slouch said.

"No," Slim said.

The two rats looked at each other.

"Well, which is it?" Mouse asked.

Standing on his hind legs, Slouch moved the right one back and forth in front of him, drawing a line on the floor as he avoided eye contact. "I'm sure Wilber wouldn't mind that we came to help you and would want us to look out for you."

"Right," Slim said, clapping his paws together. "We decided that we should do something for you to help, after all you've done for us. Please don't make us go back."

"We want to be part of the adventure," Slim said.

"You do?" Mouse asked.

"Yes," Slim and Slouch said in unison.

Just then, Carl flew in through the doorway and landed right by Mouse.

He lifted his left wing, brushed it, and checked it and then his right wing. "Corporal?" he called out, and one of the pigeons stepped forward.

"Yes, Sergeant Major."

"Please fly back and give the first report. We made it to the train ... hmm ... without serious incident. Remember to give the report directly to Ladie so that Chief will know."

"Roger," the corporal said, and Mouse watched as the pigeon went to the doorway and flew out.

Mouse turned back to Slim and Slouch.

"What do we have here?" Carl asked.

"Seems these two want to join our adventure," Mouse said.

"Is that so?" Carl said. "Didn't you two have a motto of 'Never try, never fail' or something like that? And didn't you also have a philosophy about not working too hard?"

"He's got us," Slim said.

"Wait," Slouch said. "That used to be what we said. We're reformed now. We've been working in the kitchens for Wilber for months and keeping our noses clean. Right, Slim?"

"I've been working hard," Slim said. "You, kinda."

Slouch put his paw over Slim's mouth. "That's enough. I don't want you to hear how much I've been reformed or else you'll tell me I don't have to do anything because I've been working so hard. In fact, you'd probably tell me I could just tag along as an observer."

"Not going to happen," Mouse said. "You want to come with us; it's not going to be an easy trail."

"You did notice we were traveling with a bunch of cats," Carl said.

"Which is exactly why you need us," Slouch said, pointing back and forth between him and Slouch. "With all these cats, who you gonna turn to when you need a second opinion?" He raised his eyebrows. "Also, we're great foragers; we can find all kinds of stuff that you might need. And Slim, here, he's got lots of muscle." Slim nodded. "And me, I got lots of talents."

"Such as?" Mouse asked.

"Say we come into contact with someone who tells you something, but you ain't sure you can trust the fellow. Well, ain't no one can smell a rat—you know, a con—like another rat."

Slim nodded. "He can smell a lie like a fart in an elevator."

"Carl?"

"I have an aversion to animals that live in sewers," Carl said. "The decision is all yours." Carl took leave and went over to where the pigeons were located.

Mouse turned to Slim and Slouch. "If you can keep up, you can go, but we aren't waiting for you. And you're responsible for finding your own food." She didn't want to be too hard on them but still didn't trust the two, as they easily had switched loyalties in the past.

"Deal," Slouch said.

Mouse noticed that Streets was scowling, so she asked him, "Do you have a problem with this?"

Streets sighed and said, "I dunno. I just don't trust those two." They both watched Slim and Slouch as they meandered around the rail cart and finally settled by Tattle. The other animals appeared to have settled down, except for Jinx, who watched Mouse.

Mouse went over to Jinx. "See? We made it just fine. Soon you'll be in a place where you can feel at home. I'm sure of it."

"That cat is all kinds of crazy," Sikes said as he secured his position on a flat railcar and hung on as the train pulled out of the station.

Rascal nodded. "You see how she was going to take on those dogs back there. Then she comes in here and jumps onto a moving train, causing us to have to do the same to keep up with her. I don't think she needs anyone to watch over her. See what she's got us into?"

"I see," Sikes said. He started laughing. "I see. That kid has some kind of luck." He grinned.

"What's wrong with you?" Rascal said. "Why are you so happy?"

"This … this is some of the most exciting stuff I ever done." He kept laughing. "You thought chasing pigeons was fun. This is *crazy*!"

Rascal chuckled. "You got me there." Suddenly, he ducked down as something swooped by his head and then came back around, landing a few feet in front of him. "Colonel Wellington?"

"Yes," Colonel Wellington said. "Happy you remember the rank. I was out on reconnaissance and spotted you two following us. May I ask what you're doing here?"

"We're here to keep an eye on things," Rascal said. "We got a stake in this too."

"That's right," Sikes said. "And don't you go telling anyone about us.

We're incognito. In disguise. Undercover. By the way, how'd you know we were out here?"

"This isn't like the park, where you two can hide under a tree or a bush," Colonel Wellington said. "Despite your clever disguise, it was easy to spot you two jumping on this railcar that has no covering, leaving you completely exposed. But I will say, you jump with such skill."

"Thanks," Sikes said. "But you won't tell Mouse about us?"

"Why shouldn't I?" Colonel Wellington said.

"Chief was worried abouts Mouse, and we about the boys, so here we are. Just in case, though. We don't want to, you know, interfere. We wouldn't want that little kid to think we don't trust her and all."

"Quite interesting," Colonel Wellington said. "So you do trust her?"

"After seeing what she just did tonight," Rascal said, "I'm not sure she needs anyone looking after her."

"Yes," Colonel Wellington said. "She does seem to have quite the charm when it comes to dangerous situations. She seems to know when to be calm and when to be brash."

"You aren't going to tell, are you?"

"No," Colonel Wellington said, raising his right wing. "I'll keep your secret. In fact, we can use this to our advantage. A good commander always has a rearguard or reserve forces. Now that I know you're here, I can call on you, if needed."

"How's that?" Sikes said.

"You two don't want to reveal yourselves unless you're needed, right?"

"Right," Sikes said. "We don't want to ruin the kid's confidence."

"And you don't want her to know you're following her, correct?"

"Hey, this pigeon is some kind of psychic or something," Sikes said.

"I can help with that," Colonel Wellington said. "You can keep your distance so you aren't discovered, and I can let you know the route and let you know if and when you're needed."

"You would do that?" Rascal asked.

"Of course," Colonel Wellington said. "We're allies, after all. There's just one thing I might have to do."

"What's that?"

"I might have to tell the Sergeant Major."

"Sergeant Major?"

"You know him as Carl, the cockatoo. He's also keeping watch from the air, and he might spot you. He might inadvertently expose your situation if he doesn't know about our little pact."

"Just make sure he knows not to tell Mouse."

"Agreed," Colonel Wellington said. "It's time for me to get to the car the others are riding in. I'll check back with you shortly."

"When does the train stop?" Rascal asked.

"Oh, it won't stop," Colonel Wellington said. "When it comes time, you're going to have to jump to get off. Until then, I would suggest you find some cover."

CHAPTER 6
DANGER AHEAD

I t was early morning, and Chief finished his rounds in the first building he was patrolling and went back to his home building, where he hopped in the elevator to save time. Although he wasn't used to doing the patrol the way Mouse did it, he figured he would follow her method, as he needed to make certain stops—first, to check on Miss Doris and to see Ladie to find out if she had heard any news; second, to check in on Little Foot because he had promised Mouse he would do so.

He exited the elevator on the fourteenth floor and went into Miss Doris's apartment, where he headed to the bedroom. He hadn't been in the room for almost four months, as Mouse had been taking on his duties. He still remembered how he used to check on the elderly lady by going to her bedroom and listening to make sure she was breathing normally. One time, he even had to summon Sam because she wasn't breathing right. He had saved her life, as she was in distress, something Miss Doris had rewarded him for numerous times.

"Sounds normal," Chief said to himself. He turned and went through the kitchen and into the living room, a favorite room of his in all of the apartments. While Sam had made his apartment comfortable with cat toys and cat beds, Miss Doris's apartment sparkled with colorful crocheted afghans and blankets on the chairs and couch; it represented what he considered a look of pleasant comfort. The room beckoned those who entered to be calm and relax.

"Good morning, Ladie," Chief said as he entered.

The yellow canary stirred in her cage. "Good morning, Chief. It's nice to see you."

"You'll be seeing me a lot over the next few days until Mouse gets back."

"Yes, well, it will be a welcome event," Ladie said. "Speaking of that, I have some news for you."

Chief jumped to the stool across from Ladie's cage to be at her level. It was not something he was accustomed to doing, but knew it was where Mouse sat when she spoke to Ladie. "Is this okay?" he asked to make sure it was appropriate.

"Yes, of course," Ladie said. "I'm just not used to you being there."

"I know," Chief said. "And I'm sorry. I told Mouse that birds and cats were not supposed to be friends. But she showed me."

"Yes, the little darling has a way about her with making friends."

"You had some news," Chief said.

"Yes. I've already heard from the Pigeon Brigade. A corporal stopped by and said they had made it safely to their first point without incident. Everyone is safe."

"Good," Chief said. "Let's hope that's the start of continuing good news."

"I'm sure it will be."

"Now, if you'll forgive my short stay, I have a lot of extra work to do," Chief said and hopped down. "I'll see you later today when I make my evening patrol."

"I look forward to it," Ladie said.

Chief went down the hall and took the stairs to the next level, sniffing and listening for any signs of trouble. He did this until he reached the fifth floor, where he stopped outside the furniture-storage room. He thought back to the time when Mouse and Little Foot had just become friends, and Mouse suggested Little Foot hide in the storage room to keep anyone from knowing about her. Chief still had sensed the small mouse around the apartments, but he had ignored the scent because Little Foot wasn't a normal, potentially rabid mouse but was a fancy mouse who had once been a pet. Because of a careless owner, she had been left in a pile of laundry, where Mouse had found her. Since that encounter, the two had become best friends.

Chief stepped through the door into the storage room. "It smells clean in here," Chief said.

"We keep it clean and even use some of the housekeeper's deodorizer," Little Foot said as she came out from underneath a couch. "It's a fall breeze scent." She lifted her nose and sniffed the air.

"It's got a nice appeal," Chief said. "I told Mouse I would check on you. I see you made it back safely."

"Yes," Little Foot said. "In the most fantastic way. One of the pigeons flew me home. Have you ever been flying, Mr. Chief?"

"Can't say that I have," Chief said.

"Well, it was really fun and kind of scary."

"I can see how that would be exciting," Chief said. He glanced around the room and wasn't sure what else to say or ask. The awkward silence made a loud sound in the quiet room. "I'll be coming around a couple of times a day to check on you," he said. "Just let me know if there's anything you need." He turned to leave but heard Little Foot's voice.

"I was kind of wondering ... if maybe ... you might, well, have some time later—or if not today, then tomorrow—to, you know, perhaps, if you're not too busy and all, play some hide-and-seek?" She raised her eyebrows and ears. "Mouse and I often work on our skills, you know, since she's a Protector and I'm a Junior Protector."

Chief hesitated; he didn't know what to say.

"You do know how to play hide-and-seek, right?" Little Foot asked. Her front paws came together, and her eyes got bigger. "If not, I can teach you; it's really easy."

"I know how to play," Chief finally said. He was having trouble saying no to such a cute face. "I'll tell you what. Let me finish my patrol and give Charlene the news about Mouse, and then I'll come back. But I won't be able to play for long. I've got a lot of extra patrols to do with Mouse gone."

Little Foot clapped her hands and did a circle. "It will be so much fun. I'll show you some of the places Mouse likes to hide."

"Okay, why don't you practice hiding until I get back."

He left the storage room and went through the next three floors and checked the basement before returning to his apartment. As he went down the hall, he caught the sound of Sam's voice, but he could not identify the person with whom Sam conversed. He hurried his pace, curious to see this person.

"Oh, there you are," Sam said when Chief entered the kitchen. He bent down and lifted Chief off the ground, something he rarely did. "Chief, meet Myra. She's going to be our new maintenance person while I take on my new tasks as facilities manager."

"Oh, what a beautiful cat," Myra said and put her hand out to pet Chief.

Chief looked at the lady, who was shorter than Sam by a foot and had dark hair, brown eyes, a high nose bridge, and shallow cheeks. As she petted him, he noticed her hands were somewhat calloused like Sam's.

Sam let Chief down, but Chief remained close to observe.

"The new building will take several months to finish," Sam said. "That'll give you some time move into your new apartment, which will be in the third building of the complex. Once you move in, we'll do the rounds together and make sure you know where all the maintenance points are."

"That sounds exciting," Myra said.

"And you do like cats?" Sam asked.

"Why, yes," Myra said. "Will I need one?"

"You don't have one?"

"Not at the moment," she said. "My little one passed away over a year ago." She put her hand to her eye to catch a tear. "I haven't had the heart yet to get another one."

"Well, we'll find you one," Sam said. "One that's suitable to patrol the building. See, here we don't use poisons or traps. The cats keep the vermin out. It's been highly successful with our residents."

"That sound nice," Myra said.

"The cats also serve to keep security tight. In fact, Chief here even alerted me when one of our elderly residents needed help, and it saved her life."

"Really?"

"Yes, that's something Miss Sorenson didn't tell you. I don't think she likes cats. Let me take you on a tour of the buildings, then," Sam said, and the two left the apartment.

Chief headed to the bedroom, where he found Charlene napping.

"Care to join me?" Charlene asked.

"Maybe later. I still have more things to check on. Was Miss Sorenson here?"

"Yes," Charlene said. "She was in there talking with Sam and Myra just a few minutes before you arrived. Why?"

"I thought I smelled her in the hallway is all. I just wanted to make sure there wasn't someone else smoking in the building. It's a fire hazard."

"Yes," Charlene said. "But if she quit smoking, we wouldn't be able to smell her, and then we wouldn't be able to avoid her."

"Except to listen for those high-heeled shoes she wears. I can hear them coming down the hall from the next floor." Chief and Charlene laughed at his description.

"Anyone home?"

Chief heard Baxter's voice.

"In here," Chief said and went out to the living room as Baxter entered the apartment. "Hi, Baxter," Chief said. He went to the water dish to drink and then ate a few pieces of fish that Sam had just put out.

"You're so lucky," Baxter said. "Sam is still feeding you so well, giving you fish. I mainly get dried food where I am."

"Maybe that will change," Chief said. "I just saw him walking with the new maintenance lady, and she seems to really like cats."

"Is that so?" Baxter said.

"I hope so," Chief said. "I also hope this person takes some pressure off Sam. He sure works a lot of hours now to keep up with all the maintenance stuff. He works more hours than us."

"Speaking of that," Baxter said, "I came by to see if you need any help with the extra patrols and stuff since Mouse is gone."

"I got the buildings covered, but if you could take a few extra rounds outside, that would help," Chief said, "especially the back alley, since Sikes and his boys are gone. It would be a perfect time for some rats or someone to move in without them there."

"Sure, I'll start this afternoon," Baxter said. "Have you heard anything?"

Chief noticed Charlene's ears rise at Baxter's question. "Yes. The first pigeon brought news back this morning and said they made the first leg of their journey without incident. See, everything is going to be just fine. The world isn't that tough out there."

"That's great news," Baxter said.

"Hey, Baxter," Chief said. "Can we go to the alley for a minute, just to make sure we're clear on what needs to be checked?"

"Sure, but I think I know what—"

"Just to be sure," Chief insisted. "I'll be right back," he told Charlene as he headed outside with Baxter.

Once they were out in the hall, they went to the side exit out of the building and into the alley.

"What is it you wanted me to check?" Baxter said.

"Nothing," Chief said. "I just wanted to get out of there for a minute. I didn't want Charlene to see how worried I was."

"You said everything was going fine so far. Is that not the whole story?"

"No, of course everything is fine. That's the report anyway. But it's the rest of the stuff I said about it not being too tough out there."

"Yes, I know. I haven't been to the country, but I know the city isn't a good place—full of rabid dogs that chase cats; full of cats that have turf wars and nasty, vile rats everywhere in trash piles. For being so intelligent, humans leave a lot of abandoned buildings, junkyards, and trash all around. What?"

Chief waved his paw at Baxter. "Stop describing things; you're making it worse."

"Sorry," Baxter said. "Just have some faith in Mouse and in the others who are with her. I'm sure they'll work it out."

"You're right. Come on; let's walk the perimeter together and get some air."

"Walk?" Baxter said. "Let's get some exercise." Baxter took off sprinting, and Chief followed him.

Mouse drifted in and out of sleep through the rest of the night and watched as it became day. She was more awake than the rest so that she could keep an eye on the doorway and on the others. Although Streets kept close to the other rats, she noticed they didn't talk that much to him. She considered it was because he was independent. Slim and Slouch seemed to like Tattle, and they were up most of the night, while the other cats and Butch and Jochs slept soundly. Carl sat down by Mouse and even leaned on her when he fell asleep. He suddenly woke as Streets approached them.

"Sorry, there," Carl said as he moved a step away from Mouse. "Didn't mean to lean to get so close. It was probably the motion of the train and all that shifted me."

"It's okay, Carl," Mouse said. "My fur probably makes a better pillow than the hard floor."

"Well, I didn't mean to impose."

"You didn't get much sleep," Streets said.

"I'm not used to much sleep, and I also get a lot of exercise with my patrols, which keeps me fit."

"I guess that's probably why you aren't as tired as the rest," Streets said. "We should be getting close to the next rendezvous point."

"Rendezvous, yes," Carl said. "The colonel and I will do an immediate reconnaissance when we arrive."

Mouse watched blocks of houses and businesses go by that slowly gave way to more open areas. "So when the train stops, we get off and meet Midnight?"

Streets didn't have time to answer her question, as Tattle had walked over to them.

"Why doesn't anyone like me?" Tattle said. "I've tried to make friends here, and no one on the train will talk to me, except the rats."

Mouse didn't respond right away. She didn't know how to tell him what was wrong without hurting his feelings. Luckily, she didn't have to because Streets blurted out his answer.

"Because you're always talking, noisy, telling everyone everything, even if they don't want to hear it," Streets said. "You jabber and go on and on, and you don't listen to others. Oh, I'm sorry. Were you asking her and not me?"

Tattle's eyes teared up.

Mouse frowned at Streets.

"What?" Streets said. "Someone's got to tell the kid or else he's in for a lot of disappointment. And given that he's already a weasel, he's got enough against him."

"You don't have to be so rude about it," Mouse said.

"No," Tattle said, wiping the tears with his paw. "I want to know why everyone avoids me."

"I'm not an expert," Mouse said, "but I'll tell you what I know. It's okay to talk and have a conversation, but sometimes when someone tells you something, they don't want you to blab it all over. And when someone does something, you don't have to tell everyone else about it, especially if it was something that might embarrass them. Unless you're trying to compliment someone, they don't always want everyone to know what they do. It's called respecting privacy."

"What if it's something they shouldn't be doing?" Tattle asked. "Shouldn't I tell someone?"

"You mean like being a rat?" Mouse said.

Her comment drew a cross look from Streets.

"Yes," Tattle said.

"I've always differed on that point," Carl said, "if you don't mind my participating in your conversation. The railcar is awfully small, and although my ears appear little, I hear a lot."

"No," Mouse said. "I'd like to hear your view on the matter."

"If it's something that's not going to hurt anyone, then it really doesn't hurt to look away. Kind of like Mouse, here, being friends with a bird. Many cats won't accept another cat that is friends with a bird, but why? What's the harm? Now, when you have a situation that threatens or puts others in danger"—he cleared his throat—"then it's my hearty opinion that we all have a responsibility to inform the proper authorities. That's the way the world should work."

"Sounds like something my dad would say," Mouse said. "He's smart like Carl and in charge of a lot of things."

"Thank you so much," Tattle said. He ran back to where Slim and Slouch were sitting and started talking to them.

"Let's hope he heard us," Carl said. "Your dad's not the only one in charge of a lot with this mission and all."

"Speaking of that," Mouse said, turning back to Streets, "when the train stops, that's when we're getting off, right?"

"It doesn't stop," Streets said. "When we get close to the rendezvous, we're going to have to jump."

"Hah!" Chief exclaimed as he pounced around the corner of a chair, sure he'd found where Little Foot was hiding. True to his promise, he had returned to play hide-and-seek with the little mouse. He was wrong again at finding the location where she'd hidden. It surprised him that she was so good at hiding. The little giggle from a nearby cushion gave away her true position in the chair behind him, where he found her tucked between the side of a seat cushion and the chair frame. "There you are."

Little Foot scrambled out. "I gave myself away again, didn't I?"

"I guess I'll just have to try harder to find you," Chief said. "And you'll have to try harder not to laugh."

His comment made Little Foot laugh even more, and she rolled across the top of the chair.

"You're just pretending," Little Foot said. "I think you're just trying to make me feel better by not finding me so fast."

"No," Chief said. "You're really good at hiding. And you keep yourself clean so I can't smell you."

"I thought that you were a Protector," Little Foot said. "Doesn't that give you special senses?" She sat down on the chair and looked down where Chief sat facing her.

"I didn't know my father," Chief said. "So I only know so much about being a Protector because no one explained all of it to me. We have senses that help us when something bad is about to happen or when we detect bad things in an animal or person."

"Wow, you can really do that?"

"Yes," Chief said. "That's why the Protectors were put here—to help."

"So, am I good inside and that's why you can't find me?"

"You're definitely good," Chief said. "A good little mouse and good at hide-and-seek. Now I need to be going. I have to do another patrol and see if Ladie has had any new news. I won't be back to check on you until tomorrow. No tenants are moving into this building, so you should be safe as long as you stay in here."

"Thank you for playing hide-and-seek with me," Little Foot said as Chief exited the room. "Maybe tomorrow we can work on pouncing or power-sliding."

"Sure thing," Chief said. He went down the hallway and up the stairs to Ms. Doris's room. When he entered, he sensed right away that she wasn't there and knew that meant it was later than he expected.

"She's playing bridge now," Ladie said from the other room.

Chief entered the living room. "Yes, I remember her always playing at this time," Chief said. "I just wanted to come by anyway and see if you've heard any more news."

"No," Ladie said. "But it's still only the first day."

"I know," Chief said. He considered jumping on the stool across from Ladie's birdcage but remained on the carpet instead, thinking he would just stay for a short visit. He had already done two patrols and really didn't need to do another until later in the night, so he wasn't sure what he would do next. He realized he was still standing in front of Ladie, who watched him.

"You're really worried about her, aren't you, honey?" Ladie said.

"Is it that obvious?" Chief said.

"After all that she has done and shown you, you should know that child is blessed."

"It doesn't make it any easier," Chief said. "Even the luckiest will one day press their luck. It was the same for me." Chief jumped to the stool, where he could see Ladie better than from the floor. Mouse took this position with her all of the time and had many conversations with the small yellow canary;

Chief had stood outside the door and listened on occasion. He knew that although Ladie was petite, she had loads of wisdom.

"Tell me," Ladie said. "What happened that you worry so much?"

"When I was young and on my own, I could have easily ended up somewhere bad. Instead, a solitary man, Sam, took me in. He found that I was useful. I always had a sense about me. I didn't know at the time that it was because I was a Protector. When I worked at the motel, there were lots of alley cats, clans of rats, and even a few snakes. I took them all on; not at the same time, mind you, but each time I took on a bigger challenge and always managed to come out on top."

"Sounds like you passed that ability on to your daughter," Ladie said.

"No, not at all. Mouse is entirely different. See, I didn't have allies. I did it all through speed and toughness. I wasn't the biggest cat, but I could whip any of those alley cats. I thought I was invulnerable. That's how Sam and I got this job. Between Sam being good at fixing stuff and me being good at keeping out the vermin, his boss promoted him to this nicer building. That's when it happened."

"What?"

"My luck ran out. Not right away. I mean, I made a truce with Wilber and met Charlene and all. Things were good until that hoodlum rat came along."

"Is that what this is about?" Ladie said. "You getting hurt by Bragar?"

"No," Chief said. "I knew there was danger when I faced that rat. I should have waited for Baxter and the others, but I wasn't used to asking or waiting for help. I charged in, confident that I could handle anything. I was wrong."

"But your daughter came through," Ladie said. "She defeated Bragar because of the courage you instilled in her."

"Oh no," Chief said. "She's smarter than me. And her defeating Bragar may have made her more dangerous to herself. See, with every adventure that she's had, she's pushed her luck just a little more."

"And you think eventually that luck will run out, and she'll get hurt, just like you did?"

"Exactly," Chief said. He crossed his paws in front of him as he lay down, satisfied he'd finally made sense of what he was thinking.

"You may have a point," Ladie said. "Only Mouse isn't like you."

"What? What do you mean?"

"Oh, she's brave and courageous just like you. But she also realizes she's not as strong or big as you. She relies on her friends more and trusts them to see her through. She has plenty of friends watching out for her. I understand you even made it more for this trip."

"How so?" Chief said.

"Oh, I have my way of knowing," Ladie said. "Streets may be the rat that knows everything that goes on around the streets, and Wilber may rule the underground, but I'm the queen of the castle when it comes to these buildings. I know that Sikes and Rascal went to keep an eye on Mouse."

"So you think I shouldn't be so worried?"

"No," Ladie said. "I think we both should be worried. We have a lot of our friends out there doing a brave but dangerous task. But we should also wish them the best and have confidence in them."

"You're right," Chief said. He stood and jumped down from the stool. "I've learned my lesson as well. I rely on Mouse to keep her patrols, Wilber to watch the sewers, and the alley cats to keep the alleys clear. I learned from my daughter that the more allies you have, the more you can enjoy life—you know, instead of trying to do everything yourself."

"That you did," Ladie said. "I'm sure she would be proud to hear that. How are you holding up without her around?"

Chief didn't want to seem overly concerned. He knew Mouse and Ladie were good friends, and anything he said would probably get back to Mouse. He did his best to cover how much he worried. "I trust that she's doing fine or else I never would have agreed to let her go."

"I'm glad you are handling it so well," Ladie said. "I know I'm worried every time a pigeon comes calling until I see who it is. If they have the insignia, I know it's one of Colonel Wellington's pigeons and that we may get some news."

"What do the other pigeons come here for?"

"I've lived with Miss Doris for some time. She's a wise old lady and that has rubbed off on me. These pigeons come to me for advice."

"Oh," Chief said. "Thanks for the talk."

"It's my pleasure, honey."

Chief headed back to his apartment, hoping that all was well with Mouse.

The hours passed quietly on the train as it headed north, out of the city. After being awake most of the night, many of the animals rested through the day. However, all of them were wide awake and alert when Mouse told them how they were getting off the train car.

"You did say we were going to jump?" Slouch asked. "As in hurl our bodies out the door from a fast-moving train?"

Mouse nodded. "Yes, Carl and Colonel Wellington already left to recon the area and make sure our landing site is secure."

"Landing site? We don't fly; it'll be more of a crash site," Slouch said. "If we jump, we're going to have a very bad landing—very bad."

"Don't worry," Streets said. "You aren't the first ones to do this. There's a big patch of soft grass alongside the track that will act like a big pillow. You'll slide right down a small hill. Just make sure you jump when I tell you."

"What if we don't? What if we delay?" Slouch asked.

"If you don't make the hill," Streets said, "then the train goes over a bridge. You don't want to jump off the bridge. And if you don't get off before the bridge, then there's a wall. After the wall is a bunch of pavement and rocks that will make your landing extremely uncomfortable. If you don't get off before all of that, then the train heads into another station. At this time of day, there'll probably be people about. You don't want them to find you. As for you, Mouse, the next station isn't run by rats who know Wilber. I don't know how they'll react to you bringing a group of cats there."

"We better make it off, then," Mouse said. "We'll jump in groups. Butch, you take the first group with Scratch and Dazzle. Jochs, the second group, and I'll take the final group with Streets."

"Oh no," Streets said. "This is where we part ways. I go through to the station to catch a train back."

"What about meeting Midnight?" Mouse asked.

"You'll meet him by the bridge," Streets said, "but he won't be there until it gets dark. Just wait for him."

"Not until tonight?"

"Yeah, he won't agree to meet anyone new unless it's dark outside. Don't worry; he'll be there. He's got a reputation to protect, just like me. Wait in the meadow at the base of the hill. He'll find you. Get ready; it's time."

Mouse went to the door, and Butch took the lead. The train did slow down some as it started to climb an embankment to the bridge.

"Now," Streets said.

Butch and three cats jumped with Scratch and Dazzle. Then Jochs and three more cats jumped. That left Mouse, Jinx, Slim and Slouch, and Tattle.

"Ready?" Mouse asked.

"Wee-e-e!" Tattle yelled and jumped.

Slim and Slouch went to the edge. "We're going to die!" Slouch said.

"Oh, don't be so dramatic," Slim said and pushed him out ahead as he jumped.

"We'll go together," Mouse said to Jinx, and the two went to the edge.

"Good luck, kid," Streets said as Mouse and Jinx jumped.

The landing was soft in the thick green grass. It was a sensation Mouse had never felt before as she slid down the hill; she enjoyed the smell and texture. At the end of her slide, the other animals, all on their feet, were waiting and smiling.

"Let's go again," Tattle said, jumping around in a circle.

Mouse spotted Slouch bent over, looking at his legs. "You okay?" she asked the thin rat.

"What, me?" Slouch looked surprised. "I was just pretending back there. This is nothing. I just was checking to make sure I didn't break my leg."

"So what do we do now?" Butch asked.

"We wait here until night," Mouse said. She spotted something of interest right behind Butch. She wasn't the only one. Many of the cats and Weasel noticed a difference in their surroundings, something they hadn't seen up close. "What are those?" Mouse said as she moved forward to the big, tall, brown and green plants.

"Those are trees," Butch said.

"Trees? We have some in our park but not this big."

"Not many in the city. Go ahead and touch them. In fact, I believe cats like to climb in them."

"Climb?" Mouse ran to the closest tree, stuck her claws in the wood, and found that she could climb it, just like the furniture or carpeted areas of the stairs. She raced to one of the branches and crawled out onto it. "You have to come up here," she said to Jinx.

For the next hour, she ran around the meadow and climbed in the trees with the other cats and Tristan and Tattle, while the dogs and Slim and Slouch napped in the tall, soft grass.

"You don't have trees where you live?" Jinx asked as the two cats sat on a branch looking over the meadow.

"Not like this," Mouse said. "We have some really small ones in the front parking lot and in a nearby park, but they don't have this many leaves and aren't this tall."

"You can see far from up here," Jinx said.

"Where I live," Mouse said, "there are a lot of tall buildings that are taller than these trees. I can get on the roof of them and see farther than from up here."

"That must be awesome," Jinx said.

"It is," Mouse said, "but this is too. It's so quiet here, and everything smells so … fresh. I never get that where I live except when Little Foot sprays deodorizer. I always smell car exhaust, perfume, and Miss Sorenson's smoke."

"Are we going to your building where you live?" Jinx said.

"No," Mouse said.

"Why not? It seems like a neat place."

Mouse thought for a moment before she replied. She remembered what her father had told her about having too many animals in the alley and about Miss Sorenson.

"I think it's because there are already enough animals where we live, and my dad—he's in charge—said if we brought all of you there, the people who live there would get upset."

"I just don't understand," Jinx said. "I was in a pet store, and a family adopted me for a little girl. I thought I had a home and that they would love me. But everything I did went wrong. They traded me to some girl who always took me everywhere but left me in the car all of the time."

"I don't think that's going to happen where we're going."

"Tell me about where we're going," Jinx said. "Are there a lot of trees?"

"I've never been there," Mouse said. "But I know someone who went there, and he said it's a great place with plenty of space and food. He used to live in the complex where I live, and he retired there, so it must be a great place to go."

"Anything is better than staying locked in a cage forever," Jinx said. "They fed us good, but we never got to go out."

Mouse looked down and noticed Butch was stirring. "I'm going to scout around and see if I can find us something to eat." She moved to a low branch and jumped off, startling Butch.

"Sorry," Mouse said.

"How long are we supposed to wait here?"

"Streets said our guide, a cat named Midnight, only meets people at night. So we have to wait until it's dark. I was hoping we could find something to eat before then."

"Eat?" Scratch said as he came over to Mouse and Butch. "We're close to the bridge right there. A lot of fishermen throw out what they don't want. We can probably find some fish right along the bank. Dazzle and I will go round up some and be right back."

"If your guide doesn't show up," Butch said, "maybe we could live right here in this little patch of grass and trees. It seems so peaceful."

"It is nice here," Mouse agreed. She didn't tell Butch that she sensed a human presence close by and other animals that probably frequented the area. She suspected that if they stayed too long, someone might find them, or some other animal that wasn't friendly would come along. She smiled as Scratch and Dazzle approached, both carrying a fish in their mouths.

"Dinnertime!" Scratch called out. All the cats ate well, and Butch and Jochs joined in. Slim, Slouch, and Tattle went off on their own and found a trash can to raid, bringing some scraps back that were too foul for the others to eat but that they seemed to enjoy. In all, the group was happy as night fell. Another train went by, and the noise it caused, along with the ground shaking, let Mouse know why no one had settled in the meadow.

"Yo, Rascal, we needs to get back to the bridge before we lose track of Mouse and the group," Sikes said as the two cats moved through the wooded area that ran adjacent to the train tracks.

"Sorry," Rascal said. He limped, favoring his left front paw. "That landing back there was a little hard, and my leg is a little sore. If we could've jumped out when they did on the soft grass, I would've been okay."

"You know we had to jump after them so they wouldn't see us, right?" Sikes said.

"We just didn't know that there would be a bridge and a wall and then rocks and stuff," Rascal said.

"At least we got off before the station back there," Sikes said.

"And we know what we'll pass along the way back." Rascal smiled. "A big concrete slab, a bunch of rocks, and then a bridge."

"Your leg hurt bad?"

"No, just a little sore. I'll be okay as long as it doesn't stiffen up."

"Then a good walk is whats you need," Sikes said. "Besides, I don't think there will be any more train rides from here. We gots to be close to the country after that long train ride."

"I hope we don't have any more trains," Rascal said as he limped along. "Or else I'll just have to jump in the river next time and take my chances."

Sikes laughed.

"You ever been this far out of the city?"

"No," Sikes said. "I've been around many places in the city that was farther away from the apartments than we are now but not out to the country. We took a different direction than I ever been too. How about you?"

"No," Rascal said. "I like the city, where it's safe. Out here, there's supposed to be wild things—dogs running loose, coyotes, big raptor-type birds, rabbits."

"Rabbits?" Sikes stopped walking. "Why would you be afraid of rabbits?"

"Out here they aren't just any rabbits, like the fluffy, cute ones people keep in cages," Rascal said. "They get big out here and lose their minds in the wild."

"Then that makes it even more important for us to get back to the bridge before Mouse moves out. We're supposed to be watching out for her and the boys."

"That's not what has me worried. Who's watching out for us?"

"I guess we's just going to take our chances," Sikes said. "Rabbits?"

"The size of dogs, I'm telling you. And crazy."

"It's getting late," Butch said. "Maybe he's not coming."

Mouse stood and looked directly at the bridge. She sensed a presence under it—not a bad presence but something that reminded her of a feeling she had when she first had the calling. A dark shadow moved out from under the bridge. She remembered the shadow that had called to her when she first discovered she was a Protector. Could this be the shadow again? No, this shape took physical form as it came closer. It circled around the group, and Mouse thought it did so in a manner that suggested it thought they couldn't see it.

"I can see you," Mouse called out.

"Don't worry," a voice said to her from the direction of the shadow. "I'm the one you've been expecting."

"Midnight?" Mouse said.

"Yes," said the solid-black cat.

By his size, Mouse judged he was a young cat, not as big as her dad but slender, with short black fur that glistened in the moonlight.

"They call me Midnight because I only come out at night. I see better in the dark. Night is my time, and the moon is my sun."

"Oh boy," Dazzle said. "Do we have a song for you."

"Not now," Mouse said. "We've been waiting for hours. We need to get these animals to the country. We've already lost a lot of time."

"You sound like a parent," Midnight said. "Look, we've gotta take precautions. First, I'm the leader. Second, whatever you think you're doing, I'm in charge. We're going to a place I've staked out for us and will rest there tonight. Then we leave at first light."

"I thought we'd travel tonight," Mouse said. "We've rested most of the day."

"We don't have very far to go, but it's not safe at night in the woods," Midnight said. "Daytime's not much better, but with the dogs, we should be okay. Are those birds coming along?"

"That's Sergeant Major Carl there"—Mouse pointed—"and Colonel Wellington of the Pigeon Brigade."

"Here to do air reconnaissance," Colonel Wellington said and saluted with his right wing.

"Well, at night around here there're a lot of owls. Small ones and big ones. Some of the big ones will even take after a cat if you're not careful. And during the day, there're a lot of hawks. So you better stick close to us if you want to live. Oh, and the rats and the weasel probably won't make it. We should just leave them behind, or they'll slow us down."

Mouse stepped closer to Midnight. She crossed in front of him and then turned and did so again. He wasn't as big as her dad but was bigger than she, and his legs were muscular, revealing that he must use them often, but he had no marks on him that showed he was a fighter. "We don't leave anyone behind. We all go together. If you can't handle that, then just point me in the direction, and I'll lead."

"You?" Midnight said. "I thought he was in charge." He pointed to Butch.

"No," Butch said. "She's the boss. She's the one who broke us out and got us here."

"Well, have it your way," Midnight said. "It'll take us two days to get there, and the trail isn't easy." He turned and started walking. "If the owls or hawks come after your friends, don't expect me to stick my neck out for them."

"Come on, everyone," Mouse said. "We're going. Scratch, Dazzle, would you lead them. I'll be along shortly." She went over to Carl and Colonel

Wellington. "Sounds kind of dangerous for you two to continue. You don't have to keep going if you don't want to. You can fly back."

"Nonsense," Colonel Wellington said. "We have hawks in the city all of the time. I can out-fly them, and if they get too close, I'll just dive in next to you and the other cats. However, I'm going to send the rest of the volunteers back. I wouldn't want to be responsible, should something happen to them." He went to the group of remaining messenger pigeons. Mouse watched as they departed.

"How about you, Carl?" Mouse asked.

"I'm staying right here by you," Carl said. "One of them bigger birds might take on a single cat but not a group. Every mission has risks. We'll just have to keep looking out for each other is all."

"I guess it's good we're traveling together, then," Mouse said.

Colonel Wellington rejoined Mouse and Carl. "I sent the others back. I told them to get word to Chief that we've met our guide and we're now headed to the country, but he won't get any more news from us until we get to the farm and I go back."

"Thank you, Colonel," Mouse said and saluted him. "We should catch up to the others."

Colonel Wellington and Carl kept their flying at a low level as they stayed close to Mouse, who ran until she was even with Scratch and Dazzle.

"Looks like your plan is working," Dazzle said. "We're out of the city and headed for the good life in the country. Too bad Sikes and Rascal aren't here to see this. I've never seen so much grass and trees, and the air is so fresh. It's probably going to be a smooth ride from here."

Mouse held her tongue instead of saying anything to Dazzle. She didn't want to let her guard down but didn't want the others on edge. Every step they were taking took them farther from home and brought new sensations that she was trying to process. So far, none of them seemed harmful, and she hoped Dazzle was right.

CHAPTER 7
CLOSE CALL

C hief woke earlier than usual so that he could do the extra patrols he needed to accomplish and have enough time to stop by to see Little Foot. He finished the building that used to be Paggs and headed to his home building, going straight to the fourteenth floor. There, he went into Miss Doris's room and checked on her and then proceeded to see Ladie.

"Good morning, Chief," Ladie said as Chief jumped to the stool, no longer hesitating to take the time to speak with her. "I have some good news for you."

"You've heard from group?"

"Yes," Ladie said. "Right before you arrived, one of Colonel Wellington's pigeons brought news that they had made the rendezvous safely and met the guide who was to take them to the farm."

"That's great news," Chief said. "Should be two more days for them to get there and then a few days to get back, depending on how long they stay. With any luck, Mouse will be back early next week."

"You look a little tired today," Ladie said.

"It's my back leg," Chief said. "It still hurts when I overuse it. I don't think it has healed all of the way."

"And you've got all kinds of extra ground to cover without Mouse and the alley cats around," Ladie said.

"Yes."

"Is there anything I can do? I can come out and help with the patrols." Ladie lifted the door on her cage. It was a secret, but Chief knew Ladie could get out of her cage any time she wanted.

"You talk to all of the pigeons, right? They come in here and get advice from you every day?"

Ladie nodded.

"How about keeping your ear open for anything out of the usual. Maybe even ask a few of them to do some reconnaissance in the adjacent areas, and let me know if you hear anything."

"You've got it, Chief. You sure there isn't something more I could do, like take a patrol for you?"

"I'll only be doing it for a short time. Mouse will be back soon. Well, I got to get going."

"Promise me you'll consider getting some help if you need it," Ladie said.

"I'll consider it," Chief said. "Baxter has offered to help if I need it. Just let me know if you hear anything."

Chief left the apartment and ran along the floors one by one, checking the hallways and laundry room, and then stopped in to say hello to Little Foot before he went to the side door and entered the alley between the two buildings. Everything seemed in order until he entered the back alley.

Chief rounded the corner where the dumpsters were located and stopped. Something was different; he could smell and sense it. It was not necessarily threatening but different. He looked around, knowing that Sikes and the other alley cats were gone, and he wondered if this was the reason that his senses were off. "No," he said to himself, "that's not it." After scanning for a few more minutes, he decided he'd mark the area for further investigation and finish his patrol. As he went down to the end of the alley, he sensed the presence again—a recent passing of a cat not from the area but no longer there, or at least he hoped not. As he rounded the corner to the front parking lot, he got the strange feeling that he was being watched but couldn't locate the source.

"Maybe I do need some more help," Chief said to himself. "This extra patrolling has me fatigued, and I'm sensing things that aren't there." He decided to go back to his apartment and get some food. He entered, finding that Sam was gone, and Charlene was in their room. He nuzzled next to her in a greeting before he went to the food dish.

"Did you really play hide-and-seek with Little Foot?" Charlene asked.

Chief stopped eating for a moment. "Of course I did," he said. "I told Mouse I would check in on her and keep her company. How did you know?"

"I wasn't sure how much you would check on her, so I did," Charlene said. "You think I sit around this apartment all day just waiting for you to come back and give me news about your patrol?"

"No, I don't think that at all," Chief said.

"No?" Charlene said. "Since you let Mouse start patrolling this building, there's no one around. In between her patrols, she spends the morning with Ladie and the afternoon with Little Foot. I don't usually see her until evening, which is the same time you usually show up."

"I guess I wasn't paying attention," Chief said. "With Paggs gone and all, I've just been trying to keep up with the patrols."

"Did you ever think of asking me to help?"

"Uh, well …"

"I know you're supposed to be the Protector and all, and you're probably worried about me."

"Yes," Chief said, but he wasn't sure what else he could do to get himself out of the conversation safely.

"It's not like there are a lot of dangerous things going on out there," Charlene said. "Besides, before you came along, I was running around this building and did just fine."

"Yes," Chief said. "I suppose so." He lowered his head. "My dear Charlene, I would be grateful if you would help patrol the buildings with me, if you would be willing."

"Of course." Charlene smiled.

"Then it's set," Chief said. "We'll go on the afternoon and evening patrol together, and then tomorrow, you can take this building, and Baxter and I'll handle the other two and the perimeter." Chief wanted to make sure he didn't let her do the perimeter, not until he had more time to follow up on what he had sensed. He hoped it would turn out to be nothing of importance.

After resting for a few hours in the morning, the group of animals that Mouse was helping began to trek through the forested area. They came upon picnic spots where they stopped and searched the trash bins for scraps and went around the drinking fountains for water. A few people spotted them and watched, but no one bothered them. They crossed a few roads and went through a new development of houses still under construction, but they remained in unpopulated wooded areas for most of the day, traveling at a moderate pace.

Mouse drifted back and forth from the front to the back, checking on all of the animals to make sure everyone was keeping close. Other than Slim and Slouch, who wanted to rest more often, none of the other animals had issues. Mouse was toward the back of the group, prodding them along, when Midnight came back to see her.

"What is it?" Mouse asked. "Are we going too slow?"

"No," Midnight said. "It's nothing."

"Then why do you keep looking back. Do you sense something?"

"Yes," Midnight said. "Don't you?"

"No. And I have pretty good senses. Of course, the sounds out here are different. It's quiet, but there are rustling sounds all around. Most of the time when I've heard something, it turns out to be a squirrel or something like that. I didn't realize there were so many of them out here."

"The squirrels are harmless," Midnight said. "I've been traveling these paths for a few years now, and I can tell when something isn't right. Maybe it's nothing, but I keep hearing sounds, and it's not squirrels."

"There are over seven cats, two dogs, two rats, a weasel, and a raccoon following you," Mouse said. "You sure you're not just hearing them?"

"No," Midnight said. "The hair is standing on the back of my neck, and that's a sign that something is following us. You didn't have any stragglers in your group? Someone who didn't want to come along and perhaps changed his mind?"

"No," Mouse said. "I have a good sense of danger; something I inherited from my dad. Besides, after the run-in with the dogs and the train ride and how we jumped off, it would be hard for someone to keep up with us."

"Dogs?"

Mouse shook her head. "Yes, we had a run-in with some dogs, but we handled it. If something is following us, it could be something from that meadow we were in. I sensed other animals around when we were there." She stopped and turned around. She closed her eyes and reached out with her senses. "You're right; there is something out there. I just don't sense danger."

"We're not going to solve anything by being in front of the group,"

Midnight said, coming up beside her. "It's nearly time for us to stop, and we can't do that if it's not safe. Let's hide on the side over there on that low branch. Let everyone pass us. Then we can wait and see."

"What if something is following us?"

"That's what we need to find out," Midnight said. "You any good at pouncing?"

"It's my specialty," Mouse said. "We can have Butch lead for a while. They are used to doing what he says."

"Sounds like a plan. Should we tell the others what we're doing?"

"No," Mouse said. "Until we find out what's out there, I don't want to cause a panic. Butch was in charge at the shelter and the other animals listen to him." She trotted to the front of the group with Midnight, and they told Butch their plan. Midnight told Butch to keep going forward at a reduced pace. Then Mouse and Midnight positioned themselves on a low branch and watched as the group passed by.

"I have a friend named Baxter," Mouse said. "He is almost all black, with just a small white speck on his chest. It gives him the ability to hide better in the dark, just like you. Is that why you only like to meet at night? So no one can see you?"

"That's part of it," Midnight said. "I do it so I can watch who I'm supposed to meet. I was under the bridge where you got off the train. I observed your group all day to make sure I knew what I was getting myself into. Let's just say I fell in with the wrong group one time, so now I have a built-in safety factor."

"Sounds like a good philosophy," Mouse said. Then she went silent as Midnight put his paw to his lips, indicating the need to be quiet.

In a few minutes, she heard the sounds that Midnight had spoken about, something moving carefully through the woods.

Although the daylight had fled and turned to night, Mouse could make out the two forms that came along the trail. She could also tell they were cats. She looked to Midnight, who nodded and pointed to the far cat, and Mouse nodded back. Her job was to take the closer cat. The two pounced out of the tree and landed on their foes.

"Help!" one of the cats called out. "We's being ambushed."

Mouse recognized the voice. "Sikes?"

"Yo, Rascal," Sikes said as he rolled away from Mouse. "Looks who's it is; it's Chief's daughter. What a coincidence."

Midnight had Rascal pinned, and he just lay there, not fighting back.

"You can let him up," Mouse said. "I know them."

Midnight moved from where he had pinned down Rascal. The two cats righted themselves and brushed off the leaves and dirt.

"That was a great move," Sikes said. "You really know how to get a guy."

"Why are you out here?" Mouse asked.

Sikes and Rascal exchanged glances and didn't answer right away.

"We was just out roaming the countryside and stuff," Sikes said. "Who would have guessed us and you would be heading in the same direction?"

Suddenly, there was a movement in the air, and all of the cats reacted with exposed claws and fluffed postures to the pigeon that landed among them.

"Colonel Wellington!" Mouse said. "You should let us know you're coming or something."

"Sorry," Colonel Wellington said. "Didn't know it was you lads until I got closer. Besides, you and Midnight didn't tell us you were off on a mission; these things really should be coordinated."

"I'm sorry," Mouse said. "We didn't know what we were up against and didn't want anyone to worry."

"That's quite all right," Colonel Wellington said. "But in the future, I might remind you that we're all in this together. Perhaps the civilians need not know the details of missions, but all military personnel should know."

"What is he talking about?" Midnight asked. "You're lucky one of the owls didn't come out and chase you or worse."

"Humph!" Colonel Wellington walked to where Sikes was standing with Mouse. "So, she discovered you, eh? Guess there's no need for secrecy anymore."

"I guess there isn't now," Rascal said.

"You knew they were following us?" Mouse asked.

"Of course," Colonel Wellington said. "I spotted them when we boarded the train."

"*On the train?*" Mouse paced back and forth between Colonel Wellington, Sikes, and Rascal. "So you two have been following us all along, haven't you?"

Sikes and Rascal nodded.

"Did my dad put you up to this?"

"It was sort of like a mutual agreement," Sikes said. "He was worried about you; I was worried about the boys. We ain't hurt nothing, except maybe Rascal's paw."

"Is my dad out there somewhere too?" Mouse said, looking down the trail where they had come from.

"No, of course not," Sikes said. "He stayed back to watch the place and all."

Mouse stopped pacing in front of Colonel Wellington. "And you," she said. "You're supposed to be a leader, and you just lectured me on not providing you with information. *Ha!* Just whose side are you on, keeping secrets?"

Colonel Wellington lowered his head. "Yes, of course you're correct that I should have told you."

"You two." Mouse went to Rascal and Sikes. "I can understand my father doubting me; he's my father and always will be insecure. But you two were there when I took on Bragar; when I freed Scratch and Dazzle. Yet you still treat me like I'm a little fluffy cat. Well, thanks a lot. I expect you to leave first thing in the morning. Got it?"

Sikes nodded.

"Come on, Midnight," Mouse said. "Let's get back to our mission." Mouse walked at a fast pace to catch up to the group.

"You okay?" Midnight asked.

"I don't know," Mouse said. "Maybe when this is all over, I'll join up with you, since no one trusts me at home." The two cats trotted to the front of the group.

"Everything okay back there?" Butch asked.

"We just gained two more cats is all," Mouse said.

"Really," Butch said. "We're just a regular caravan, aren't we?"

"How much longer till we stop?" Mouse asked.

"We didn't go too fast today," Midnight said. "If we go a little farther tonight, we could probably make it there by the end of the day tomorrow."

"Scratch, Dazzle," Mouse called out, and the two cats ran to her. "We're going to keep going a few more hours before we rest. It's dark out, so would you pass it along for everyone to keep in tight so no one gets lost?"

"Sure, we can do that," Dazzle said.

"And another thing," Mouse said. "You might want to go all the way back to the end of the group and say hi to your friends." Scratch and Dazzle looked puzzled. "Seems like Sikes and Rascal didn't trust us out here all alone, so they've been trailing us."

Dazzle did a dance step and spun around. "See? I knew those two cared about us. Let's go, Scratch." The two cats headed down the trail and relayed the message to the others.

Mouse kept to herself for the next hour, upset at the thought of her dad sending Rascal and Sikes to look out for her. Then she remembered her conversation with Little Foot and how she had felt about protecting her. "He was just looking out for me," she said to herself.

"What's that?" Midnight asked. He was too far away to hear what she had said.

"Nothing," Mouse said. "I was just talking to myself."

"Are you and your dad close?" Midnight asked.

"Very," Mouse said. "He's taught me everything, and I think we're a lot alike. When he was young, he used to be more adventurous, and I think I'm just like him. How about you?"

"I was close to my dad. He taught me a lot too, until I found out he wasn't who I thought he was."

"What do you mean?"

"The stuff he taught me was useful; it's just that he used it for the wrong reasons, and I couldn't live with that. So I went out on my own." Midnight didn't say anything further, and Mouse didn't want to pry.

"Are you ready to stop now? You seem to be slowing down."

"No, that's not it," Midnight said. "It's just …" He paused and looked around. "I must've gotten turned around back there when we ambushed your friends and let Butch lead."

"Oh no, don't tell me we're lost," Mouse said.

"No, I'm sure we're headed in the right direction. It's just that everything looks different at night. We haven't made it as far as I would like. But maybe we should stop for the night, just in case."

Mouse turned, and as everyone approached, she told them to hunker down for the night and stay within sight of each other. She checked to make sure everyone was okay, except for Sikes, Rascal, and Colonel Wellington, who brought up the rear. Carl was also with them, but after a while, he came over to see Mouse.

"They informed me what happened," Carl said.

She sat down and looked at him. "Did you know about all of this?"

"No," Carl said. "Colonel Wellington said he was going to tell me, but he forgot. I know I'm only a sergeant major, but I let the colonel have it. And by the way, he, Sikes, and Rascal are sulking. I'd say what you said is really weighing on them."

"Maybe I should go talk to them," Mouse said. "After all, they were just looking out for me."

"Oh no," Carl said. "They deserve what they get. They schemed and planned behind your back without telling you. Looking out for you? They were worried you couldn't handle the mission."

Mouse didn't say anything, but the words he said hurt her feelings because they were true. Carl was right; Chief, Sikes, Rascal, and Colonel Wellington were still under the impression she was a small, fluffy cat who couldn't handle the dangerous mission they were on. The proof was in the fact that they sent Sikes and Rascal to look out for her. She kept to herself through most of the night, as did Midnight.

Moats watched from his position across the busy street of the apartment complex as the two cats walking the outside finished their round and went back inside. He had been watching them for two days now, ever since the other cats that lived in the alley had left. It was dark, and he knew this was the best time for him to get a closer look around.

"I'm going to go into the alley this time to see if those other cats have all left," he said. "Stay here, Rocko." He darted out across the street and made his away along the side of the complex to the back alley that ran across the two buildings. He carefully walked down the alley. "Mmm-mmm," he said to himself as he smelled the leftover food in the dumpsters. He walked past the first set and then glanced down the alley between the two buildings to make sure it was clear. Behind the first building he'd come upon, he studied the construction site and noticed a lot of materials around that would be good hiding places for him and the other cats.

"Only two cats and all of this turf," he said to himself. He jumped on top of one of the dumpsters and pushed the hard plastic lid open slightly to get his head under it. He emerged with a leftover piece of chicken. He glanced around to make sure he was clear before going back down the alley to the side of building, where he went across the street to Rocko.

"What did you see?" Rocko asked.

"Here." Moats dropped the leftover chicken, which Rocko quickly grabbed. "I saw plenty. There's all kinds of food in those dumpsters and lots of places to hide. I don't know why those other cats left, but it seems there's only the two of them now, and it looks like they live in the buildings."

"The two we saw earlier?" Rocko asked.

"We haven't seen any others, have we?"

Rocko shook his head.

"I think they must be guarding the place or something," Moats said. "But they let those other cats hang out in the alley. It might be due to all of the construction. Looks like another building is going up. I say, what's wrong with us moving in back there? There's plenty of food."

"What if those two cats give us trouble?"

"Then we'll just have to explain the situation to them—that we outnumber them. In fact, if they don't like it, maybe we'll just take over the buildings and everything."

"That's why you're the boss," Rocko said, licking his lips. "That sure was good chicken."

"There's more where that came from."

"When do we move in?"

"How about tonight?" Moats asked. "Get the others. We'll move in while it's dark out, before they do the morning patrol. We even have time for a midnight snack."

"Mmm-mmm," Rocko said. "I can't wait to get more. What should I tell the others? Should I mention the two cats guarding the place?"

"Tell them we found an alley full of food, and that's all you need to say. I'll keep a lookout until you get back. If we move in now with the others, it'll be too late for them to stop us."

"They ain't going to like it if we have to fight to stay in that alley," Rocko said. "They didn't like it when you surprised those rats the other night."

"Why?"

"Because the rats weren't doing anything but minding their own business."

"If they aren't willing to fight to stay, maybe they should just go hungry, then," Moats said. "I think when they get motivated the right way, they'll protect what's theirs. Just go get them already."

"Right," Rocko said.

Moats watched him as he ran toward the park, where the other members of the group waited. "Only one thing left to do," he said to himself. "Once we get settled in, I'll have to show those other cats who's the boss."

Chief checked with Charlene to see how her day had gone and then ate a late dinner with Sam before he went to bed. He didn't sleep well and woke up during the night. He sensed something wrong, a feeling he hadn't experienced since Bragar. Unable to shake the uneasy feeling, he decided to investigate.

Earlier, he had sensed something in the alley, and for a few days he'd felt like he was being watched. He needed a way to patrol without being seen; then he remembered the comment he'd made when he and Mouse were sitting on the roof looking down: *"I can see the grounds from there."*

Chief ran to the roof of the complex and began walking along the edge, looking down at the parking lot and then the sides of the building before he settled on a place that overlooked the back alley. He sat close to the edge, trying not to expose himself, and he watched the alley below. He heard footsteps behind him and turned to see Baxter. He raised his paw so Baxter didn't come to the edge, and he slowly backed away.

"What's going on?" Baxter asked.

"How did you know I was here?" Chief asked.

"I was on the roof of my building and spotted you walking around. You looked like you were watching something below."

"You go on the roof this late often?"

"On a warm night, it's the best place to be. With the starlight in the sky and the city lights below, you can't beat the view."

"I know," Chief said.

"Are you going to tell me what's going on?"

"I don't know," Chief said. "I sensed something different in the alley but couldn't pinpoint it, so I was taking a bird's-eye view."

"Do you see anything?"

"Not yet, but there's something there; my senses are never wrong."

"You think it's because Sikes and the boys are gone?"

"That could be part of it. But there's more than that. I sense a presence. Maybe something passed through there last night, and I'm just getting the scent."

"Here, let me have a look," Baxter said and cautiously approached the ledge to the right of Chief. "Well, your senses were right. Look over there at the west entrance."

Chief went to the ledge and looked over. He spotted three cats entering the alley, all of them large-framed. One was black; another mixed with white, black, and brown; and the third, which caught his attention due to its size, was black with some brown and white stripes.

"That's clearly the leader," Baxter said. "The big one out in front. He looks like he's a fighter too. Maybe they're just passing through."

"We can't count on that," Chief said. "And with everyone gone, it's just you and me, and my leg just isn't as good as it used to be."

"Then let's hope they're just passing through."

"If not?"

"We can go meet them, try to reason with them, and let them know who we are. Heck, we might even tell them to stay until Sikes and the others get back. As long as they keep a low profile, it might help keep any other vermin from moving in."

"That's not a bad idea," Chief said. "Just in case, we need to make other considerations."

"Not until you're healthy, we don't," Baxter said. "I've been in some situations before. Not as many as you, but I can handle myself. Those cats down there look tough, and I know you're pretending it's not bothering you, but you're in no condition for an all-out brawl. There might be more of them than we can see. I suggest we make peace at whatever cost until Sikes and the boys return."

Chief shook his head. "That's the second time this week someone has pointed out to me something I already know. I'm better off with allies. I guess I never realized how important Sikes and the boys were to protecting this place."

They watched the cats pick through the dumpsters and eat. Two more came down the alley, making the total five. Chief hoped they would leave after they ate, but his fears were realized as they went to the construction site directly behind his building and hid in some of the pipes.

"Looks like they found a source of food and are sticking close," Baxter said.

"We're going to have to deal with this," Chief said. "The sooner the better."

"Just remember your leg is still healing," Baxter said. "You better be diplomatic about it."

It was late morning when Mouse woke to the warm sunlight filtering down through the leaves. Although she was in the woods, her internal clock had gone off multiple times to let her know it was time to get up and patrol. She went around the camp, noticing Midnight wasn't around. She stretched out, enjoying the peaceful surroundings as she talked to everyone and checked on them. Finally, she came to a stop by Butch. "It's so nice out here. No cars, no people running about everywhere. No Miss Sorenson barking orders or smelling like smoke."

"Yes," Butch said. "The air is quite pleasant."

"Have you seen Midnight?" Mouse asked.

"He went out scouting," Butch said. "Said something about being behind schedule and off track."

"I don't think I like schedules anymore," Mouse said. "I would be happy if we didn't have to look after everyone and could just roam around and explore."

"Sikes and Rascal came to say goodbye when you were sleeping. They didn't want to wake you."

"Did they leave?"

"That's what they said they were doing."

"I'll take a look around later to make sure they aren't following us again," Mouse said. "Everyone still looks tired."

"That they do," Dazzle said as he approached. "I'm not sure we can keep this pace here. I'm an alley cat, used to living on the street, and even I'm tired."

"What do you mean?" Mouse asked.

"These animals were sitting in cages for the last month, eating well and doing nothing. You can't just take them on a twenty-mile road hike, spending nights on the hard ground and without the daily food handed to them, and expect they'll keep up."

"What do you suggest?"

"We need to get more food for everyone," Dazzle said. "They need to get a good breakfast to travel today. How far until we get where we're going?"

"I don't know," Mouse said. "I think we're off our course, and that's what Midnight is trying to figure out. Did you see Sikes and Rascal leave?"

"They did," Dazzle said. "They were pretty upset after what you told them last night. They think they let you down."

"They did," Mouse said. "I just hope my dad wasn't behind it. He said he trusted me."

"Sikes has been looking after us for a long time," Dazzle said. "Makes me feel kind of special that they cared. I wouldn't dwell on it. We all do stupid things when it comes those we care about. We don't always think straight."

"I'll keep that in mind," Mouse said.

Slim and Slouch approached Mouse, walking slowly. Slouch rubbed his stomach. "When we going to eat? I don't smell any trashcans around here."

"I don't know," Mouse said. "We're waiting for Midnight to get back."

"What? He left us out here alone?" Slouch said. "What if he's abandoned us?"

Mouse reached out her paw and put it in front of Slouch to get his attention. "Look, keep it down. I don't need you to start a panic." Then she noticed someone missing. "Where's Tattle?"

"Why would we know?" Slouch said.

"Weren't you hanging out with him?"

Slouch turned away from Mouse and started whistling.

"Slim?"

"We, uh, we kind of"—Slim moved his front paw back and forth in the dirt—"ditched him."

"Why did you do that?"

"Do you know what weasels eat?" Slouch said, returning to the conversation.

Mouse shook her head.

"They eat the same thing as cats. And we're in the wild now. I didn't like the way he started looking at me. In fact, I'm not liking how the cats are looking at us either."

"We need to stick together," Mouse said. "I hope Tattle isn't lost."

Just then, Tattle appeared from behind a fallen tree off in the distance. "Hey, Slim, Slouch, you guys gotta come over here. I've found some grubs, and they're really good." He had one in his paw and put it in his mouth.

Mouse shivered at the sight.

"Yum," Slim said, and he and Slouch headed toward the tree.

"Looks like all is forgiven," Butch said. Mouse and he laughed at the sight of the rats hanging out with the weasel, eating grubs.

Mouse noticed Tristan approaching and realized she hadn't paid much attention to him since they left the train.

"I overheard you talking about food. There's a picnic area over there," Tristan said.

"We've been lucky so far," Mouse said. "But picnic areas have people in them, and sooner or later, we're going to attract attention."

"Getting around picnic areas and campgrounds is my specialty, along with being able to get into anything."

"Maybe we can send a small group over there and check it out," Mouse said. "Would you be willing to take them?"

"You can count on me," Tristan said.

"Tattle, Slim, Slouch, come here."

"What?" Slouch said as he came to the area where Mouse stood with Tristan and leaned against the nearest tree.

"I'm sending this team on a mission to get food from the picnic area and bring it back to the camp. Tristan is in charge."

"Sounds like a chore to me," Slouch said.

"Come on and quit complaining," Slim said as he grabbed Slouch by the arm and moved out with Tristan. "We're going to get some real food. Maybe there's a leftover churro in those trash bins." The comment seemed to motivate Slouch, who ran to the front of the group.

"You want us to go with them?" Dazzle asked.

"I'd rather everyone stick together. If they are not back in a few minutes, you can go check on them," Mouse said.

It didn't take long for the misfit patrol to bring back a bucket of leftover chicken pieces and other food scraps that they shared with the rest of the group. Mouse sat back, watching the interaction, and felt glad that Tattle appeared to be getting along better with the others. She noticed Jinx looked more at home with the group instead of staying in the background. When they finished eating, the cats grouped around Mouse.

"When are we going to start moving again?" Jinx asked. "It's already late in the afternoon. Are we going to go out at night again?"

Mouse didn't know where they needed to go without Midnight there, and she was worried what she was going to tell them. Then her ears picked up a sound of something heading toward them, and she sensed Midnight approaching. At first she was relieved that he had returned to take control of the group. Then, a different sense warned her of danger by the speed of his approach.

"*Run!*" Midnight said as he headed through the group. "Follow me, and *run!*"

Mouse spotted what looked like two dogs following Midnight and quickly ordered the group to run. It was a hectic order, and the group scattered. She waited until everyone was moving before she turned to follow Midnight. She looked back to see the two animals had stopped, distracted by the scents of animals and food, and were sniffing around the campsite.

"What are those things?" Mouse said as she came alongside Midnight. Jochs and Butch were in close proximity, and she could see a few of the cats but not all of them. "Slow down; we might lose someone."

"If we slow down, we're going to lose someone; those things are killers," Midnight said. He didn't slow down but kept dodging and making turns until they came to a small clearing. Then he turned back to look in the direction where they had just come from.

"I told you I thought we were off track," Midnight said. "Well, I went out before daylight to see if I could find the path, and I stumbled upon some coyotes out hunting. I thought I lost them, but they gained on me right before I got back to the group."

"Coyotes?" Mouse said. "What are they?" She scanned the area, trying to spot the members of the group.

"Like dogs, but they're wild, and they think we're food. We might be able to outrun them. They don't like crossing roads, and there's one up ahead. I can hear the traffic."

"Wait," Mouse said before Midnight started running again. "I can't tell if we have everyone. Carl!"

Carl and Colonel Wellington flew down and landed by Mouse as she came to a halt.

"Did we lose them?" Mouse asked.

"If you're speaking about the two coyotes," Carl said, "they're still on our trail, but they're stopping to sniff a lot."

"If they get sight of us again, they won't be sniffing," Midnight said. "We need to keep going,"

"Okay," Mouse said. "Everyone get together, and try to keep up. Carl, can you and the colonel do anything to slow them down?"

"We can try to make some sounds in a different direction and see if that throws them off your trail. But they're attracted to your scent," Carl said.

"Whatever you can try, do it," Mouse said. "And then find us. Wait. Where's Jinx and Slim and Slouch? Anyone see them?"

No one answered.

"Keep the group going forward to that road you were talking about," Mouse said to Midnight. "Keep them safe."

"Where are you going?" Carl asked.

"I'm not leaving anyone behind." Mouse headed in the direction they'd come from, straight into danger, with Carl and Colonel Wellington high overheard.

It was late afternoon, and Chief knew people would be returning from work soon, and the cafeteria would be busy. It was during this time that the trash was unloaded, and he needed to make sure the alley was kept clean. He took the long way around the building through the parking lots and came at the alley from the west side, leaving Baxter and Charlene in place to come down between the buildings. He did so, hoping that if the new cats did flee, they would go his way to the open lots behind him. He also wanted Charlene to be closer to the side entrance of the building. If the new cats did try to follow her, he could get Sam or even Miss Sorenson to drive them out, something that was a last resort because he didn't want to give an impression that he wasn't on top of his job.

He positioned himself carefully to hide the fact that his back left leg was still sore. He didn't expect any fighting, but his history had taught him to be prepared. Once he spotted Baxter and Charlene at the other end, he started walking slowly toward the dumpsters.

"I know you're out here," Chief said. "I know that there are five of you. My name is Chief. I'm in charge of protecting these buildings. I'm not here to fight, just talk. Come out."

Four of the cats emerged from the dumpsters. Three looked like they'd just woken up. The fourth was the large black cat that Chief recognized had been with the cat he'd assumed was the leader. He didn't see the white, brown, and black cat.

Baxter and Charlene closed in from their side, and the four cats noticed as they looked in that direction and then back to Chief. Exposed, they sat down, which was a good sign to Chief and meant they weren't looking for trouble.

"I'm Rocko," the solid-black cat said, facing Chief. "We're just trying to find a place to be. We don't want no trouble. It's just people keep chasing us away everywhere we go, and this alley looked like it had plenty of food an' all."

Chief then spotted the one who had been out in front the night before; he was coming from behind one of the dumpsters.

"Oh, there you are, Moats," Rocko said. He moved over as Moats passed him and headed toward Chief.

"Looks like you have it pretty good here. I know; I watched you for a few days before we decided to come over. I also know the other cats left, and there's only you and—" He noticed Charlene. "Oh, so there's three of you now."

"I've been watching you too," Chief said, trying to get Moats to focus his attention on him. He didn't want Moats to get too good a look at Charlene; her being a Persian cat didn't make her look intimidating in any way. "We do have it good here," Chief said. "It's up to me to keep it that way. I don't want any trouble either, so I have an offer for you."

Unlike the other four cats, Moats stood ready to fight and even walked a few paces toward Chief, but when Chief said this, he sat down.

"I'm listening," Moats said.

"There were some alley cats here. This is their place, and you're right in what you witnessed—they left, but they'll be back. Until then, you're welcome to stay. In fact, it's better that you do."

Chief noticed Moats's eyebrows raise.

"With you in the alley, I won't have to do so many patrols, and you guys will keep other cats, rats, and vermin from moving in; for that, you can help yourselves to the leftovers in the dumpsters."

"See, Moats? I told you we should just go and talk to the guy," Rocko said.

Moats held up his paw, and the other cats stopped celebrating. "What's the catch?" Moats asked. "There's always conditions."

"You have to keep a low profile," Chief said. "Stay hidden during the day. Don't leave food scraps out in the open where the maintenance people or the sanitation services suspect you. Don't leave any trace that you're out here, and stay out of the buildings, and no one will notice you."

"You mean, act like we don't exist?" Moats said.

"No," Chief said. "Like you aren't around. As hard as that may seem, I can't change it. If the complex manager finds you out here, she'll drive you out. She doesn't even like me being around."

Moats stood and turned to Baxter and Charlene. "What about you?" he said, looking to Baxter. "What do you have to say about this?"

"He's in charge," Baxter said, standing just a few steps in front of Charlene. "In case you don't know him, he's Chief, the Bronx Bruiser. You may have heard of him from downtown. It looks like that's where you came from."

Moats didn't flinch, but Chief noticed his tail flicking back and forth in a sign that Baxter had hit a nerve.

"One other thing," Baxter said. "He's also a Protector."

Chief watched the reaction as Baxter's revealing his secret spread through the cats. The four cats with Moats seemed to soften their eyes as they looked upon him. The expression as they studied him was one of awe, and he sensed they were reluctant to engage him, an impression he did not sense from the leader, Moats. The cats remained sitting, and Moats was the only one standing as he faced Chief.

"A Protector?" Moats said. "I didn't know there were any still around. I thought they were a myth."

"Not a myth," Chief said. "You're looking at one."

"I heard they had special senses," Rocko said, "and lightning reflexes."

Moats narrowed his eyes as he looked back to Rocko and then to Chief. "They were supposed to be the best of us," he said. "But they had one flaw; they served people. In case you haven't noticed, people haven't been exactly good to us. So don't expect too much from us."

"Do we have deal, then?" Chief said. He felt like he had the upper hand with the four cats knowing he was a Protector. He wasn't sure where he stood with the leader.

"Sure," Moats said. "We can keep a low profile and all. Looks like there's some construction going on back here and plenty of places to hide. And you're right about us keeping the vermin out. We have a lot of experience there; in fact, we already paid some of them a visit on the way over here last night."

Chief walked to where Moats stood and stuck out his right paw. Moats stuck out his paw, and they tapped them together. He tried not to break eye contact while his peripheral vision took in as much as it could about the cat in front of him. He noticed several scars on Moats's right leg and that he had trouble lifting it very high. He also noticed damage to both of his ears, the signs of doing battle.

Moats moved in and whispered to Chief, "I've been around plenty of cats that make deals and break them. You do anything funny, and it won't matter that you're a Protector."

"The kitchen staff will be out here dumping trash after dinner. You need to hide until it's late, or they'll see you and report you."

Chief wanted to send a clear signal, so instead of turning around, he walked beside Moats and past the other cats, measuring each one as he did, before going to Baxter and Charlene. "Let's go before they change their minds," he whispered.

The three walked around to the alley between the two buildings, away from the dumpsters and out of range of the other cats.

"That went well," Baxter said.

"Better when you told them who I am," Chief said. "You didn't have to do that."

"Hey, I say if you got a reputation, use it," Baxter said. "Do you think we're okay?"

"For now," Chief said. "You can go in if you want to," he said to Charlene. "I'm going to stay here with Baxter for a minute and make sure none of those cats comes around the side here." He waited until Charlene was inside before he started talking again. "Don't let your guard down, though. That

Moats—he's a big cat, and by the look of him, he's been in some scraps. He favors his front right paw and can't lift it very high."

"Really?"

"Just letting you know in case. If he comes at you, go to his right and attack from there."

"Attack? You really think it might come to that?"

"I hope not," Chief said. "But he doesn't seem like the type that likes to take orders from anyone. I think it's only a matter of time before we have a problem. I'm also worried about what he said about vermin."

"What do you mean?"

"I hope he didn't get in a tangle with any of Wilber's rats. It'll jeopardize the truce, and that's all we need right now."

"How would we know?"

"I can find out," Chief said. He knew that Mouse and Little Foot kept in contact with Wilber, and he was hoping Little Foot could contact him. "Just keep your guard up, and if anything happens, don't try to take them on your own."

"You either," Baxter said.

"Agreed."

Chief went to the apartment and found Charlene waiting for him right inside the doorway.

"I can see Sam's not home," Chief said, looking around Charlene, who wasn't letting him go past her.

"If they cause trouble, you're going to let me know, right?"

"Of course," Chief said. "But there's five of them and only three of us, so I'm hoping to avoid a fight."

"Then you're going to get Sam?"

"Not yet," Chief said. "I don't want Sam to know. He might think I can't do my job around here if I can't keep a few cats out of the alley. I used to handle tougher situations than this back at the motel."

"That was before your injury," Charlene painfully reminded him. "I know you're already thinking of a plan, maybe even more than one."

"Of course," Chief said. "Right now I'm hoping Sikes and his boys will be back soon, and that will solve everything. Can I get by you?" He moved forward into the apartment, and Charlene let him by but followed him into the living room.

"What if they don't get back soon?"

"Then I need a way to get more leverage over the new alley cats, a plan that I'm thinking about that comes from my new way of thinking."

"Oh?" Charlene said.

"Something my daughter taught me, and it included allies."

Midnight stopped the group at the edge of the woods. In front of them was a busy two-lane road.

"The traffic is steady," Midnight said. "We should cross. The coyotes don't like people or traffic; it's too dangerous for them."

"We know more about crossing roads than anyone," Scratch said. "We can help lead the others across, but that road is really busy. Some of them might not make it."

"Ah, laddie, I see we've come to an impasse," Jochs said as he approached the group. "We need to get to the other side; is that it?"

Midnight nodded. "We should get across the road and stop at the first clearing," he said. "Is everyone here?"

"I think so," Butch said, breathing heavily as he came forward. "Except for them rats and that one Jinx cat."

"You take them across and stop at the first clearing, and I'll find Mouse and catch up to you," Midnight said.

"You need us to go back with you?"

"No," Midnight said. "I'm faster alone. Now, how do we get the others across?"

"Allow me," Jochs said and went to the side of the road. "You see, cars won't slow down for cats, rats, raccoons, or weasels. But they always fall for this." He dropped his ears down, lowered his head, and started limping on the side of the road. Almost immediately some of the cars started to slow. Jochs hollered back, "But for a dog, these people will do anything."

After the cars started slowing, Jochs pointed himself across the road and limped into the path of the oncoming traffic as the cars in each direction screeched to a halt.

"Now, everyone cross quickly," Jochs said, "before they find out I'm bluffing."

Midnight watched in amazement as the animals all crossed. He spotted a lady and young boy getting out of their car and heading toward Jochs.

"Poor hurt doggy," the lady said. She put her hand out to pet Jochs. He leaned in and let her pet him, and his ears and tail went up.

Midnight watched the scene unfold before him as the lady reached around and picked up Jochs. "You're coming home with me. I'm going to call you Precious."

Joch's face was full of excitement, and he licked the side of her face and smiled at Midnight.

"Good going, Jochs," Midnight whispered to himself. "You found a home."

Confused people returned to their cars and started moving until traffic returned to a normal pace.

"That's going to be a fun story to tell one day," Midnight said as he ran back through the trees and shrubbery, listening and looking for Mouse.

Mouse hadn't gone far when she spotted Jinx, stopped between some trees. "This way!" Mouse yelled out, but Jinx didn't move and didn't look at her. Mouse went forward and noticed why Jinx was frozen in place; in front of her was the animal Midnight had described. It was mostly brown in color and snarled as it faced her. It didn't move forward but seemed to be waiting. Instincts took over, and every lesson her dad taught her about defense flooded back to her as Mouse went toward it, hissing, with her tail fluffed in full action to make her look larger. The move had its effect, and the coyote hesitated as Mouse took a position next to Jinx. "We need to get out of here," Mouse said. "Can you run?"

"It's not me that can't run," Jinx said and nodded toward the tree next to her.

Mouse barely noticed the two forms that had plastered themselves against the back of the tree, hiding their faces. Slim peeked out at her, but Slouch didn't move.

"Okay, listen," Mouse said. "Slim, Slouch, I'm going to cause a diversion, and you two and Jinx need to run the way I just came. Don't stop until you get to the road." Mouse continued to keep her face toward the coyote, and she hissed loudly to keep his attention on her. The coyote lowered its head and growled but didn't move forward.

"What are you going to do?" Jinx asked.

"Never mind that; get ready." She moved closer to the coyote, hissing as she did. "Look, name's Mouse."

The coyote's eyebrows rose as she said this.

"I know; I'm a cat, but that's my name. I'm also a Protector. I don't know if you know what that means, but if you don't stop chasing us, you're going to find out." She stopped when she knew she was within pouncing distance and flexed her claws, making sure they were visible to the coyote.

He remained still but revealed some sharp teeth as he spoke. "They call me Slash. Two of my friends are right behind me, cat," he said. "It's you who better worry."

"Can't we talk about this?"

"I don't think so. You're in our woods, and we're hunting. You know what that means?"

"I'm sorry you feel that way. Run *now!*" Mouse called out, knowing that time was limited if more coyotes were coming. Jinx, Slim, and Slouch started running, which caused the coyote in front of Mouse to look away from her and toward them. As its head still was lowered and to the side, Mouse pounced on its back and dug her claws in. The animal jerked left and right, but Mouse held on, shifting her weight as it bucked. Once she could see that Slim, Slouch, and Jinx were clear, she jumped off the animal and immediately faced it again, expecting it to attack, but it didn't. Instead, it shook his head and snarled at her.

"You better go back where you came, or I'll do that all day," Mouse said, slicing her right claws in front of her body.

The coyote stepped forward and tried to bite her when she did this, but her paw knocked his mouth to the side as it made contact. Mouse moved quickly out of the way and dodged the teeth. She noticed there were two more coyotes approaching from behind the one, so she swiped one more time as a diversion and ran slightly left of where the rest had gone. The coyote came after her and was faster than she expected, but she had a plan.

She turned and ran toward a large tree. She moved to the left of it, as though she was going to run completely clear. Then she executed her power-slide and turned, at first letting herself slide and then digging her claws to change direction. She was so close to the trunk of the tree that the coyote could not correct and overshot, stumbling as it did.

"Great power-slide," Carl said as he flew right over Mouse in a dive.

Mouse ran, looking back just once to see Carl and Colonel Wellington dive-bombing at the coyotes, trying to distract them. She caught up with Jinx, Slim, and Slouch and spotted Midnight heading toward her.

"They're right behind me!" Mouse called out.

Midnight changed direction and ran beside her until they were at the edge of the road.

"The others have already crossed," Midnight said. "Come on; follow me." He ran across the road, making it safely, but no one else followed.

"How are we going to cross that?" Slouch said. "We can't go that fast, and the traffic is too heavy. We're doomed"

"The coyotes are right behind us," Jinx said. "We're running out of time."

"Save yourselves, then," Slim said. "We're done for." He smacked Slouch on the arm. "This is all your fault."

"Jinx," Mouse said, "grab Slouch and follow me. I'll get the other one. Hold on, Slim." She grabbed Slim by the back of his neck. Jinx did the same thing to Slouch, and Mouse looked for an opening as she darted across the road, dropping Slim as soon as they were clear.

"Yuck," Slouch said, wiping the back of his neck after Jinx put him down.

"You're welcome," Jinx said.

"What took you so long?" Midnight said and turned into the forest and kept running.

"Follow him," Mouse said. "I don't know if those things will stop at the road, but we better not chance it. And you two"—she motioned her paw at Slim and Slouch—"keep up!" She took the group forward, and after an hour or so, they caught up with the rest of the animals in a small clearing. She was happy to see Butch, Scratch, and Dazzle.

"Looks like everyone's here now," Scratch said as Mouse came to the middle of the group. Carl and Colonel Wellington landed.

"Any sign of them?" Mouse asked Colonel Wellington.

"No," Colonel Wellington said. "Looks like they weren't willing to cross the road, like Midnight said, and we've made good our escape. What is your next order?"

"Where's Midnight?" Mouse asked. "He was just ahead of us a minute ago."

Scratch pointed. "He's over there with Butch."

She looked around and spotted Butch and Midnight but noticed someone missing. "Where's Jochs?"

"You're not going to believe this," Scratch said and relayed the story of how Jochs helped them get across the road and got himself adopted.

"Well, that's great news," Mouse said. "He found a home." She jogged her way over to Butch and Midnight, who had stepped away from the group. "Why don't we all take a break? We all made it across. Looks like those coyotes didn't have the will to cross the road and follow us."

Midnight didn't respond. Butch shrugged and walked back to the rest of the group, leaving Mouse and Midnight alone.

"Did you hear what I said? The coyotes didn't cross the road. Just like you said they wouldn't."

"They didn't used to be around these parts," Midnight said. "I think they're getting closer and closer to the cities now because of all of the food and trash people leave around. They hang out in groups, and they aren't scared of cats. I should've been more careful. We got lucky."

"It was touch-and-go there for a minute, but we made it," Mouse said.

"What?" Midnight said finally, looking at Mouse. "You think we've made it? We almost got everyone killed back there. Between the coyotes and the cars! This was a bad idea all along. There are too many of you, and you … you city cats … you don't belong out here. We're hungry and lost, and it's only a matter of time before something else goes wrong, and we don't get so lucky."

Mouse didn't know how to respond to Midnight; she sat down, trying to consider what to do. Her heart was racing from the recent encounter with the coyotes and all of the running, and she felt light-headed.

"Keep everyone together," Midnight said. "I'm going to scout around and make sure we're in the clear."

Mouse watched as Midnight left the area. She looked back at the group of cats, rats, and dogs that she was leading. Midnight's words rang in her head: *It's only a matter of time before something else goes wrong, and we don't get so lucky.* Mouse closed her eyes and wished she was back at the apartment complex, where it was safe.

It was the end of the day at the complex, and Chief finished the inside patrol and headed out through the side door. So far, Moats and the other cats had stuck to their end of the bargain and remained out of sight. He still walked across the back alley, just to check that none of them was around and that they didn't leave any signs of their presence. He spotted Moats on the dumpster in broad daylight, a clear violation that could easily be noticed if Miss Sorenson or Sam was about. He went to the dumpster where Moats was half sticking out, with his head and front legs under the large plastic lid.

"Moats," Chief said, "it's still light outside and worse, it's almost time for the truck that dumps these containers to come back here. They're going to see you."

Moats stuck his head out from under the lid. "Sorry, Chief," he said, "but Rocko's fallen in there, and I think he's hurt bad. He's not answering me. I can't keep this lid up and at the same time jump down there to save him. The other boys are off in the junkyard. I can't just leave him here."

Chief glanced around the alley. "Okay, what do we do?"

Moats backed away from the lid. "I'll hold the lid enough for you to jump in and see if you can help him get up." With great effort, he raised the lid enough for Chief to jump in.

Chief didn't trust Moats and sniffed the air to see if the other cats were in the area, but he didn't sense any. The foul smell of the dumpster blocked his ability to tell what was inside. He knew the dumpster was usually full and that Rocko couldn't be too far down in it, so it probably wouldn't be a difficult task.

"What are you waiting for?" Moats asked.

Chief knew he could show Moats he was willing to help him and gain his trust, but trusting him was another matter.

"Hold on, Rocko. We're coming." Chief leaped to the edge of the dumpster, only to have the lid drop on him, forcing him down to the bottom. "What?" Chief was surprised to find the dumpster nearly empty, causing him to fall farther than he'd expected. "I should've known," he said.

"For you being a Protector, that seemed awful easy, Chief," Moats said from the other side of the lid.

"I've been working on my trust issues," Chief said. "Thanks for setting me back again."

"I had my boys empty this dumpster last night. In fact, they are probably all still carrying some of the bags now. I'm the only one around. Rocko's fine."

"Moats, what's this all about? We had a deal," Chief said.

"Not really," Moats said. "You see, in case you didn't get the impression the first time, I'm not the kind of cat that likes following rules, especially those I don't make. So I'm renegotiating. In fact, I just might be taking over. I watched this place for some time before we showed up. I also know what day the trash is dumped, but thanks for confirming that trash day is today. I'll bet that as low as you are in the dumpster and as heavy as this lid is, you can't get out by yourself. So I'm just going to assume when they dump the trash, you'll be gone with it. And on the chance that you do somehow escape that crushing thing they have in the back of the truck that compresses the trash, just remember who put you there because I can do it again."

"Does the rest of your group know what you're doing?"

"Let's just say there's followers and leaders, and they'll follow what I tell them to do."

"Don't do this, Moats," Chief said. "You and the others have it pretty good right now, and you don't want that to change, do you?"

Moats didn't reply; he jumped down off the dumpster. "Maybe I'll see you again someday, Chief. But I hope not."

Chief waited a few minutes until he was sure Moats was gone. Then he jumped at the lid but to no avail. Moats was right; the lid was too heavy for him to move it. He was trapped!

The group traveled a few more miles to make sure they weren't being followed before stopping at a clearing. The sounds of traffic were distant, so Mouse knew they were far from the road. The trees were not as thick where they settled, and the ground was full of rocks. She remained separate from the group all day as they remained in the clearing until night fell.

Mouse held her head down as Carl approached her. "I should've known they were right. I shouldn't be out here. I've led all of you to trouble."

"That doesn't sound like the cat I know," Carl said. "Not the one I witnessed earlier today, jumping on the back of a coyote to save her friends."

"You jumped on the back of a coyote?" Midnight said as he walked over to Mouse.

"She did," Carl said. "In order to save Jinx and the rats, she gave that coyote something to think about."

"Wow," Midnight said. "I'm sorry about the things I said earlier."

"No," Mouse said. "You were right. It's getting dark, we're lost, we failed to get food for the group, and we don't know what's out there."

"Colonel Wellington is making sure the coyotes are not behind us," Carl said.

"It's what in front of us that I'm worried about," Mouse said. "We don't know where we're going, and there may be more dangers ahead."

"Sounds like we're in a bind," Carl said. "Kind of a bad situation."

"Yes," Mouse said. "And it's all my fault."

"No, it's my fault," Midnight said. "I was supposed to be leading you."

"Hold on there," Carl said. "We can't have you two battling about whose fault this is and trying to outdo each other as to who is the biggest failure. What's that going to solve?" Carl raised his right wing and pointed to Mouse and then Midnight. "You're both brave and competent, as shown by your deeds. We need you to put your heads together and get us out of this mess." Carl turned his head. "Scratch, Dazzle, can you come here?"

The two cats came over to Carl. "What is it?" Dazzle asked.

"Nothing," Carl said. "I just wanted you to hear what I'm about to say. I'm going to tell you all and remind Mouse about $S = IP^2$ because she has forgotten. It goes like this." Carl cleared his throat. "Hmm, hmm."

> When you find yourself in a bad situation,
> You just call upon your imagination
> To think outside the box
> And find a better way.
> It's a simple mathematical equation—
> $S = IP^2$ the calculation.
> It's the key to overcome,
> So make this notation.
> You will find it useful in many situations.

"$S = IP^2$?" Dazzle asked.

"Yes," Carl said. "Mouse, please explain."

"It means," Mouse said, "success is the product of imagination times perseverance squared."

Carl continued:

> When you find yourself with a losing proposition,
> You just have to find a better disposition.
> When you think the door is shut
> And you say you're in a rut,
> Just consider a brand new relation
> With your own imagination.
> Let your creative side do the talking, and your ideas will be
> up and walking,
> The outcome of a splendid combination.

Mouse joined in the next part and sang with Carl:

It's a simple mathematical equation,
A statistical, magical relation
You can use it in any situation:
$S = IP^2$ ... the calculation.

Scratch and Dazzle erupted in applause, as did several other cats that had heard the song.

"Thanks, Carl," Mouse said. "I needed that."

"I see," Midnight said. "We just need to consider options. Is that what you're saying?"

"Yes," Mouse said, feeling better than she had before Carl's song. "There has to be a way. Can you tell where we are?"

"I think I can find my way back to the trail that will take us to the farm," Midnight said. Before he could say more, he was interrupted by Tattle's scared voice.

"There's something out there!" Tattle jumped between Mouse and Midnight with his eyes dilated and his fur fluffed out. "There are three of them, and they have glowing eyes, and they're wearing masks."

"The coyotes must've crossed the road," Midnight said. "We'll never outrun them in the dark."

"Butch, Scratch, Dazzle," Mouse said, "we're going to make a stand. Tattle, where are they coming from?"

"I'll show you." The group followed Tattle, but when they got to the edge of the camp, they didn't see any coyotes. Instead, they spotted three raccoons watching them.

"Hey, where's Tristan?" Mouse asked.

"I'll get him," Tattle said.

"Who is Tristan?" Carl asked.

"The raccoon," Mouse said. She walked forward to get closer to the raccoons. "Can you hear me?"

"Yes," a voice answered.

"What do you want?"

"We saw that you had one of our kin with you. It's unusual for one of us to be traveling with a group of cats, so we were just checking on him. Well, I'll be! Tristan, is that you?"

"It is," Tristan said as he came alongside Mouse and headed toward the other raccoons. "I thought these woods seemed familiar. I'm so glad to see all of you." The raccoons hugged Tristan as the oldest one stared at Mouse.

"Tristan, what are you doing out here with a bunch of cats?"

"It's a long story, but we can talk about that back at the lodge," Tristan said. He ran back to Mouse. "Thanks for breaking me out." He hugged Mouse. "Bye all. Safe journey."

Mouse watched the raccoons disappear into the night. Then she turned to Midnight and the others. "See? Things are already looking up. Just think; if those coyotes hadn't chased us, we never would have been off course, and Tristan wouldn't have found his family."

Colonel Wellington landed. "The coast is clear. No sign of them."

"The only problem is, when the traffic dies down later tonight, they might follow us," Midnight said. "They'll probably be holding a grudge after what you did, and if they figure out that we're just a group of cats and some old dogs, they won't be afraid to attack."

"Then we have to be ready," Mouse said.

"We might stand a chance with Butch," Midnight said. "Still, it's risky."

"Fighting them will get someone hurt," Mouse said.

"What then?"

"Carl, do you remember what we did to Slim and Slouch that time they were with Bragar's rats, and we led them into the apartment at night?"

"You mean when we acted like we were dead with the fake blood stuff and all?"

"Hey," Slouch said as he stumbled into the middle of the group. "I remember what you did. It wasn't funny. I had nightmares for weeks."

"But it worked," Mouse said, "without anyone getting hurt. Except for the nightmares; sorry about that."

Slouch nodded to Slim and then to Mouse. "Can we help?"

"We're going to need some supplies if our plan is going to work. Ketchup and some of those white tablets people use for heartburn, the ones that foam up when you get them wet," Mouse said.

"Where are we going to get that kind of stuff out here?" Carl asked. "There are no people around."

"Those raccoons said they were at a lodge, right? Carl, do you think you can catch up to them?"

"I'm on it," Carl said, saluting. "Colonel Wellington, will you be my wingman?"

"I would be proud to be your wingman, Sergeant Major."

The two birds took off in the direction of the raccoons.

"What do we do until they get back?" Slouch asked.

"We practice," Mouse said.

Chief kept his ears open for the trash truck. He knew the driver rarely got out to check the bins; instead, he would stay in the truck and work the machine with its long arms that automatically picked up the bin and dumped it. He knew his one chance to escape would be when the truck started moving the trash bin over the area where it dumped, inverting the container. Right before the container would go upside down, the lid would open. It was then he needed to jump out.

"Mr. Chief?"

Chief heard a voice from the alley.

"Mr. Chief."

The small voice came again and Chief recognized it as Little Foot.

"*In here!*" Chief called out. In a moment, he heard scratches on the outside of the dumpster as Little Foot scurried up. Her head peeked in through the lid.

"What are you doing in there?" Little Foot asked.

"What are you doing out here?" Chief said from within the dumpster.

"I've been keeping an eye on you, trying to help. I'm a Junior Protector, and you don't have much help with everyone gone. I saw you talking to that other cat, and when he left and I didn't see you anywhere, I waited. Now I'm coming to check on you."

Chief smiled, but his joy with Little Foot disappeared when he considered the danger she was in. "That cat you saw me talking to is a part of a new group of alley cats out here. You better watch your surroundings. I don't think they can be trusted."

"They're all gone," Little Foot said. "What are you doing in there?"

"The leader, a cat named Moats, tricked me in here. They emptied the dumpster, and I'm too far down to open it. I can't raise the lid."

Little Foot strained against the lid. "It's too heavy for me."

In the distance, Chief heard the distinctive sound of the trash truck coming. He knew he was running out of time.

"I can go get help," Little Foot said and began backing out from under the lid.

"*No!*" Chief said. "Wait. By the time you get help, it'll be too late. We have but one chance."

Little Foot moved forward; her face was in full view. "Tell me what to do."

"When the truck comes in to lift the dumpster," Chief said, "it will raise over the top of the truck. There is a brief moment when the lid will start to open. I'll have to try to jump out of here before it goes all the way over, or I'll fall in the back of the truck."

"What happens if you don't make it?" Little Foot asked.

Chief didn't answer.

"Oh my," Little Foot said. "There must be some way I can help."

Chief heard the truck entering the alley. "There is," Chief said. "Get down and get clear. If I don't make it, you have to tell Charlene and Baxter what happened." He watched as Little Foot backed out from under the lid and disappeared. Then he waited.

Soon, the truck made contact with the dumpster, and he heard the forks come out and engage the sides. The dumpster began to lift, and he tried to keep steady to position himself for his escape. He knew he would have to act quickly and cursed the weak leg he had and the injury that caused it. The dumpster lifted higher, and the lid began to open. Chief transferred from the bottom to the side as it went over the truck and began its descent to an inverted position.

With a sudden thump, Chief was jarred and stumbled forward. The movement stopped, and the dumpster lid was cracked open enough for him to get through. He raced to the opening, spotted a place to jump, and easily leaped out while the dumpster was stationary. He only stayed there a moment before he jumped to the concrete wall and moved along it until he was even with the front of the truck. He looked in to see what had caused the driver to stop the dumpster in midair, where it still remained. He spotted the driver frantically moving about the front of the truck as a little black-and-white mouse ran along the dash.

Little Foot had created a distraction and caused the driver to remove his hand from the control button, which had stopped the dumpster over the truck and allowed Chief time to get out. But now she was in mortal danger as the driver rolled up a newspaper and was readying to use it as a club. Chief hurled himself through the slightly opened window and landed on the passenger seat. He hissed at the driver, who drew back in surprise, dropping the newspaper.

"Jump out through the window behind me, Little Foot!" Chief yelled. He watched the mouse go by him and jump to the fence. He turned to the driver, who had leaned back from him, confused, and gave a soft *meow* before jumping to the wall. Little Foot joined him there, and Chief and Little Foot stayed atop the wall for a few feet before they headed to the side of the building.

"Stay still," Chief said. He bent down and grabbed Little Foot by the back of her neck. He ran to the fire escape and jumped to it, going to a second-floor window, where he entered the building. "If we see any people, act like you're dead." Chief continued to the fifth floor and into the furniture-storage room, where he let go of Little Foot.

Little Foot stretched her neck and shook her head. "That was a little uncomfortable."

"Sorry," Chief said. "It was all I could think of at the time and seemed the best method, given the situation."

"I guess so," Little Foot said. "What? Why are you looking at me like that?"

"Because I owe you a great amount of thanks," Chief said. "It's hard to believe you're so small but so brave."

Little Foot sat back on her hind legs, curled her tail in her front paws, and blushed. "You really think I'm brave?"

"One of the bravest I've ever met," Chief said.

"I guess it's because although I'm small, I don't think small."

"No, you don't," Chief said. "Now I understand why Mouse and you are such good friends."

"She was right," Little Foot said.

"Who was right?" Chief asked.

"Mouse. She told me I needed to stay behind to help you because you were taking on so much and might need help. She was right."

"Yes, she was," Chief said. "If it hadn't been for you out there, I might not have escaped. Things might get worse with those cats in the alley. I'm going to ask you to be extra careful until I figure out what we can do about it."

"Yes, sir." Little Foot saluted. "What are we going to do about it? That Moats cat you were talking about—he's gotta go."

"I agree," Chief said. "We're going to have to think of something. And we might need help."

"That's going to be hard," Little Foot said. "I mean, with everyone gone on the adventure and stuff. I haven't even seen Sikes or Rascal around. I wonder if those alley cats chased them away."

"I wouldn't worry about them," Chief said. He didn't want to tell Little

Foot that he knew where Rascal and Sikes were. "We just have to think of our options."

Little Foot put her paws together under her chin and close her eyes. "Mouse, Sikes, Rascal, Scratch, Dazzle, Ladie, Carl, Baxter, Wilber ..." She opened her eyes. "Yep, out of the people I know, most of them are gone."

"You keep thinking, and I'll see you tomorrow," Chief said. He headed out of the room and down the hall, and as he did, one name that Little Foot had mentioned caught his attention: Wilber.

Mouse watched the path where the raccoons had left and where Carl and Colonel Wellington had gone out searching. The plan she put together to deal with the coyotes was ready, except for the supplies they hoped the raccoons would provide.

"It's getting late. Maybe they won't make it back," Midnight said. He stood with Mouse, Butch, and Dazzle.

"Okay, we may need a backup plan just in case. We will attack from multiple sides to confuse them. Butch, you and I will take the left, and Dazzle, you and Scratch take the right." She noticed Midnight looking at her.

"What about me?" he said.

"Midnight, you will lead the group as far away as possible, if that's okay with you. You're the most qualified to get them back on track and find our friend."

Midnight nodded. "Let's hope they don't come." The words had barely left his mouth when an alert came from Scratch, who was out on the perimeter, watching.

"Something's coming!" Scratch ran over to the group but came from the opposite side of where they were expecting the coyote.

"They got around us somehow," Butch said.

"No, wait," Mouse said. "That's the direction the raccoons left." She heard a familiar sound in the air, closing in on them. "It's not the coyotes coming; it's Carl and Colonel Wellington."

Carl appeared, and under him along the trail were three raccoons, hauling items.

"We heard you needed some help," one of the raccoons said. "You brought our cousin back, so here you go." They proceeded to haul in two ketchup bottles and several packs of the white tablets Mouse needed for her plan.

"Tristan couldn't come; he was busy saying hello to everyone. Also, his mom grounded him."

"Thanks a lot," Mouse said as the raccoons scurried away. "Now we have everything we need to finish our preparations." Mouse discussed the details with those involved in the plan.

It was late night, with three quarters of the moon showing, allowing plenty of light, when they heard the sounds of something approaching the clearing. As part of the plan, Mouse had let a few of the animals go up and down the trail to make the scent fresh, hoping it would lead the coyotes right where they wanted them: a small clearing surrounded by trees and laid out according to her plan. Mouse gave careful instructions to all of the players, and Midnight helped position them to take advantage of the moonlight.

From her position behind a group of trees, Mouse spotted the coyote she had pounced on, who called himself Slash, leading the group directly into the clearing.

"What's that?" Slash said.

"Looks like a dead rat," one of the other coyotes said as they stood three abreast. "Two of them, from what it looks like. We're on the right trail of those cats. They probably killed them."

"You sure they're dead? I thought the cat was traveling with them."

"Look at the blood. Besides, nothing alive could smell that rank. The cat was probably traveling with them to have something to eat."

"No, that cat came back and saved those rats like they were friends," Slash said.

"I don't think you saw what you think you saw, Slash. Those cats probably turned on them when they got hungry."

"I know what I saw," Slash said.

Mouse cued Carl and Colonel Wellington by waving her paw.

Carl and Colonel Wellington limped out from each side and in front of the coyotes. Both of them were covered in ketchup to make it look like they were bleeding. "She did turn on us," Carl said.

"She wasn't our friend; she was our keeper. We were just food to her," Colonel Wellington said. He put his right wing to his chest, let out a long sigh, and plopped down, playing dead.

Carl took a few more steps. "Run, if you know what's good for you. She's infected, rabid. Rabies or worse." He didn't go too far before he fell down. He flapped his wings. "Run. Run for your lives." He went completely down and then raised his head one last time. "Oh, the *petmanity*." He gasped and went limp. This was Mouse's cue.

"Follow my lead," she whispered to Midnight as she popped a piece of the white tablet in her mouth and gave the other part to Midnight. "Now remember, Tattle, you're supposed to play dead." Once Mouse could tell the tablet was working by the saliva running out all over her mouth, she grabbed on to Tattle with her mouth as lightly as possible and came out from behind the tree, hissing.

The coyotes looked stunned as they watched Mouse. One of them turned sideways as though it was about to run away. Mouse hissed and approached Slash. She dropped Tattle, who did a good job staying limp as he hit the ground. "I'm hungry. Kill, food, hungry ..."

Midnight came out with the ketchup all over his side and looked at the coyotes. "She bit me, and now I'm infected too." White foam ran out from his mouth. "We're coming for you next." He and Mouse moved forward slowly.

"Slash, I don't care what that cat did to you. I'm not dying here," one of the coyotes said and took off running the way it had come.

"Me either," another one said and bolted, leaving but one left—the one Mouse had scratched.

"Join me, Slash. Let me bite you, and together, you and I can roam the woods and hunt," Mouse said. She started closing in on Slash and reached deep insider herself, creating her worst snarl, which was made even more horrible when some of the white foam went down her throat, causing her to choke and almost vomit as she emitted a sound that scared even her.

"If you're infected, you won't be around for long anyway," Slash said as he turned and ran away down the trail.

Mouse stopped moving forward. "Hold your positions, everyone," she said. "Wait until I give the all-clear." She spit a few times, trying to get the foaming to stop, and then she reached out with her senses and tried to follow the coyotes to make sure they had cleared out.

"Let's go check," Midnight said.

Mouse followed the trail alongside Midnight to make sure the coyotes had kept going.

"No sign of them," Mouse said. "Let's get back."

"We're clear, everyone," Mouse said as the two returned to the camp.

"That stuff is disgusting," Midnight said as he tried to spit out the foam and shook his head.

"But it works," Mouse said. "Just don't ever swallow the tablet."

"It sure was nice to be on the other side of the plan this time," Slouch said. "Wait, where's Slim?"

"He was over there last I saw." Mouse pointed.

"I'm going to patrol the perimeter," Midnight said. "Make sure nothing else is out there. I'll be right back."

"Be careful," Mouse said. "Carl, Colonel, you guys all right?"

"Fine," Colonel Wellington said as he shook the ketchup from his wings. "Another successful mission. You're a great strategist. In the corps, we call that psychological warfare."

"I just thought it was a good trick," Mouse said, "but thank you." She turned her attention to Slouch, who had run over to Slim and was making a fuss. She went over to where he was standing by Slim, who remained still on the ground.

"I think something's really wrong with him," Slouch said. "He's not moving."

Mouse carefully examined Slim, and when she looked at his face, she spotted him peek at her and wink. She took a step back.

"Talk to me, buddy," Slouch said as he put his paws on Slim and shook him. "Don't go into the light; come back."

"Slouch, is that you?" Slim said in hushed voice.

"Yeah, little buddy. What is it?" He leaned over by Slim's head.

"Slouch ... come closer."

Slouch looked to Mouse, and she shrugged her shoulders. He moved closer to Slim. "What is it?"

"Slouch, you need a bath."

"What?"

"Got you, old buddy," Slim said as he rolled over and stood, laughing.

Mouse laughed along with the joke. Slouch frowned for a moment, and then he started laughing as he went over to Slim and hugged him.

"Okay, everyone, let's get some rest," Mouse said. "We've got a long day ahead of us tomorrow." As the other animals settled down, Midnight and Carl joined Mouse.

"Did you see anything?" Mouse asked.

"The coast is clear," Midnight said. "We should keep everyone close tonight."

"Good idea," Mouse said.

"I suggest we do some scouting early in the morning," Carl said. "Colonel

Wellington and I could go out. Owls will be in bed at that time, and the hawks won't be flying yet."

"We'll go out too," Mouse said, pointing to Midnight. "This time together."

"You want me to go with you?" Midnight said.

"If we would have gone out together today, my senses would have warned us about those coyotes before you stumbled on them."

"Oh, I see," Midnight said and turned to walk away, but Mouse walked in front of him.

"That's not what I mean. We need you. I don't know where we are or where we need to go, so we need to work together. It's time for you to learn a lesson I had to teach my dad: You need to trust others. You need allies."

No one spoke for a few minutes.

"I'm sorry," Midnight said. "I'm not used to trusting so easily. I told you about my father."

"Not really," Mouse said.

"Oh, that's right," Midnight said. "He was smart, quick, and a good fighter. I used to admire him. But he used his ability to get his way. He would lie and mislead others. I didn't notice at first, but when I did, I asked him about it."

"That must have been hard."

"He tried to convince me it was okay, but I saw the way he hurt others. So I left. Went out on my own and have been that way since."

"And now, you help others," Mouse said and smiled. The smile returned to her let her know she'd won a trusted friend in Midnight.

"Tomorrow, we go out together," Midnight said.

CHAPTER 8
DINING WITH RATS

"**A**re you here to play hide-and-seek again?" Little Foot asked as Chief entered the door.

"How did you know I was coming? Did you sit there watching the door all morning?"

"No," Little Foot said. "I mostly sit in the back over there"—she pointed—"where the sun comes in and makes that chair seat warm. It's the best place to take naps. I knew you were coming because I could hear you. I have excellent ears."

"Is that so?" Chief drew closer and examined the little mouse closely. "Yes, I guess those are quite large ears." He considered his words after they left his mouth. Little Foot was always polite and nice, and he didn't want to upset her, especially when he needed her help. "I mean, your ears are perfectly placed and shaped to accommodate a great level of hearing. I'm sure they are of the best examples of ears I've seen."

Little Foot's eyes widened, and she sat back and ran her front paws over the outline of her ears. "You really think so?"

"You bet," Chief said. "I would have never made you a Junior Protector if I didn't think you could handle the job. And that's what I'm here to talk to you about. I have a mission for you. It's has to do with the plan we spoke about last night and needing more allies."

Little Foot quickly stood at attention. "Yes, sir!"

"You and Mouse both go to see Wilber, correct?"

"Yes, sir! Do you need me to go see him?"

"Yes. And I need you to take me to him," Chief said. "Do you know how to get to where he is?"

Little Foot put her paw to her chin. "Yes, sir, but it could be dangerous."

"More dangerous than venturing out into an alley full of cats or jumping into an operating trash truck?"

"I meant it might be dangerous for you," Little Foot said.

"What?"

"You may not know this, but there are hundreds of rats in the sewers. They're all over the place."

"That's why we're going together," Chief said. Little Foot smiled at him. He considered that she might have a point; he had tolerated Wilber and his legion of rats as long as they remained underground and away from the complex, but he wasn't exactly best friends with Wilber and didn't know how many rats existed underground. The situation with the new alley cats above ground wasn't safe either, but it was a chance he was willing to take.

"Are you going to ask him for ideas on how to get rid of those mean cats?"

"Yes," Chief said. "I'm going to ask Wilber for help. I figure if he helped Mouse get rid of Bragar, he might help me get rid of Moats."

"I'll take you to see him, but I want to be part of the plan."

"Of course," Chief said. "We need to keep a low profile during the day so no one will suspect what we're doing. Remember Moats thinks I'm gone."

"Got it," Little Foot said.

"We'll leave as soon as it's dark."

It was early morning at the camp in the woods, and all the animals were awake and stretching in the small clearing where they'd slept for the night. Mouse and Midnight had scouted ahead and found a direction they wanted to try. They returned to the camp and gathered the other animals around.

"We know we can't go back that way," Midnight said, "not with those coyotes around."

"What do you suggest?" Scratch asked.

"We scouted ahead of us, and I think it goes to the farms," Midnight said. "We're just going to end up a little off course. But I'm sure the farms are in this direction."

"What are we waiting for, then?" Butch asked. "The sooner we start, the sooner we get there."

"Mouse," Midnight said, "will you stay in front with me? That way we can both keep an eye open."

"Sure," Mouse said. "Lead the way."

Well rested and still boasting about the success of their plan the night before, the group traveled with light hearts and little complaining for hours before the weariness of the trip started to show.

"Looks like we're starting to get strung out," Mouse said. "I might have to motivate some of them to keep up."

"Don't take too long," Midnight said. "I see a clearing up ahead. Looks like the tree line is about to end."

Mouse remained still as the group passed her. "Come on, everyone; we don't have much farther to go," she said, hoping it was true.

After a few minutes, most of the group had passed her, with Slouch, Slim, and Tattle in their normal space in the rear.

"You guys need to keep up," Mouse said.

"What?" Slouch said. "You expect us to give up our perfect view from back here? The way I see it, if you run into trouble up there, we can see it from here and still have time to get away."

"Oh," Mouse said. "I thought you were being brave and staying back here in case those coyotes were still following us. That way, you could warn us in time." The words took a moment to sink in, but Slouch reached over and grabbed Slim's arm as he pulled him along.

"Come on," Slouch said. "We need to be somewhere in the middle."

Mouse watched as Carl flew overhead and pointed to the front, causing her to notice that the group had come to a halt. She sprinted to the front of the group, where Midnight was crouched down.

"Everyone, down," Mouse called out to the rest of the animals. She slowly approached Midnight. "What is it?"

"A large dog up there. Moving slow. He might have spotted us."

"Dog?" Mouse said. "Maybe we can ask him for directions?"

"I'm not sure that's a good idea," Midnight said.

"Oh, don't worry. Butch!" she called back. "Can you help me?"

Mouse and Butch went out into the open in clear view of the approaching dog; he was light brown with black ears and nose and much larger than Butch.

"Any impressions?" Mouse asked as the dog approached.

"He seems friendly enough," Butch said. "His ears are floppy, and his tail is wagging. He doesn't look like a fighter."

"We're about to find out," Mouse said as the dog was in sight of them.

"I'll be," the dog said. "I thought I smelled something out here. Guess my nose isn't as old as I thinks it is. Higgledy-piggledy, what are all of you doing out here?"

"I'm Mouse; this is Butch," Mouse said. "We're looking for a friend of ours who lives on a farm. Perhaps you know him?"

"There are a lot of farms out here," the dog said. "Big ones, small ones, dairy farms, apple farms, cherry farms, hay farms. Lots of farms. I'm Dandee."

"That's a fine name," Mouse said. She realized how much she sounded like Little Foot, always being polite. She considered it a good habit.

"Ask me how I got my name," the dog said. "Go ahead; ask me."

"How'd you get your name?" Mouse asked.

"Ask me how I'm doing?"

Mouse looked to Butch, who shrugged his shoulders.

"How are you doing today?" Mouse said.

"Just dandy," Dandee said. "That's what I used to tell everybody all the time. So they all started calling me that."

"Pleased to meet you, Dandee."

"Oh, it's great to meet someone new, isn't it?" Dandee said. "Now, what are you all doing out here?"

"Like I said," Mouse said, "we're looking for a friend of ours. He's a cat named Paggs."

Dandee's tail wagged, and his eyes were wide. "I know Paggs. Why didn't you say so? This way, this way." He started running back the way he'd come from.

"Wait!" Mouse called out.

Dandee ran back to where they stood. His tail went low, as did his ears. "What? Do you see something?" He scanned around and sniffed.

"No," Mouse said, "but there are more of us." Mouse took a few steps toward the edge of the trees. "Come on out, everyone."

The rest of the group came out of the forest and walked to the line of grass where Mouse stood with Dandee and Butch.

"I'll be," Dandee said. "There's a whole lot of you. I didn't know Paggs had so many relatives. We have plenty of room in the barn for you to rest and visit. Follow me."

Mouse stood back while she made sure everyone was out and following Dandee. Then she noticed Midnight at the edge of the woods. She went over to him. "Are you coming?"

"I don't know," Midnight said. "It seems my part of this mission is done, and you've found your friend."

"You don't want to come with us and get some food and rest? Or hang around to make sure everything works out?"

Midnight didn't respond.

"How about sticking around for the return trip. Some of us are going back. We could use your help."

"You seem capable of finding your way," Midnight said. "You don't need me around."

Mouse sensed something wrong that Midnight wasn't telling her. She thought about it for a moment and then took a chance that she understood what Midnight was feeling.

"You're feeling let down, aren't you? I get that way too when the adventure is over." Mouse put her paw in the air. "It's like, what do I do now?"

"You feel that way too?" Midnight said.

"All the time," Mouse said. "That's why I keep planning new stuff. I can't stand to be still."

"Me either," Midnight said. "I get a hollow feeling inside. I really should stick with you to see this through."

"You definitely should," Mouse said.

"It's just …" He looked back at the woods behind him.

"What?" Mouse asked. She moved closer to Midnight. "After what we just went through, you can tell me."

"That's the thing," Midnight said. "With what we just went through, I feel I let the group down. I led the coyotes back to the group and got us lost."

"Not everything goes right all of the time. I think you're forgetting $S = IP^2$. We wouldn't have made it this far without you. You're part of this adventure. Now come on; I can't even see the group anymore. Let's catch up before we get lost, and they all make fun of us. That is, unless you have some place better to be." She lightly swatted Midnight on his shoulder, turned around, and ran. What she said had its effect, and he followed her.

"You know," Midnight said, catching up to Mouse, "I really don't have a home. I kind of just wander around and help other animals here and there. It must be nice to have someplace to go back to."

"You don't have a home?" Mouse asked.

"I kind of have some alleys that I call home. But the city changes so much that I have to keep moving around."

"That doesn't sound like a lot of fun." Mouse could see the rest of the group ahead.

Jinx slowed down and joined her and Midnight. "I just wanted to thank you both for all that you're doing," Jinx said. "I'm sure the others would say that too."

"Let's just wait until we really get somewhere safe before we start saying stuff like that," Midnight said.

The surroundings changed from the wooded areas to wide-open spaces of grass and crops.

"I've never smelled so many pleasant things," Jinx said.

"Me either," Mouse said. "Where I'm from, it's usually trash, smoke, cleaners, or something like that. The air is so clean out here that I can smell the flowers and the … wait. What's that?"

Midnight laughed. "That's the cows. Now it's more like the city, eh?"

The three enjoyed the walk to the farm. They crossed another road that was paved and only two lanes. It wasn't busy or hard to cross like the road on the previous day. Dandee led them around the side of the place, which had three outer buildings and one large house. Of the outer buildings, two were holding areas—one for pigs and the other a shed full of tools. The large barn in the middle was where they entered. The wood barn was two stories high and as large as the lobby in Mouse's complex. She looked around and noticed some horses to the left of a large open area. The chickens that roamed about didn't take kindly to all the cats coming in, as some ruffled their feathers and ran out of the barn. A stairway on the right side led to a loft, where Carl and Colonel Wellington flew in and landed.

"Well, I think we've arrived at a safe place," Mouse said as she stopped and breathed a sigh of relief. "Maybe we can get some rest and food here and take time to make a plan."

"That would be nice," Midnight said.

Mouse ran up to the loft and stood by Carl. She surveyed the surroundings and felt happy that they had made it this far.

"Your dad would be proud of what you've done," Carl said.

"Thanks, Carl," Mouse said. "I'm sure he would have liked to have come along if he hadn't had so much work to do. I bet you he's bored back at the apartment."

Chief slowed his pace, waiting for Little Foot. The two had left the apartment complex under cover of darkness to keep the alley cats from seeing them; they were heading to see Wilber. Although Little Foot was pointing the way, she was having trouble keeping up with Chief's pace. He tried to remain patient but wanted to get the trip over and get back to the apartments as soon as possible.

A couple of miles from the complex, they had entered a back alleyway of a business district that was under construction. Some of the buildings were new, while others were being renovated.

"I'm sorry if I'm not going fast enough," Little Foot said. "I'm not used to traveling here like this."

"What do you mean?" Chief asked.

"I usually ride on Mouse's back, and she can go much faster than me. No one ever notices unless they look really close because we're the same color."

Chief considered the need to save time, and then he lowered his shoulders. "I'm just doing this to get there and back. There will be none of this around the complex. Understand?"

"Fully," Little Foot said and climbed on his back.

"Hold on," Chief said. He felt the little paws grab onto the back of his neck as he sprinted down the road and down the alley to the rear of an abandoned storage building.

"Wow, that was cool!" Little Foot said. "Mouse is fast, but you're faster and taller."

"Glad you enjoyed that. Where to now?"

"In there," Little Foot said. Once they entered the room, Little Foot jumped down and led Chief to an open floor drain. "This is where Streets usually hangs out. Streets?" she called out, but no one answered. "He might not be back yet."

"What do we do?" Chief asked.

"We can get to the sewers through that drain. Just watch your head."

"How much farther, once we enter?"

"Just a few turns, and then we have to cross a river."

"A river?"

"It's okay; the rats built a bridge to cross. Then we'll be in Wilber's den. He lives under an Italian restaurant."

"Of course he does," Chief said. "Anything else I need to know?"

"You might want to take short breaths and not inhale deeply because it really stinks down here."

"Lead the way."

Little Foot led Chief down a floor drain to a long pipe; he had to duck down to enter. The pipe ended at a larger tunnel that had water flowing down the middle. There were enough dry ledges in the concrete tunnel for them to make their way in what increasingly became a dark path. After two turns, they emerged at an even larger section, where the waterway was flowing heavier and light trickled in from manhole and side-drain covers above.

"This is where we cross," Little Foot said.

Chief looked in both directions but couldn't see a way to cross. Then he went still as his senses detected a presence that alarmed him. "We're being watched," he said.

"It's Wilber's rats," Little Foot said. "They're probably on the other side, trying to figure out who we are."

Chief looked across the water to the other side and slowly started picking out the forms of large rats, staring at them but not moving. "There are five of them," he said. "All large."

"That's more than usual," Little Foot said. "Probably because of you."

"I always wanted to draw a crowd. So what do we do now?"

"Hey, over there," Little Foot called out across the water. "It's me, Little Foot, Mouse's friend. I know it's not time for a meeting or anything, but I have Mouse's dad, Chief, here, and he wanted to speak with Wilber. Can you please raise the bridge?"

"They aren't moving," Chief said.

"It's important," Little Foot called out.

"Still not moving."

"When Mouse comes back, I'm going to tell her you wouldn't help me. Then she's going to tell Wilber."

"That got their attention."

"Anyone else with you?" a voice came from the other side.

"No," Little Foot said.

"If anyone else but you two tries to come across, we're going to drop the bridge, and you two are going for a swim. Understand?"

"No one else is with us," Chief said.

He watched and marveled as a dozen large rats emerged and split into two groups. Each group pulled on a small rope, which caused a wooden walkway to rise out of the water and settle a few inches above it to create a path to cross. The wooden bridge was held together by scraps of twine, zip ties, and wire.

"You've done this before?" Chief asked.

"Many times," Little Foot said. "It's much safer than it looks."

The two walked across the bridge, which was about five feet in length, and made it to the other side. The rats immediately lowered the bridge. One of them approached Chief and addressed him.

"Just remember, before you try anything, you're on our side now," the rat said. "You might be able to make that jump, but the mouse there never would."

Chief heard Little Foot gasp. "Don't worry," he said to her. "I won't let anything happen to you." He went forward as the rats led him to another opening in the wall that was protected by a set of wood-crafted double doors that they opened in front of him. Chief ducked down and went through the opening; he found himself in large tunnel that angled downward. Slightly inside, the room opened wider on both sides and was full of rats, sitting at makeshift tables. The room was lit by a strand of small light bulbs that ran across the center and above a walkway that split the room in half; the tables were located on either side.

At the other end of the room, which was about seven feet long and five feet wide, there was a platform with a master table. There, Chief spotted Wilber. All movement stopped as Chief entered the room. Little Foot remained slightly behind him.

"I was hoping to have a moment of your time," Chief said as politely as possible. He noticed the rats on both sides of him stood from the tables and came forward to line the walkway. Several of them formed a line in front of Wilber, making it hard for Chief to see him. He slowly ventured down the aisle to get closer.

"Congratulations. You've found my hideout," Wilber said.

"I didn't know it was a secret," Chief said. "Don't worry; you have nothing to fear from me."

Chief noticed several injured rats as he slowly walked to the table where Wilber sat. He remembered the conversation with Moats and what he had said about dealing with vermin. He hoped the cats hadn't done too much damage because he needed Wilber's help. He caught a glimpse of Wilber between the rats, who increased in number as he approached.

"You boys seen some action lately?"

"Funny you should notice that," Wilber said. "One of them new cats you allowed into the alley did all of this. Came down in one of our outer tunnels and tore up some of my guys. I don't remember discussing any new terms in our truce, but I would say this jeopardizes it."

"No," Chief said. "The truce still stands. That's what I've come to tell you. I'm not associated with those alley cats and didn't want them to stay." Chief made it as far as he could go; the rats in front of him prevented him from getting closer. He could see Wilber better now on the platform in front of him. He raised his head above the rats in front of him to get a better view.

"So why are they hanging out in your alley?"

"You know Mouse went on her adventure, or mission, or whatever. Scratch and Dazzle went with her."

"Yes, I think a couple of my guys went as well," Wilber said. "A few I asked to help and some stragglers that are probably causing problems. But that's another matter."

"I was convinced that Mouse needed more looking after and was going to go along and keep an eye on her from a distance, but Sikes, Rascal, and Baxter wouldn't let me go."

"They shouldn't have," Wilber said. He stood and raised his arms. "Without you, this place would have no order and would fall apart. You're the Protector!"

"Lot of good it's doing now," Chief said.

"I don't understand."

"We still wanted to look after her, so Sikes and Rascal went to keep an eye on Mouse and the others."

"Let me get his straight." Wilber put his elbows down on the table and leaned forward. "You left the alley completely empty, with all of those dumpsters full of trash and food scraps? You're lucky that only a few alley cats have wandered in. There are hordes of vile rats in this city that might be tempted by that. We could have another Bragar pop up."

Chief nodded. "I thought I could control it with extra patrols, but it's only Baxter and me watching the place. There are five of these alley cats, and all of them, I'm afraid to say, are big. In the past, I'd just take out the leader but—"

"So are you here to apologize for letting these new cats in?" Wilber said.

"Now, hold on there," Chief said. "I had nothing to do with that."

Wilber slowly walked to the end of the table and started coming around to the front. "Don't want a battle on two fronts, I guess. I never thought I'd see you come down here. I still remember our first meeting; you were tough, all right. Toughest I've ever seen. Your daughter comes down here; she seems more pleasant and open-minded." He moved around the table and put his paws on a few of the rats in front of Chief. The rats moved and cleared the way. Now, still on the platform, Wilber faced Chief eye to eye.

"She's a different"—Chief searched for the word he wanted to use— "spirit. You and I, we're from a different time and still stuck in our ways." He sensed the rats around Wilber were jumpy, so he sat back on his hind legs and relaxed. The rats didn't budge.

"Stuck in our ways," Wilber said. "Old-fashioned, I guess."

"That's one way to put it."

"I guess she's teaching us both, then," Wilber said. "So why are you here?"

"You think once a cat, always a cat. I'm telling you those alley cats aren't with me. But they outnumber us, and I didn't want to risk a fight."

"Yes, I noticed you still favor your leg."

"Is it that obvious?"

"Quido, did you notice anything different about Chief, here?"

A tall, fit-looking rat dressed in a black outfit, spoke. "No, he looks fit and lean, boss."

"Thank you, Quido," Wilber said and pointed to his own eyes. "See? You aren't the only one who has abilities. I'm in charge not just because I'm strong but because of my skills. I can perceive what others miss."

"You're right about my leg," Chief said. "Those boxes Bragar's boys dumped on me injured me more than I'd like to tell. If I take on those cats, I could lose, and with me goes control of the apartments—and the truce as well. If you trust my daughter, you should know that I'm not here to cause trouble."

"I didn't think you were. But I've had trouble convincing the others here. I knew you weren't behind it because we think alike." Wilber tapped his head and then pointed to Chief. "We're both in charge and have a lot to lose if something goes wrong."

"Yes," Chief said. "It's not easy being in charge."

"Not at all," Wilber said. "I remember a simpler time, when things were where they were supposed to be. Roles were not confused, and the young respected their elders."

"I know what you mean," Chief said.

"We used to teach respect and responsibility."

"Both are in short supply these days," Chief said.

Wilber started singing:

Many are unhappy
Because they want everything for free,
But you've got to work to earn a living—
It's a simple reality.

I've got something to say about
Two things that are near and dear to me,
And it's very clear to me
That what we need is more.
It's time to say it for all to hear it,
Can't steer clear of it.
We may agree that we disagree.

Respect,
Responsibility—
They can take you far.
You can take it from me.
Respect,
Responsibility—
It's what you do to earn it.
You just don't just get it free.

It takes guts to be the boss.
It's not an easy road
To be in charge, make the tough calls.
It's quite a heavy load.
Others that are jealous of the top,
Think it's all fortune and fame,
But when things go wrong,
I'm the one they blame.

Respect, responsibility—
It's about doing what's right,
Not what's in it for me.
It's something you learn and earn;
You just don't get it for free.

Is it hard to imagine
A world where these two qualities
Are earned and cherished,
Exist in harmony.
Without them we don't have—
Really have—
A civil society.

Respect, responsibility—
It's what you do to earn it.
You just don't get it for free.
Respect, responsibility—
It's what keeps us together.
You can take it from me.
Respect, responsibility.

Wilber moved back to the other side of the table where Quido stood and pulled out a chair.

Applause erupted from the rats, and any that were still sitting came to their feet. Wilber took a bow and then sat down in his chair.

"You wants I should bring him a plate?" Quido asked.

"We were just getting ready to eat. Your daughter likes the pasta. Care to join us?"

"I will," Chief said. Several rats cleared away from the place across from Wilber. Chief moved to the table and sat back. He looked to his right and confirmed that it was Streets sitting at the table. Little Foot approached; she took a place to Chief's left and sat on a large spool of thread the rats used as a stool.

Wilber took his seat, and then all the other rats sat down. "Yes, Streets was just telling me about his journey with your daughter."

"I didn't realize you were back already," Chief said to Streets.

"I only went halfway," he said. "You have one brave daughter." He recounted the night of the breakout and how Mouse dealt with the dogs in the shelter and the others she handled on the way to the train.

Plates of pasta with a little sauce on top were served to the main table. Chief watched in amazement as a row of rats emerged from a set of double doors behind Wilber and continued to serve every table in the room while they began eating. Chief took a bite and found the noodles softer than expected.

He was not particularly fond of the taste, but with the sauce, it wasn't as bad as he'd expected. Little Foot nudged him, and he looked down at her.

"Like this." She put one of the noodles in her mouth and slurped it down. "That's how you do it."

"That Colonel Wellington," Streets said. "He usually doesn't brag much about anyone but himself, but he was sure telling a lot of stories about your daughter."

"I guess that's a good thing," Chief said.

"It sure is," Wilber said. "Makes me jealous."

"Really?" Chief said.

"Of course," Wilber said. "We might be rats, but we have a lot of respect and dignity. I respect what she has accomplished and wish I had a kid that I could brag about so much."

"Sorry," Chief said. "I guess I never thought about it. Do you have any children?"

The sounds of eating went silent, and Chief was worried he'd said something wrong.

"Did you hear that, Quido?" Wilber smiled. "I have over a hundred children," Wilber said. "Many of them are out there guarding my territory and some are in the seats around you. And you, Quido, my oldest here, serving me and making sure I'm watched after." He turned back to Chief. "Yes, our children make us proud."

Chief ate the last noodle off his plate. He waited until Wilber was finished before bringing up business.

"All the news I've been getting about her trip has been good news. I wish I could say the same thing around here. These alley cats appeared a few days ago. I discovered them but didn't know what do. With Sikes and his boys out, it's just me and Baxter. I didn't want to risk a fight with the five of them, so I made a bargain."

"I take it the bargain didn't include leaving us alone."

"I didn't even think about it," Chief said. "It was a bargain just to buy time until Sikes and the rest got back. The leader, a cat named Moats, has been doing stuff that leads me to believe he has no intention of leaving, even when the others get back. Whatever he's started, it's only going to get worse unless we deal with him."

Wilber turned to Streets. "You know anything about these cats?"

"Only the one," Streets said. "You said his name was Moats?"

Chief nodded.

"See, I know all the stuff about cats being cats and needing to eat and all, but this one—Moats, as he's called—he's a really bad character," Streets said. "He's a fighter—cats, rats, even some dogs. He's been moving around for years. Finds a new group but always manages to get in some kind of trouble. Can't follow any rules, see. He's bad news."

"I tried to reason with him," Chief said, "and he tried to get rid of me. Trapped me in one of the empty dumpsters, and I nearly got taken out with the garbage. Little Foot, here, came to my aid."

Little Foot sat up in her chair and smiled.

Wilber picked up a napkin from the table and wiped his face. "What do you have in mind to deal with this Moats?" he asked.

"I don't think we have a problem with all of the cats. If we get rid of Moats, I think the rest will hesitate to engage us. We lure Moats into a trap and see if that solves the problem. If the others agree to the terms, we leave them alone," Chief said. "If it doesn't … well, we have one less to worry about."

"What would the terms be?" Wilber asked.

"They can stay in the alley if they keep a low profile. They have to stay out of sewers and leave you alone, and they have to leave when Sikes and the boys get back. But we won't have any trouble once they get back because we'll have numbers on our side."

Wilber leaned in. "I take it you want to use some of us to bait him, then. Is that right?"

"I want to lead him away from the alley and the other cats. That way, you and I can have a word with him."

"I'm listening."

"Thanks, Paggs," Mouse said as she moved back from the food dish where Paggs had led her and the rest of the cats. They were in a large barn inhabited by cows, some loose chickens, and a pot-bellied pig. Most of the animals seemed hospitable to the group, but the chickens kept their distance.

"I would have never expected you to make it all the way out here," Paggs said. "And thanks for bringing Scratch and Dazzle along too. How did they get out of animal control?"

"That's a long story," Mouse said. "We broke them out, and that's when we discovered all these other animals that we decided to help." She noticed Paggs seemed to have lost some weight, but his yellow fur still looked shiny.

"We'll have plenty of time to talk," Paggs said. "I hope you're staying for a while to tell me what's been going on back at the place."

"Just long enough to find these pets a home. But we can catch up on things. You look good, Paggs," Mouse said. The two walked across a floor full of scattered hay.

"I do a lot of roaming around. Probably more than what I used to do back at the apartments because there's just so much land out here and interesting stuff to see—and without the stress of worrying about so many people and cars. The only issue has been the field mice. They have been rampant, and there's a shortage of cats out here to keep them down. I'm sure your group of cats will be welcome."

"We got your message from the pigeons, including the part about the mice; that's why we came."

"Good," Paggs said. "There aren't as many pigeons out here as in the city, and they don't trust cats much, but they all seem to be kind enough to carry a message when I need it, if I mention Colonel Wellington's name. Speaking of pigeons …"

Colonel Wellington flew into the barn and landed by Mouse and Paggs.

"What is it, Colonel?" Mouse asked.

"Seeing how we've completed our mission and found these animals a farm to live on, I'm ready to depart and head back to the brigade in the morning. That is, unless you need any further assistance."

Mouse glanced at Paggs. He didn't say anything to her, so she turned back to Colonel Wellington. "No, Colonel," Mouse said. "We won't be needing anything further. You should return tomorrow, and please let my dad know we made it here safely. We're going to stay until everyone has a home, and then we'll be coming back."

"Very good," Colonel Wellington said, saluting Mouse with his wing to his forehead.

"Colonel?" Mouse said as she saluted back. "I would ask that when you talk to my dad, you leave out the part about the fight with the dogs, jumping on the train, jumping off the train, the fight with the coyotes, and any dangerous stuff like that."

"But … won't he find out sooner or later from one of the others?"

"Not until I get back," Mouse said. "That way he'll feel better that I'm right there by him."

"Understood. I'll consider those details of the mission classified," Colonel Wellington said. He took off and flew to the rafters.

"My, you have been busy," Paggs said. "Now, what's this about these animals needing a home?"

Mouse told Paggs the story of rescuing the animals from the animal control office. Paggs listened with the patience that comes with old age and didn't interrupt.

"That's how we came to be here," Mouse finished.

"Did you really jump on a coyote's back?" Paggs asked.

"Just for a moment to distract him," Mouse said.

"What about those two?" Paggs pointed to Slim and Slouch. "They seem a bit out of place."

"Those two worked for Wilber. They were at the train station," Mouse said. "I believe they're tagging along just to find a place where they don't have to work hard. I think they intend to hang out with the pigs and eat out of the trough."

"They'd better not," Paggs said. "The pigs will eat them. There's one thing I've learned out here above all: Don't mess with the pigs' food. The horses over there"—he nodded to the horses—"they think they're better than all the other animals because the people pay so much attention to them and comb and ride them and stuff. The cows, they don't say much. They get milked daily and don't do much else but stand around in the barn all day. The goats and chickens just kind of roam around. Dandee chases them once in a while for fun. Squeals, the Grunter, as Dandee calls him, is really nice and goes inside the house a lot."

"Squeals?" Mouse said.

"The pot-bellied pig. The little one over there."

Mouse looked to where Paggs pointed and spotted the small black-and-white pig with a long pink snout, talking to Tattle.

"She has a lot of energy, that one," Paggs said. "She's more like a pet and goes inside when she wants, just like Dandee and me."

"There sure are a lot of animals out here," Mouse said. "Do you think they want some more?"

"I don't know," Paggs said. "Dandee goes inside the most and would know. Me, they just tend to leave me outside and let me do what I want. They feed me good and all, but I'm not sure they want this many cats, as I've got the mice problem under control here. Other farmers complain a lot about all of the field mice getting in the houses, infesting the hay, and getting in the animal food and stuff. A few more cats around would solve that problem. Dandee usually comes back out after dinner. Let's talk to him when he does and see what he says. I don't think it will be a problem for you to settle in for the night."

"That sounds good," Mouse said. She was ready for a good rest after the last few nights in the woods. She climbed to the loft where Carl and Colonel Wellington were watching over everyone below. She noticed Midnight sitting with Jinx and Butch, together in a corner; Slim and Slouch and Tattle were hanging out by the barn door.

"What is the Protector looking at?" Carl asked her.

"I was just noticing the friendships that have been made during our trip," Mouse said. "Tattle seems to be getting along with Slim and Slouch, Butch and you are hanging out together, and Jinx and Midnight do well together. A lot of them didn't have anyone to hang out with, and now they have a friend."

"Yes, it looks like everything is going to work out," Carl said.

"Just like back at the complex," Mouse said. "My dad keeps everything in line and everyone happy."

"It will be good to get back to a place where things are normal," Carl said.

CHAPTER 9
SPECIAL DELIVERY

It was late at night in the apartment complex. Chief remained in his apartment all day, putting his plan in place while leaving the impression on Moats that he had been taken away with the garbage truck. He was waiting for Baxter to stop by, and then he would leave.

Sam came in the door, whistling. "Ah, there you are," Sam said.

Chief noticed he was dressed in a nice shirt and pants—clean, without the usual stains of grease or cleaners—and his hair was combed.

"I just had dinner in the cafeteria with Mr. Ryan and Myra—you remember, the other maintenance person I'm considering hiring. Well, Mr. Ryan liked her and told me to go ahead and hire her. She's going on a tour of the grounds with us tomorrow. If everything goes well, she'll be joining us by the end of the month."

Sam bent down and patted Chief on the head. "So make sure you're doing your patrols and keeping this place in shape because we'll be touring tomorrow and want to make a good impression." He went into the kitchen and took out a fresh piece of salmon and prepared it for Chief. He set the dish down on the floor. "There you go, boy. Enjoy. I'm going to turn in for the night."

As much as Chief wanted to sink his teeth into the fish, he knew he needed to stay on his toes tonight. Baxter came in through the pet door.

"Mmm-mmm, fresh fish again tonight," Baxter said, coming into the kitchen where Chief stood by the food dish.

"Sam left it for me," Chief said. "Help yourself, if you'd like to."

"What's the occasion?"

"He's bringing Mr. Ryan and the new maintenance lady on a tour tomorrow. Isn't that just great?"

"I guess your plan better work, and we better get rid of those alley cats. You sure you don't want me to come along?" Baxter asked. "Or maybe I should do it, and you stay here with the lady. After all, I'm black and better suited to be out there at night."

"Ha," Chief said. "I have the element of surprise. Moats thinks I've been hauled away with the trash. He'll never see me coming. If he even senses you, he might get suspicious. Stealth is the key here. If something does go wrong, protect Charlene and get Sam."

"How will I know?" Baxter asked.

"If I come back here, you'll know it worked. If I don't …"

"I'm sure everything's going to work just fine," Baxter said. "I'll save you some fish."

Chief left Baxter just inside his apartment, although as he headed up to get Ladie, he was considering if it would be better to have Baxter along with him to help. "No," Chief said to himself. "Wilber will come through."

He used the stairs to climb to the fourteenth floor and listened for a moment at each floor to make sure no one was stirring. The complex was quiet as he exited on the fourteenth floor and went through the pet door to his destination.

"You sure about this, Ladie?" Chief asked as he entered the dark living room of Miss Doris's apartment. "We can handle this. I don't want you to get hurt."

"Without Carl or Colonel Wellington around, I'm the best chance you have for air support," Ladie said. "They outnumber you, and you need all the help you can get. I can tell you where the other cats are and let you know when he's away from the others. Besides, I've done this before."

"What do you mean, you've done this before?"

"Your daughter and I put an entire plan together when we first scared off

Bragar and his goons. Of course, he came back anyway, so I hope your plan works better than ours."

"We're getting rid of Moats. He's going for a long ride out of the city. I don't know the details; Wilber's handling transportation. We just need to lead him there."

"Is Miss Doris asleep?" Ladie asked.

"Soundly," Chief said. "It's late enough that the halls are clear."

"Okay," Ladie said. "Let's go."

Chief watched as she moved to the door of her cage, put her beak on the bar that ran across the bottom, and lifted the door. She kept her head up, supporting the door, and twisted her neck while the rest of her body went through the opening. By the time she was out, she had completely turned her body around and gently let the door back down.

After dinner it grew dark outside, and all the animals remained in the barn. Dandee came out to the barn and listened to Paggs and Mouse recount the story of how the group came to the farm. This time, Butch, Scratch, and Dazzle listened in. Carl positioned himself high on a set of wooden crates that were in the middle of the open area where everyone gathered.

"You really jumped on the back of a coyote?" Dandee asked Mouse as the story was being told.

"Yes," Mouse said. "But just for a moment."

"Wow," Dandee said.

"There's more to it than that," Carl said from his elevated position. "You're looking at a Protector. One of the few chosen ones. Her father is also a Protector."

"What's a Protector?" Dandee asked.

"Allow me," Paggs said. "The Protectors descended from cats that were treated like gods, from Egypt. They existed before humans. They were the protectors of the spirit. When humans came, their spirit was among the most fragile, as it was younger than the other animals. Cats and humans walked beside each other as companions, as hunters. In ancient times, cats were revered as gods. They guarded the humans' temples, their homes, and their families from the carriers of death, like the snake, the hyena, and the rat."

"Uh-uhmm." Slouch cleared his throat in the distance.

Mouse walked to the edge of the barn and looked at the night sky. She could still hear Paggs as she watched the starlight burst into shapes and outline statues of cats and ancient households, with cats curled up by the bed and by the doors. She lifted her paw to rub her eyes, but it had no effect. The visions continued as Paggs spoke.

"As times changed, humans lost sight of their spiritual heritage and turned more to things they could touch: hard things, material things. Their spirits grew weak, and wars raged. The Protectors became just another animal to them. Some were discarded. Some became pets. The larger of our species rebelled and went into the wild, never to serve again. The spirit of the cat was broken. Only a few remained to serve as Protectors to keep the humans safe against the countless dangers.

"Thousands of years have passed, and the light of the Protectors has dimmed, but the spirit still remains in a few of us throughout the generations. Mouse and her father are among those chosen to carry this light. That helps explain her feats of bravery and her skill."

Mouse's visions disappeared, and the stars went back to their places. She blinked her eyes, but the stars remained still. She noticed how quiet the farm was compared to the city where she lived.

"The greatness of cats," Slouch said as he and Slim passed by Mouse and went outside. "Blah, blah, blah. We're going to find somewhere else to hang out."

Mouse went back to the middle of the barn where the animals had gathered.

"What are we going to do tomorrow?" Jinx asked.

"We're going to see if you can stay here," Mouse said. "Dandee, do you think these animals can stay on the farm here?"

"Maybe, maybe not. I don't know."

"Who would know?"

"Trevor will help," Dandee said, jumping around. "He's a nice boy. Always combs his hair. Always is polite."

"Who's Trevor?" Mouse asked.

"He's my owner; you know, a boy. Don't you have an owner?"

"I suppose Sam is my owner," Mouse said.

"Stay here," Dandee said and rushed out of the barn.

Mouse listened and heard Dandee barking. It started far away and then slowly got closer. She heard a human voice.

"What is it, boy? Where are you taking me? You have something to show me? Is that it?"

Lights turned on, causing some of the animals to scatter and hide as a tall, thin boy with short brown hair and brown eyes entered the barn.

"Oh," the boy said as he looked at the animals that remained in center of the stalls in front of him. He bent down and slowly reached out his hand to Butch. "Hey there, boy. No one's going to hurt you." When Butch didn't move, the boy slowly patted him on the head. "Now, what about the rest of you?"

"This is Trevor," Dandee said. "If anyone can help, he can."

"Come out, everyone," Mouse said. The cats that had gone into hiding slowly came out and gathered in front of the boy. To show him they were tame, Mouse went forward and rubbed against his leg and purred.

"Well, aren't you just a little fuzz ball," Trevor said and patted Mouse on the head. Then he bent down and picked up Paggs. "Are these friends of yours? I guess you got tired of trying to keep up with all the field mice and brought in some reinforcements."

Trevor sat down on a stool and counted all the cats. "I don't know where you've come from, but we've needed a few more cats. So do our neighbors. Mice have been in the hay and eating the animal food. We need some help, so they'll be glad to see you."

Trevor pulled out his electronic device that Mouse recognized as something all the people in the apartment complex had except Sam. She watched as he put it to his ear.

"Hey, Hanna, Riley, this is Trevor. You know how you were talking about getting a cat? Come over tomorrow. Just come over. Have I got a surprise for you."

He called several more friends before he left the barn, closing the door behind him.

"I guess that worked out," Paggs said. "You all get some sleep tonight. Looks like you've found a new home."

"Three cheers for Mouse," Jinx said.

"Hip-hip-hooray!" the group cheered.

"Thank you," Mouse said.

Scratch and Dazzle approached her.

"This calls for a celebration," Dazzle said.

"It's too bad I don't have my guitar," Scratch said.

"Guitar?" Dandee said. "I can get you a guitar. But I get to do my song first."

"Deal," Scratch said.

Dandee ran out of the barn and returned with a small guitar and handed it to Scratch. After a few turns on the strings and a practice chord, Scratch nodded that he was ready.

"Okay, give me a tune like so." Dandee tapped his foot to give Scratch the beat and then started singing:

> Out here in the spacious pastures,
> I can think out loud
> With no one bothering me.
> I can take my time
> To notice what's going on.
> Not lost in a crowd—
> My neighbor knows my first name
> And so much more about me,
> And I know him just the same.
>
> I like the country life,
> Tired of the big-city lights,
> The noisy days
> And noisy nights—
> Can't stand the city life.
>
> Here out in the great wide-open,
> We help each other out,
> And on our friends we rely.
> Not so hard to understand why.
> I like the country life.
> Not in a hurry to have fun,
> We live life—
> Life's not on the run.
>
> And there's nothing wrong with a quiet evening
> Or a boring day—
> Plenty of time to do things right
> And do them the right way.
>
> I like the country life
> With the simple joy it brings.

More work than worry,
No reason to hurry—
It's a wonderful thing.
It's a wonderful thing.

Out here you can breathe the air
And just be yourself
Despite the clothes you wear.
We teach respect and manners.
It's a simple life;
You'll fit right in.

I like the country life,
Tired of the big-city lights,
The noisy days and the noisy nights—
I can't stand the city life.
I like the country life.

Applause erupted from the audience of cats, dogs, rats, and chickens as they all gathered on the barn floor around Scratch and Dandee.

"That was really good for a country boy," Dazzle said.

"Thank you," Dandee said. "That's some good guitar playing by your friend there."

"Yes, it is," Dazzle said. "Now let me tell you a little about myself and where I come from. Hit it, Scratch."

Now you might think I'm just an alley cat,
That I don't know this from that,
But I'll tell you they got me all wrong.
Listen to me; I'll sing you my song.
I never knew my mama, my father, or my kin—
Born into a world
That I didn't fit in.
I learned the alley cat;
He knows where it's at.
I said the alley cat;
He knows where it's at.
So I took to the streets

And struck out on my own,
Knowing that I'd spend my whole life alone.
I was down and out, not a bite to eat,
Head down low, watching my own feet.
When I heard this tune, put me in a trance—
My feet went crazy, and I started to dance.
I went to the left.

Then Scratch joined in. "He went to the left."
"And I moved to the right," Dazzle sang as he danced.
"He moved to the right," Scratch sang.
"A little bit a grooving, then I realized ... that the best time of day."
"Best time of day."
"Is the middle of the night."
"The middle of the night."
"The best kind of sun."
"The best kind of sun."
"Is the bright starlight," Dazzle sang, and then he finished:

So I sleep all day.
They call me lazy and ignore me,
But I don't let it get me down.
The ladies they adore me
Because I got these moves.

He tapped across in front of Dandee and the other animals. "And I got these grooves."

He danced to Scratch and Mouse and held his paws out. "And with friends like these, I just can't lose. Yes, the alley cat."

"The alley cat," Mouse joined in.

"Knows where it's at," Dazzle sang again.

"Knows where it's at." They repeated this several times until the tune faded.

The barn erupted in applause; even the horses whinnied from their stables behind the rest.

"That was great," Dandee said. "Now I've got to skedaddle. If get don't get inside, Trevor will wonder where I am. You just sleep tight tonight, and after Trevor gets home from school tomorrow, we'll see about getting you settled."

All the animals went to sleep except for Mouse, Scratch, and Dazzle. They went up to the loft where Carl had gone.

"What a party," Scratch said. "That old dog could really sing."

"So, what now?" Carl said.

"We stay hidden up here tomorrow," Mouse said. "Make sure everyone gets a home, and then we head back."

"I'm not sure we're heading back," Dazzle said.

"What?" Mouse said.

"Sikes has been taking care of us long enough. It's time for us to head out on our own, and this seems to be the time and place to do it. The complex is getting busier with the new building going up. There's going to be more people and fewer places to hide. We'll never get another chance like this. You'll let him know for us, right?"

"I will," Mouse said. She watched as the two cats headed back down to the ground floor. Then she turned to Carl. "Are you flying back tomorrow with Colonel Wellington?"

"I was planning to do so. But with Scratch and Dazzle staying, that leaves only you to go back. I can't leave you to make it back all by yourself," Carl said. "I can wait another day. We'll travel together."

"I won't be by myself," Mouse said. "I'm sure Midnight will help me find my way back."

"You sure about that?" Carl used his wing to point down to where Midnight was sleeping, cuddled next to Jinx.

"I noticed they've been hanging out together," Mouse said. "At least he seems more content that he was earlier."

"All of us need someone," Carl said. "I'm sure he's happy he's found someone to talk to. You did good. You helped out all of those animals, and you gave us a great adventure to talk about."

"It wasn't easy," Mouse said. "And the adventure's not over; we still have to get back."

"I'm sure it will be easier without all the others to worry about."

"I hope you're right," Mouse said. "It'll be nice to get back to the complex and my dad. Where it's safe."

Back at the apartment complex, Chief continued with his plan to get rid of Moats. "Follow me to the second floor," Chief said to Ladie. "That's where I always leave a window cracked open by the fire escape. We can exit the building there. I'll go to the alley to meet Wilber's rats. They're going to draw Moats out of the alley. You stay above us and keep an eye on the street, and call out if you see any people."

Chief led the way down the hallway and to the stairs. Little Foot met them at the fire escape, and Chief lowered his shoulder as Little Foot jumped on his back. Ladie took off and flew to the alley while they made their way down the fire escape to the side of the building. It wasn't long before Ladie came back and landed in front of them.

"Looks like it's just two cats in the alley," Ladie said.

"What do they look like?" Chief asked. By the description Ladie gave, it was Moats and Rocko. "That's perfect," he said. "We only have one to get rid of, but if we get Rocko too, it might not hurt our cause. Now remember, Wilber said he would take care of drawing them out and to the rendezvous point."

"Then what?" Little Foot said.

"Then you do your stuff and lure Moats into the delivery truck. You're the only one small enough to get back out through the ventilation system. If anything goes wrong, I'll be standing by. Now, we just need—*ow!*" A small rock hit chief in the back, and he whirled around. "The rats. And they're here."

"Sorry," Quido said from down the alley. "Are we ready to start?"

"Ready," Chief said. He jumped back to the fire escape with Little Foot and stayed above the alley in the darkness as he watched the rats get into position.

Quido went to the end of the building and stood out in the open. Then he picked up a small stone and threw it down the alley.

"*Ouch!*" Rocko yelled. "It's them rats from the other day."

"You cats got yours coming," Quido said. "Now we know where you live."

Quido turned and ran, and a few seconds later, Moats and Rocko came around the corner, following him. As soon as the two cats ran past Chief and Little Foot, Chief jumped down and followed them. He was amazed at how the rats kept just a few paces ahead of the cats and lured them along the street, away from the complex. Chief recognized the route they were taking as the same he had taken to go to Wilber's hideout. Once he was sure they were on the right track, Chief turned the Little Foot. "Hold on tight." He felt the mouse grab his fur, and he increased his speed, taking a shortcut to the small restaurant above Wilber's hideout. He immediately smelled rats around him on the street. He spotted Wilber by a fire hydrant in front of the restaurant and went over to him. Most of the businesses on the street were closed this early in the morning, and the street was empty.

"You made it," Wilber said.

"They're on their way," Chief told him.

"That's the truck there," Wilber said, pointing to a truck parked on the side of the road. The truck had pictures of cows and milk bottles on it. "This is his last delivery, and then he heads back upstate to the dairy farm. I've sent a few of my boys there. It's a long ride."

"If it's his last delivery," Chief said, "how do you expect to lure the cats in there?"

"Don't worry," Wilber said. "The driver always keeps some milk for himself. Watch."

Chief took cover and watched as the driver pulled all but one carton that had four bottles in it out of the back and closed the door, just like Wilber said he would. He headed inside the restaurant with his delivery.

"Now he'll sit in there and drink some coffee and give us time to do our thing. See, timing is everything."

"Great," Chief said and headed to the truck. Wilber's rats were already opening the back and left the door wide enough for him to jump in with Little Foot. Once he landed, the rats scattered. Ladie came in for a landing right beside Chief.

"They're right around the corner," Ladie said.

"We've got it from here," Chief said. "Get back to the apartment. Thank you for your help."

"No way," Ladie said. "I'm going to stick around just in case you need me."

"Get someplace safe, then," Chief said. He watched Ladie fly to one of the rooftops and then went to the shelf in the truck where the four containers of milk were placed. He used his paws to tug on a bottle, pushing it over until it crashed down, breaking open. "There you go," he said to Little Foot. He jumped down off the delivery truck just before Moats and Rocko came around the corner. Chief ducked behind some construction materials on the sidewalk. He positioned himself so he could see the alley and watched as Moats and Rocko drew closer.

"Where'd them rats go?" Moats said.

"I don't know," Rocko said. "But look what's over there; there's a mouse in the back of that truck, drinking milk."

Both cats ran toward the truck, but Moats stopped just before he was going to jump in. "Wait," he said. He looked around. "Doesn't this seem a little suspicious to you?"

"Oh, come on," Rocko said. "That's fresh milk up there. I haven't had any for a long time. And there's a live mouse as a bonus."

"There's plenty up here," Little Foot said, sticking her head over the edge of the truck to look down at the cats. "Unless you're too scared to come up here."

"What? Did you hear what that mouse said? Come on, Moats; let's get him."

"Wait a minute," Moats said, putting his paw on Rocko and preventing him from moving forward. "I'll check this out." He jumped into the back of the truck.

Chief pounced from his position as soon as Moats landed at the back end of the truck. He knocked Rocko to the ground with this accurate jump and then pounced a second time, landing his front paws squarely on the truck's back door handle and rode it down as it closed. Little Foot darted around Moats and jumped out the back of the truck, just clearing the door as it came shut. She landed in front of Rocko. Little Foot froze.

Chief heard the door click shut and knew Moats was stuck inside. He bounced from the bumper of the truck to the ground and faced Rocko, but he was on the opposite side of Little Foot. Rocko smiled as he prepared to swipe at Little Foot. A yellow flash was all Chief saw; Rocko missed his mark when Ladie swooped in and bounced off the black cat's head, distracting him. Chief pushed Little Foot out of the way and tackled Rocko again. He lay motionless as Chief held him down.

"I don't have any issue with you, but we're sending Moats on a long trip out of here. You better split before I change my mind about you," Chief said. He moved so Rocko could stand.

"Rocko, what's going on out there? Get me outta here," Moats said from inside the truck.

Chief noticed a multitude of rats closing in from both sides and nodded left and right. He watched as Rocko brushed himself off and took note of the beady eyes that were coming toward him.

"Geez, this place is infested," Rocko said. "I never liked him anyway." He turned and bolted down the street, back toward the apartments.

"You okay?" Chief asked Little Foot.

"I've been pushed harder," Little Foot said.

Chief patted Little Foot on the head and turned back to the truck. "Hey, Moats, can you hear me?"

"Chief?"

"Yes, it's me."

"So you made it back. Hey, I was just trying to get a point across."

"That's funny," Chief said. "I thought you were trying to get rid of me." There was no response from inside the truck. "But you see, I've got a lot of allies." He winked at Little Foot and at Ladie as she landed beside him. "It's something I learned from my daughter. When you mess with one of us, you mess with all of us."

"No hard feelings, right?" Moats said from the other side of the door.

"No, no hard feelings," Chief said. "But you better get my point, Moats. In a minute, that truck is going to start its engine and take a long trip out of town. If you make any noise, the driver is going to look back and think you were the one who broke that bottle in there. By the way, that was milk for his family, and he's probably not going to like that you're back there. If you stay quiet and wait until he stops, you may be able to jump out and get away when he opens the door. Wherever that is, which I hope is far away from here, you just need to stay there and remember who sent you there because if you come back … well, let's just say if I find you back here, my friends and I won't be so nice next time. Capisce?"

Moats didn't respond. The door to the restaurant opened, and Chief quickly grabbed Little Foot and ducked under cover. He watched as the driver entered the milk truck and drove away, with Moats securely in the back.

"Capisce?" Wilber's voice came from behind Chief. "Those are good words."

"You know for a rat who uses a cane, you sure get around okay," Chief said as he turned to face Wilber.

"I ditched the cane," Wilber said. "But you weren't around for that adventure. So are we square again?"

"You bet," Chief said.

"Then I'll see you next Thursday?"

Chief raised his eyebrows, not knowing what Wilber was speaking about.

"You know, for spaghetti? At my place."

"Thursday it is," Chief said. "Come on, Little Foot, Ladie; let's get back home."

"Oh," Wilber said, causing Chief to pause. "Bring the mouse."

Little Foot smiled at the invitation as Chief lowered his shoulder for her to climb on his back.

"Hold on," Chief said to her. He ran down the street at top speed, with Little Foot riding low. The night was coming to an end, and it was almost daybreak by the time they got back to the apartment complex. Chief dropped Little Foot off in the furniture-storage room. Then he headed to the fourteenth floor and peeked his head in to make sure Ladie was in her cage. Ladie winked at him to let him know she was fine.

"What was that move you did in the alley tonight," Chief said.

"I guess I've been hanging around Sergeant Major Carl too much," Ladie said. "I got inspired by all his stories of adventure."

"Well, thank you," Chief said. "I'm glad everyone made it back safely."

He left the apartment, satisfied that the mission was over for the night but still worried about the remaining alley cats. As he headed back to his room, he thought he might pay them a visit and see if Rocko had told them what had happened, but he wanted to take Baxter with him and check in on Charlene first.

"Sorry, I'm so late," he said as he entered the apartment. Other than Sam snoring in his bed, he found the apartment empty. Warnings went off in Chief's head, and he immediately ran outside to the alley, worried that something had gone wrong. After a night with so much action, he felt an ache in his leg but pushed past the pain as he rounded the corner to the back alley. He came to an abrupt stop at what confronted him.

"I guess those guys ain't so tough now, eh, Baxter?" Sikes said. "Yo, hey, Chief, it's goods to see ya."

Chief stood still as Baxter, Sikes, Rascal, and Charlene approached him.

"Since Sikes and Rascal came back," Baxter said. "Charlene and I figured we'd take care of the rest of those bums for you. Hope you don't mind."

"You must have shook up that one cat," Sikes said. "Rocko, Socko, Taco—whatever his name was. He was all messed up when he came running, telling the other cats that a thousand rats or something like that was chasing him. We scared 'em good. At night, your missus looks really tough and all, Chief. She gots all that fur and stuff. Makes her look really big. I mean no offense by that."

"I know what you mean, Sikes," Charlene said.

"How'd things go with Moats?" Baxter asked. "Did the plan work? Chief? What's wrong?"

Chief took a breath, surprised that Sikes and Rascal were back and glad that Charlene was okay. He decided he had nothing to worry about but needed to catch his breath in the moment.

"Chief?" Baxter said. "What is it?"

"I'm fine," Chief said. "Everything is fine. I just came from the apartment. When I didn't see the two of you there … well, I thought something was wrong."

"Come on," Baxter said. "You know I wouldn't let anything happen. Now, did you get rid of Moats?"

"Moats is on a long trip out of the city on a delivery truck," Chief said. "Call it a special delivery, compliments of Wilber. He and his rats executed the plan perfectly, and so did Little Foot. I don't think that cat will be back."

"If he does come back, we'll show him," Rascal said.

"When did you guys get back?" Chief said.

"Just a little while ago," Rascal said. "We got caught following the group. Your daughter was too smart and set an ambush for us. I mean, she didn't know it was us at first, but I guess we were following too close."

"Yous got nothing to worry about," Sikes said. "That kid is tough. She's got ol' Scratch and Dazzle and some other cat and a bulldog helping her. She'll be fine, Chief. And now that we's back, the alley will be kept clear."

"Now that you two are back, I can get some rest tonight," Chief said. "We can patrol in the morning and make sure those other cats are really gone. Thank you, all of you. It's great to have so many friends."

With that, Chief went inside with Charlene.

CHAPTER 10
A NEW BEGINNING

The usual quietness of the barn was interrupted by the events taking place center stage in the early morning. Mouse and her friends were reenacting the story of her battle with the hoodlum rat Bragar. Mouse played herself, while Slouch drew the role of Bragar, and Slim and Tattle played various roles throughout. They were near the ending scene, and Mouse watched from the side, waiting for Carl to cue her part.

In order to make himself look taller, Slouch had tied pieces of wood to his legs, and he carried a rusty fork in his right paw as he went out from behind the wooden crates they were using as their backdrop.

"Now, I've finished Chief the Protector. He's gone, and there's no one left to stand in my way of absolute rule," Slouch said.

"It's true," Carl said. "Chief has fallen, and there's no one left to stand in the way of the cruel and devious Bragar the Horrible."

"Oh, what will we do?" Slim and Tattle pleaded to the audience of cats, cows, and dogs. Even the horses rested their heads out of their stalls to listen to the tale.

"You'll do what I say," Slouch said, waving the fork awfully close to Slim's head.

"Watch it," Slim whispered.

"It's all part of the drama," Slouch whispered back. He spoke louder. "No one can stop me. Not man or cat or mouse."

"Here's when our story takes a curious turn," Carl said, narrating from his position atop the crates. "See, Mouse was born the runt, which means smallest, of her litter. Because she was so small, her father, Chief the Protector, called her Mouse. The name was not to be confused with the amount of courage that existed in her." Carl pointed toward Mouse, and she knew it was her cue.

Mouse took one step out from the side of the crate, to the far right of where Slouch was standing. "I can't stand by and let this bully Bragar take over my home. I must believe that although I'm just a small, fluffy cat, I can make a difference. I've just got to round up my courage and think up a plan. It's time to make a stand." Mouse moved across the floor, closer to Slouch, and came behind Tattle and Slim. "You two join me, and we'll stand against the bully. You help me take on his evil minions, and I'll stand up to him. We just have to have courage!"

"How dare you challenge me!" Slouch said and pointed the fork at Mouse. The barn went quiet as Slouch approached Mouse. "I'll make you pay."

Mouse looked at the audience of animals, turned from Slouch, and ran back across the floor as though she was fleeing. She executed a loop behind the wooden crate and went out of sight for a moment as she crossed behind it.

"See how brave your hero is? She has fled in my presence."

Mouse came out from the other side of the wooden crate and passed behind Slouch, where she executed her power-slide by digging her front left claw into the ground and letting the rest of her body slide. She turned and kicked forward with her back legs to gain momentum as she crouched and pounced.

The surprised look on Slouch's face went beyond acting. He dropped the rusty fork and raised his hands above his head as Mouse came down on him, being careful to use her paws to catch herself so the full weight of her body didn't land on him.

"Hurray!" the animals cheered as Mouse came down on the evil rat.

"You've had your last day to bully us," Mouse said. "Surrender, or you'll feel the fury of my claws!" She raised her right paw above Slouch, who lay on the ground.

"I ... I surrender," Slouch said.

Mouse leaned in to Slouch. "You're doing a great job; keep it up." She moved away from him, and Slouch slowly came to his feet.

"We've joined together to stand against you," Mouse said. "Now you're banished forever, and if I ever see you here again"—she smacked her front paws together—"I'll be cracking skulls."

"I'm Wilber," Slim said as he completely changed his posture, signaling to the audience that he had changed character, "head of the rats. I'll honor our truce between the Protectors and the rats, Mouse. I'll take care of this vile rat who has no respect and deserves none in what he has coming to him. Come with me." Slim grabbed Slouch by the ear and escorted him out of sight behind the crate.

"And that's the story of Mouse the Protector!" Carl said as all the animals applauded and cheered.

Slim and Slouch came out and—along with Mouse, Carl, and Tattle—took a bow.

"That was a great story," Midnight said as he and Jinx approached Mouse. "Now I know why all these animals respect you so much."

"The truth is, my mom helped me in the end," Mouse said.

"It still sounds like you were the one who organized the entire plan," Midnight said. "Just like you organized the plan to get rid of the coyotes."

"Well, this has been my greatest adventure," Mouse said, "but it doesn't end until all of these animals find homes. I hope Trevor comes through with his friends."

"I'm sure he will," Midnight said. "And that's something I've been thinking about."

"What's that?" Mouse asked.

"Finding a home. Do you think if I decided to go with someone that you would be able to make it back on your own?"

Mouse wasn't sure what to say at first. She wanted Midnight to be happy, but she didn't want to get lost on her way back to the apartment complex. She'd already lost Scratch and Dazzle, who had decided to try to find a home on the farm. With Carl staying, she might have a chance, since he could fly and see the ground from high above. "I'm sure we can manage," Mouse said.

"Chief," Baxter called out as he entered the apartment. "Chief, you home?"

Chief came out the bedroom where he'd been sleeping. He stretched his legs as he walked into the living room. "Right here, Bax. Just slept in for once."

"Good. You deserve it. I came by because Colonel Wellington is back. He came by the alley to talk to Sikes and then went down to the park."

Chief went to his water dish and took a drink. "I guess I'll go talk to Sikes and see what's going on. Maybe they're all close to being back. It sure would be nice to have Mouse back and safe."

"It would," Baxter said. "After what we've been through this last week, her trip was probably a walk in the park."

Chief headed out to the alley. It was midmorning, and he knew that Sikes and Rascal would not be out at this time. They would either be sleeping somewhere out of sight or down at the park. He stood in the alley, closed his eyes, and reached out with his senses. He smelled left over garbage, gas fumes from all the cars starting in parking lot, the remnants of Moats and his group, and a faint hint of rats but no Rascal and no Sikes.

He took off down the side of the buildings and through the parking lot, where he crossed the street and headed down to the park. He didn't like to leave the complex but wanted to find Sikes or Colonel Wellington to get information. He spotted Sikes and Rascal sitting under some bushes, watching the pigeons that gathered in the park.

"Already out and chasing pigeons, I see," Chief said as he approached.

"We have a job to do," Sikes said. "We promised the colonel we'd help keep them pigeons in shape. See, theys just got those people over there tossing them food all day, making them fat. We don't catch them. We just let them know we're here. I imagine they wouldn't be able to fly after too much eating if it weren't for us."

"Good thing you're back, then," Chief said. "Speaking of the colonel, Baxter told me he was back and brought you some news. Are the others close?"

"I'll handle this," Sikes said. "You go ahead."

Rascal leaped out from the bushes and ran forward to a group of pigeons, causing them to scatter.

"The colonel came in this morning," Sikes said. "He says they made it to the farm. All the animals are planning to get homes, and all is well. But they ain't started back yet." Sikes eyes filled with tears.

"Sikes, are you okay?" Chief asked. "What is it?"

"Sorry, Chief," Sikes said. "I get all choked up when I think about it." He stood and turned his face away from Chief. "I guess Scratch and Dazzle are going to stay out there in the country. They seems to like it. They told the colonel to tell me."

Chief patted Sikes on the shoulder. "I'm sure they'll be fine. You always took good care of them."

"Thanks, Chief," Sikes said. "The colonel also said Mouse is doing fine, and she's heading back as soon as she knows the other animals have all found homes. Carl is still with her."

"Thanks, Sikes. Let me know if there's anything I can do." Chief didn't know what else to say and started to head back to the apartment. Rascal finished his round of chasing pigeons and returned to the bushes and stood by Sikes.

"Hey," Chief said, going back to the two cats. "I have an offer for you. Until Mouse gets back, I want one of you to take the patrols of Paggs's old building. And the other … well, you can see that they're building another set of apartments. That's the fourth building in the complex, and we're going to need another cat to patrol it. With the increased parking lots and perimeter, I'm going to need more help. I want you two to join Baxter and me to protect the grounds."

"You hear that, Rascal?" Sikes said. "We ain't going to be just alley cats anymore. We're gonna have real jobs and stuff. You gotta deal there, Chief."

"Good," Chief said. "As soon as Sam gets the new maintenance person hired, I'll introduce you."

"It's a deal," Sikes said. "Come on, Rascal. We gots to keep them pigeons in shape and get ourselves in shape for our new duties." Sikes took off across the park with Rascal, and Chief headed back to the apartment complex.

High in the loft above the barn floor, Mouse sat beside Carl and Paggs as they watched the scene below. Dandee and Trevor had come into the barn a dozen times that morning with different kids of all ages and even some adults that picked out a cat. Each time one of the animals was selected, he or she would look to the loft and thank Mouse. An older boy took Scratch and Dazzle, telling them they would be perfect to help him at his farm, and since they were going together, neither one of them minded.

It was a little brown-haired girl Trevor called Hanna who intrigued Mouse as she entered the barn. She took her time looking around before she went to Jinx. She carefully lifted Jinx and hugged her. As she turned around, Jinx was facing Mouse and smiled at her. Mouse waved. As the two started toward the barn door, another cat came out from the bales of hay; it was Midnight. He went in front of the little girl, causing her to stop as he meowed.

"What's he doing?" Mouse said.

"I think he made his decision," Paggs said. "He wants to go with Jinx and that little girl."

"He's going to ruin her chance of getting a home," Mouse said.

"I don't think so," Paggs said. "Just wait."

The little girl watched Midnight as he circled around her leg, purred, and worked his charm. "All right," the little girl said. "You can come along too, but you two better get along. I have a little brother, and you can be his cat."

"Whew," Mouse said as she watched the drama below. "That's about everyone but poor Tattle."

"Guess no one wants a ferret," Paggs said.

"He's a weasel," Mouse said.

"Oh, I can't tell the difference."

"Me either, but he told me so. This doesn't look good. There's no one left for Butch or Tattle."

Mouse watched as Trevor sat down on a single bale of hay and lifted Tattle in his lap. "Hey there, little fellow," he said. "Don't know why no one wanted you. You're so playful and rambunctious."

Tattle moved in and out of Trevor's hands and did loops around him. Around noon, from outside the barn, Dandee started barking, causing everyone to watch the door as he approached. He came in with his tail wagging, and a small, thin girl with long blonde hair followed him.

"I hope I'm not too late," the little girl said. "I had gymnastics this morning."

"Hi, Riley," Trevor said as he stood and struggled to keep Tattle in his grip. "All the cats are gone, but I have this little ferret here."

"See? Even he can't tell the difference," Paggs said.

"Shh," Mouse scolded and looked on.

"That's a weasel," Riley said and reached out to take Tattle from Trevor.

"Smart kid," Mouse said.

"He seems really tame and friendly," Trevor said. "And he got along with Dandee and the other cats, so you probably wouldn't have any issues with him."

"I've never had a weasel before," Riley said. Tattle crawled around her arms and on her shoulders.

"You better make sure your parents are okay with having a, uh, weasel."

Riley laughed. "Like they are in charge of anything. I'll take him." Tattle curled around her arm as she petted him on the head. "What do I owe you?"

"These animals just showed up here," Trevor said. "I didn't have to raise them or feed them or anything. No charge. Just promise me you'll give it a good home."

"I will," Riley said. "I see you got a new dog."

"He's a bulldog," Trevor said. "Oddly enough, he came with the others. I decided to keep him and see if the school wants to use him as a mascot. Go, Bulldogs!"

"Go, Bulldogs," Riley said.

Mouse watched as Trevor, Riley, and Dandee left the barn.

When they were gone, Butch said, "Hey, I just wanted to tell you thanks, Mouse."

"You're welcome, Butch. Thank you for your hospitality."

"A successful day," Carl said. "Congratulations, Mouse."

Mouse stood and shook off some of the hay that stuck to her fur. "It took all of us," she said. "Now, we'd best get moving."

"It's about time," said a voice from behind them in the loft.

Mouse turned around to see Slim and Slouch emerge from underneath a pile of hay. "Slim? Slouch? What are you guys doing?" Mouse asked. "I haven't seen you all day. I thought you left."

"We're up here, where it's safe," Slouch said as he wiped hay off his body. "Do you realize how dangerous it is out here? Last night we were chased by an owl. This morning we tried to make friends with the pigs, and they just snorted and snapped at us. We asked the chickens to spare an egg, and the rooster chased us."

"Hmm," Mouse said. "That's not what Tattle told me. He told me you guys tried to eat out of the pigs' trough without asking, and they chased you away. Then you tried to steal an egg from the chickens, and the rooster caught you."

"He told you that?"

Mouse nodded.

"Well, I'm glad he's gone, then," Slouch said. "Did he also tell you that we went out to the field to find something to eat and there was some strange person out there, standing real still, like he thought we wouldn't notice him? You can't leave us here; it's too dangerous."

"Hmm," Mouse said. "I guess maybe that's why there're not a lot of rats out here in the country. What do you say, Carl? Shall we take them with us?"

"Yes," Carl said. "We shall journey out into the wilderness with courage to face the unknown and perseverance to overcome any obstacles until we succeed in our mission. I just hope these two don't mess things up."

Mouse turned to Slim and Slouch. "Okay, you can join us."

Slim nodded while Slouch shook his head. "I can't go through those woods again. Are you crazy?"

"You're right, Slouch," Mouse said. "The journey may not be so easy."

"It's not the journey back I'm worried about," Slim said. "It's facing Wilber. We're going to be in the kitchen for months."

Mouse laughed. "I'm just hoping we don't get lost."

"We're doomed," Slouch said.

"We aren't doomed," Mouse said. "You just have to have a little confidence, and we'll be fine. I'd think, after this trip, you would have learned that." Mouse started singing:

> If it doesn't work out the first time,
> Why not give it another try?
> Change your approach—
> Ask yourself why.

Slouch looked at her. "So you're saying if it doesn't come easy, I should work harder and ask why? I say it's not worth it to try."

Mouse started singing again.

> Have a little confidence.
> Know where you're going
> And where you've been.
> Have a little confidence, and you can win.

> Some things come easy, but most things worthwhile
> Take a bit of effort and can sometimes be a trial.
> It'll be worth it
> When you look back at what you've done.
> Have a little confidence, and you've won.

"What if it just doesn't work out?" Slouch asked.

"Did you really try? Did you give it your best?" Mouse sang back.

"What if I didn't?"

"Then what did you expect?" Mouse sang the next verse.

> Just have a little confidence.
> Believe there's nothing you can't do.
> If you have a little confidence,
> It's up to you.

"Okay," Slouch said, "I think I understand now. You mean I just got to try?"

"No, you have to believe in your ability."

"What if I don't?"

"Oh ..." Mouse paused before she started the next part:

> Even the tallest tree
> Starts as a little seed.
> The greatest song,
> A simple melody.
> Have a little confidence;
> Believe in who and what you are.
> Have a little confidence;
> And you'll go far.

"Great song, Mouse," Paggs said. "Even without Scratch playing the guitar, you've got quite a rhythm."

Mouse turned to Carl, Slim, and Slouch. "Let's go. We can make that clearing by nightfall if we keep a good pace."

"I can't wait to get back to the city," Slim said. "I can almost taste the spaghetti now." He licked his lips.

Moats slowly made his way along the bank of the stream, heading back to the city. He shivered in the cool of the night; his coat was full of road grit and was wet from the stream he'd tumbled into while dodging traffic. After escaping from the enraged milk-truck driver, he had made his way to the highway. At first he tried walking alongside the road but found it unsafe because of the cars. After traveling for hours, he came to a large opening on the side of the stream—a pipe that seemed empty—and decided to crawl in and rest for the night.

"That Chief, he's in for it when I get back," Moats said. "And Rocko. I'll teach him a lesson."

Right before Moats entered the opening, he sensed something and hesitated.

"They tried to drown me, my own kind," a voice came from inside the opening.

It was too dark for Moats to see who or what was speaking to him, but he figured it must not be threatening, or it would have come at him. "How did you survive?"

"I've been through it before," the raspy voice said. "Only before, it was the humans who tried to drown me."

"Is that why you talk funny?"

"Yes. Is it something that's going to bother you?"

"Why would it bother me? I'll just go find another place if this one is taken." Moats turned to leave.

"Wait," the voice said. "I'm thinking we can help each other."

"Help each other? How?"

"Come closer."

Moats entered the pipe but couldn't see who had addressed him.

"Can you lift this grate?"

The voice came from underneath where Moats stood. He could see two beady red eyes staring back at him from under a small grate in the pipe. He put his paws under the wires and lifted the grate enough to make a small opening. He watched as a white hairball of a figure grunted and emerged from the opening. When he lowered the grate back down, he looked at what had emerged, surprised to find it was a large white rat.

"I'm Bragar."

"I'm Moats. Why would I help you, rat?"

"I heard you mention the name Chief."

"What about it?"

"The Protector?"

"How would you know?"

"He's the reason I'm here. Well, not him, exactly, but his daughter."

"And you're thinking we can help each other out to get revenge? How?"

Moats looked closer at the large white rat with beady red eyes that stood before him. He was intimidating because of his size. Suddenly, he noticed Bragar's grin—an evil, toothy grin.

"Would you look at that," Bragar said as his eyes looked across Moats to something in the distance.

Moats turned to look down the hill into the forest, where he spotted movement. About fifty yards away from them, a cat and two rats were traveling together, with a bird circling close overheard.

"You know them?" Moats asked.

Bragar nodded as his eyes narrowed, and his grin turned to a scowl. "Let me introduce you to Chief's daughter."

Moats looked at the group in front of him. He didn't know the smaller cat or the rats and was surprised that they were traveling together. He was further surprised when he spotted another cat following right behind them. This cat—a solid black cat who went by the name of Midnight—he recognized. It was his son.

Printed in the United States
By Bookmasters